PENGUIN BOOKS

ANOTHER BOUQUET ...

Andrea Newman was born in Dover in 1938, and was brought up in Shropshire and Cheshire. In 1960 she graduated from London University, where she married while still a student, and then worked as a civil servant and a teacher before becoming a full-time writer.

Her publications include *A Share of the World* (1964), *Mirage* (1965), *The Cage* (1966), *Three into Two Won't Go* (1967), *Alexa* (1968), and *A Bouquet of Barbed Wire* (1969). *A Bouquet of Barbed Wire* was dramatized by her for London Weekend Television, and this was followed in early 1977 by *Another Bouquet*. ... She has also contributed to other television series such as *Tales of Unease*, *The Frighteners*, *Love Story*, *Seven Faces of Woman*, *Intimate Strangers* and *Helen, A Woman of Today*.

Andrea Newman is divorced and lives in London.

ANDREA NEWMAN

ANOTHER
BOUQUET...

PENGUIN BOOKS

Penguin Books Ltd, Harmondsworth, Middlesex, England
Penguin Books, 625 Madison Avenue, New York, New York 10022, U.S.A.
Penguin Books Australia Ltd, Ringwood, Victoria, Australia
Penguin Books Canada Ltd, 2801 John Street, Markham, Ontario, Canada L3R 1B4
Penguin Books (N.Z.) Ltd, 182–190 Wairau Road, Auckland 10, New Zealand

—

First published 1978

—

Copyright © Andrea Newman, 1978
All rights reserved

—

Made and printed in Great Britain by
C. Nicholls & Company Ltd
Set in Linotype Juliana

Dedicated
to the memory of
Cyril Bennett
who asked for a sequel

CONTENTS

AUTHOR'S NOTE

Bouquet of Barbed Wire was my original novel which I dramatized for television. *Another Bouquet* ... was originally commissioned for television and I have since adapted it from my own scripts in order to give the reader the same impression as the viewer.

I

CHANGES

HE walked from the station. It gave him time to reflect; it was reassuring. At any point he could turn back. He would have liked to drive all the way for the same reason, but it was too frightening these days, never knowing when his mind might wander away, causing an accident. Other people might be hurt and he would have them on his conscience.

Walking up the path he told himself there was still time to choose; he was not yet committed; he need not go in. But he knew this was false. The fear was too strong: if he did not go in today he would never go in. So often he had come half way and had to get off the train. To come so near and go away again would embody total flight.

He looked over the hedge at the house. There was no feeling of ownership. It did not even look like his house any more, merely familiar, like the country retreat of friends with whom he had lost touch. But, in the middle of the lawn, there she was. On a blanket, kicking, playing with her toys, laughing to herself. His heart contracted with pain and love till he felt quite dizzy, as if he was going to black out.

He went in slowly, carefully, wanting to be stealthy, remembering how the gate creaked. It was important not to be discovered too soon. Would she cry, would she reject him, indignant at this intruder who was trying to pick her up? Whom would he see in her face?

She stopped playing as he approached her and watched him, not warily but with interest. When he was near enough he put out a tentative hand: the urge to grab her was overwhelming, to scoop her up and hold her in his arms, but he must not give way to it yet. He must not alarm her. After all, to her they were strangers. But the waiting made his chest ache. He put out his other hand and picked her up; she was heavier than he expected.

Would she cry out at the unfamiliar touch? Instead the miracle happened: she looked at him with Prue's eyes and she smiled.

Cassie, turning round from the stove to glance through the window, simply could not believe it. The routine of checking that Eve was all right was automatic: she did it a hundred times a day, far more often and more neurotically than she ever had with her own children. From the very beginning she had been quite irrationally terrified of the new responsibility, haunted by fantasies of illness and accident, sudden death, accusations of neglect in the coroner's court. Now, as she raced from the kitchen to the garden, the empty blanket stayed as a shock-image in her mind. How far could Eve crawl without encountering danger? Cassie felt hot with panic, but there was also a dreadful feeling of satisfaction that all her worst fears were justified. She was not neurotic: she had known all along that Eve was doomed. There was no thought of Gavin in her mind as she ran. It was Prue she imagined, demanding an explanation. 'Mummy. Why didn't you look after my baby? I trusted you.'

When she saw him the relief was instantaneous, mixed with astonishment. Then both were elbowed out, swept away and rage took over. She was so angry she could not speak. She would have liked to kill him.

'Why didn't you phone?' she said, pouring tea. He sat with Eve on his lap, as if he had a right to her.
'Yes.' He looked vague. 'I meant to. I should have done.'
She said smoothly, 'I might have been out.'
'I'd have waited.'
She handed him his tea. It was insufferable, this smug assumption that she had nowhere else to be, that there was nowhere else she *could* be, so it was perfectly all right for her to be intruded upon without warning at any hour.
She said, 'Would you like some cake? I only made it at the week-end.' Another week-end of wasted effort and disappointment. As if you could bribe someone to make love to you by cooking

12

for him. She was ashamed of herself, but there seemed no other way to behave.

He looked pleased. 'Yes. I would.' He actually glanced up from the child and in her direction. 'So you still bother with all that.'

She could not decide whether he made her sound dedicated or infantile. She said curtly, 'It seems to be a habit,' and cut him a large slice. She was hoping he would not be able to manage the baby, the tea and the cake; it felt odd to see him sitting there, making himself at home, after giving her the fright of her life.

'Let me take her.'

'No, it's all right, I can manage.'

He had always been stubborn, she would grant him that. In a way she admired him for not giving in to her. And he did not look well, now that she came to examine his face more closely. A sudden rush of compassion for him made her want to apologize for her anger; instead she said defensively: 'You gave me such a fright.'

He seemed surprised. More than that bemused. 'When?'

'Just now. Snatching her up like that.'

'Oh yes, of course. I'm sorry.'

She wondered if he had taken in what she said. There was something not quite right about his manner: a loose connection somewhere. More compassion flooded in, leaving no room for anger. Instead she felt resentment: she did not want her feelings assailed in this way. She could not afford to feel sorry for him again. Her resources were depleted. And yet she wanted to help him. He was her responsibility. If not, he was nobody's. But she felt she would be more willing to try if she was certain of success. Another failure, in her present state, would be unbearable.

He looked up suddenly, almost his old self, charming, relaxed. 'I should have come before.'

In the bathroom he stared as greedily as a starving man might eat. She was so lovely and she had changed: so much had happened in his absence. He wondered if Cassie even began to appreciate her. She seemed so casual, going through the bath routine. Spoilt, no doubt, by having so much time alone with Eve; she took her good fortune for granted.

He said inadequately, 'She's grown so much,' and Cassie replied at once, 'They do at this age. Don't you remember?'

She made it sound like a reproach. What had remembering got to do with it? The time was now and Eve was unique. What was the matter with Cassie? Waiting perhaps for some inquiry about herself; had he been neglectful? He could not remember.

'How've you been?' He was surprised to hear the words, did not realize at first that he had finally made himself ask them. They came out sounding diffident, unsure.

'All right,' Cassie said. 'How about you?'

He could not get used to this politeness, as if they were strangers instead of being married for half their lives.

'Oh, I'm fine,' he said. 'Much better.' He felt like someone on a train making conversation with the traveller in the opposite seat. Neither cared about the answers but it passed the time.

'Are you sleeping?' she asked, with a touch of concern.

'Yes.' At last there was some positive information he could give her to ease the silence. Relief overwhelmed him. 'I went to the doctor and he gave me these marvellous pills. It's amazing the difference it makes if you get a good night's sleep.'

After all, he wanted her to think he was all right. It was so boring to be worried about: you could feel it oppressing you, like thundery weather.

Suddenly he was aware of pressure. There was something she was expecting him to ask, something he should have said earlier, if only he could remember what it was.

'How are the boys?' That was it.

'Very well.'

Why didn't she sound pleased? Hadn't he got it right?

'Really?'

'Why don't you go and see for yourself?'

He was being chastised for negligence. He said humbly: 'Yes, I ought to.'

'Don't make it sound like a duty.' There was an edge to her voice.

He kept quiet. He had an urge – absurd, he knew – to lie down and hide. He could not tolerate anger these days; it was too dangerous. He kept his eyes on the baby and waited.

Cassie said, 'Sorry. They miss you, that's all.'

He said, eager to make peace, 'I know. I miss them too.' It was true and yet it did not mean anything. The boys were remote, not like this little creature here.

Cassie took Eve out of the bath and wrapped her in a big towel. His arms ached to hold her again.

Cassie said, 'There. There's a clever girl. All nice and clean and ready for bed. Aren't you lovely?'

He could not prevent himself. 'Let me hold her.'

Cassie said doubtfully, 'Well ... she's a bit damp.'

'I don't mind.'

She handed Eve to him; he sensed reluctance. Predictably, Eve started to cry.

'She's not used to you.' He detected satisfaction in Cassie's voice.

'She was all right before.'

He did his best to cheer her up but she wouldn't stop crying.

Cassie said, 'She's probably tired.' She held out her arms. 'Better let me have her.'

He handed her back and despaired. He watched Cassie's expert soothing; Eve stopped crying for Cassie. What was the matter with her: didn't she love him? Why should she? She didn't know him. All the more reason then ... His mind ran on tormentingly.

And then – she smiled at him. He wasn't imagining it. Swathed in her bath towel, ignoring Cassie, she smiled directly at him.

He said abruptly, 'You were right. There is a resemblance.'

Vicky studied the table. It looked all right; in fact it looked very good. She knew that. And yet there was still this awful lurking fear that she had overdone it. Perhaps Gavin would not appreciate water-lily napkins; perhaps candles were too overtly romantic. Or was it the flowers? If she took them off the table, would that make the rest of it more restrained? She caught sight of herself in the mirror and frowned with annoyance: she had on her typical look of anxiety mixed with eagerness to please, 'like a nervous puppy,' as her father had once described it. She had never forgotten. He had said it was attractive, but she did not believe he meant it. Annoyed at the memory, she decided to have the courage of her convictions and put the flowers back.

The front door slammed at that moment and she nearly dropped the vase.

Gavin said, 'You still here?' and looked at the table. 'My God, what's all this?'

The more her stomach churned as she looked at him, the harder she tried to make her voice sound flippant. 'Well ... you haven't given up eating, have you? I thought as I was here I might as well do something about dinner.' Then she went up to him and kissed him, wondering what kind of mood he was in. Sometimes he hugged her and sometimes he pushed her away. 'Hullo,' she said, to make it casual.

'Hullo.' He allowed himself to be kissed. She savoured every moment, the feel of him, the smell of his skin.

'It's boeuf bourgignon,' she said lovingly, 'and jacket potatoes and courgettes.' She punctuated the menu with kisses, thanking God that her father had at least taught her to cook properly.

Gavin pulled away. 'What the hell have I done to deserve all that?'

She said lightly, 'It's supposed to be the way to your heart. I've tried all the other routes.'

He ignored that. 'D'you want a drink?'

'Yes, please.' Too late she remembered where the bottle was. He looked for it in its usual place and of course failed to find it.

'Oh hell, we didn't finish it last night, did we?' He hated to run short of whisky.

'No, it's still –' She hesitated.

'What?'

'In the bedroom.' Now he would see her suitcases before she had time to put him in a good mood. He disappeared and she waited tensely, expecting him to shout. Silence. He reappeared with the bottle.

'Great.'

Was it possible he was pleased? 'What?'

'It's a quarter full. We're okay till Friday. Get some ice, huh?'

His tone betrayed nothing. Hadn't he even noticed? Her heart thumped as she returned with the ice. He poured two drinks and gave her one.

'What are we celebrating?'

She said nervously, 'Celebrating?'

'Yeah. You don't go to all this trouble every night of the week.'

She took a deep breath and said, 'I'm not here every night of the week.'

'No.'

The silence made her feel she was choking. 'If you want me to go, you must say so.'

'I never said anything about going.'

'You never said anything about staying, either.' She longed to remind him of their nights together, which had made her brave enough to bring her suitcases, but he was a different person in the daytime: other rules applied. It was privilege enough to have shared the nights; she must not remind him of them. That would be taking an unfair advantage. She said, 'Look, you ought to try a few weeks going to and fro on the bus with your books and your toothbrush. Everything's always in the wrong place. I spend my life going backwards and forwards to change my clothes, it's bloody tiring and a waste of money.' She heard self-pity rising in her voice and disliked it as much as she knew he would.

Gavin said ironically, 'I may cry.'

'Is it all right?'

Silence again. He enjoyed making her wait.

He said, 'That stew isn't burning, is it?'

'I can help with the rent too.'

'I bet it is burning.'

She followed him into the kitchen. 'Then Prue's father won't be able to say you don't pay enough.' His face changed; she had gone too far. 'Aren't I allowed to mention her?'

He turned away. 'Do what you like.'

'And if I go too far you'll kick me out?' She started to tremble with fear and rage. 'I did *know* her, for God's sake. It might even help to talk about her.' He didn't answer. She tried to interpret his silence. 'Gavin?'

He said eventually. 'Just don't push me, that's all. Okay?'

Relief washed over her. 'Okay.' She went over to him and hugged him. After a moment he put his arms round her.

'How long before supper?'

She said, 'An hour or so.'

'Whatever are we going to do till then?'

Coming out of their block of flats, Geoff said, 'Be on your best behaviour tonight, won't you, Pussycat?'

Sarah said lightly, 'I always am.' He had taken to calling her Pussycat since the wedding. She had liked it at first and said so (it all started with some joke about her purring after they made love and scratching his back with her claws). Now he said it too often and she was trying hard not to mind.

He went on, 'Only he's a useful contact. Could do me a lot of good.'

'If he ever takes time off from peering down my dress.' She found most of his business associates both boring and lecherous.

'It's nice to be envied.'

A flash of irritation. 'You're getting very smug.'

He said genially, 'I've got a lot to be smug about. How did I ever manage without you?'

'I can't remember. You muddled through somehow, I expect.'

They had reached the car. He opened the door for her and she got in. As he walked round she studied him: handsome, amiable, rich. She had nothing to complain about. Nothing.

He said, 'I bet his wife's nervous about cooking for us after that Cordon Bleu job you served up.' He had still not got over his surprise that she could cook, a fact well concealed during their affair.

'I like showing off.'

'Don't get too cocky. Wives are supposed to know their place.'

All her jokes were sharp edged these days. 'No wonder you didn't want bacon for breakfast. You might have been eating a relative.'

He laughed. He didn't even notice.

Pouring drinks for them both, Cassie suddenly remembered that it was a weekday and he had arrived in the afternoon. 'Weren't you at the office today?'

He looked vague. 'Everything's under control. I don't think it matters to Rupert if I turn up or not.'

'Is that good?'

'It's convenient. I haven't felt so free in years.'

She tried to put it another way. 'But isn't it dangerous – letting Rupert get too powerful?'

'Why? He's trustworthy. At least I think he is.' He looked amused. 'Oh, what's it matter? If he isn't I'll soon find out.'

He finished his drink rather quickly. Cassie studied him. She said, 'It sounds as if he's in charge.'

Manson said cheerfully, 'Oh, it's not important.'

Impasse. 'Would you like another drink?'

'Yes. Yes, I would. Thank you.'

She got up and took his glass. As if sensing her anxiety he said placatingly, 'It's good to see you again, Cass.'

'I'm glad you came.' And she was, but she felt awkward saying it.

He seemed eager to believe her. 'Are you really?'

'Yes, of course. I've been worried about you.'

'But we've never lost touch.'

'I don't call one lunch in four months keeping in touch.' She was surprised how much she still resented that. (If Gavin had not rejected her, would it have mattered so much?)

He said mildly, 'I've phoned you regularly.'

'Yes.'

'I know what you mean, though. It's different, being here. That's why I was afraid to come.' It was true but he found it difficult to say: he had not talked about feelings for so long. Yet she obviously needed to be told. 'Oh, I wanted to. I started out many times.' He tried to remember accurately. 'One time I actually got to the end of the lane but I had to turn back.'

'Why?' He had captured her interest, at any rate.

'It seemed safer. Going back is dangerous. But it's such a temptation.' Was that really how he had felt? It seemed a long time ago and the feelings blurred even as he described them. But she seemed gratified.

'I know what you mean.'

'Do you?' Now they had both said it, but was it any more than empty reassurance?

'I think so.' She paused, almost embarrassed. 'It's silly – but now you're here I don't know what to say to you.'

Relief. 'No. I feel a bit the same. It's been a long time.'

They sat and looked at each other in silence.

Cassie said, 'Would you like to stay to supper?'

Vicky lay awake, her mind racing, as always after making love. She listened to Gavin's breathing, trying to gauge if he were asleep. She would have to say it now, in any case: there was not much time left to catch the good mood before it evaporated.

'Gavin.'

'Mm.'

She summoned all her courage. 'Can we have a week-end now?'

'What d'you mean?'

'Well – now I'm here properly. We never have.'

He said, as she had expected him to, 'I go to see Eve week-ends.'

'Yes, I know you always *have*. But there's no rule about it, is there?' She was always braver when she had recently had him inside her.

'I want to see her. And you don't want her here, do you?'

That was one to avoid. 'I meant couldn't you go some other time. Like one afternoon in the week. Then we could have a week-end together.'

'What's so great about a week-end?'

'I don't know. But other people have them. They always *sound* nice. As if they ought to be fun.'

'Yeah. Like Bank Holidays.'

He sounded grumpy, but she sensed she was winning. 'Can't we try?'

'You're making it sound like hard work.'

'Just once?'

Silence. She held her breath.

Gavin said, 'I'll say this for you: as a diplomat you're one hell of a good cook. Okay. I'll go to see Eve tomorrow.'

'Thank you.' She hugged him too tight with relief and predictably he pulled away.

'Pity we didn't think of it earlier. I could have gone tonight.'

'Not when I'd made dinner.'

'I'm not very hungry.'

'You bastard.' But he was only restoring their precarious balance after her victory. She knew it so she did not mind. They started wrestling playfully and she dared to tickle him until he yelled for mercy.

Cassie said with satisfaction, 'You were starving.'

'No, I wasn't.' Instantly defensive.

She had been watching him, amused. 'Well, you've had second helpings of everything.'

'It was very good.' He looked a bit shamefaced and she felt herself smiling. 'You're not to fuss. I do eat properly. I go out a lot and sometimes I even cook.' He saw her look incredulous. 'Yes, really.'

Cassie said, 'And sometimes you forget.'

He felt guilty pleasure at being caught out. 'Yes, sometimes I forget.'

Cassie said almost flirtatiously, 'You must come to dinner more often, Peter.'

He could feel her trying to pull him back into her soft, warm net of caring, and he didn't want to resist. 'I'd like to.'

'I didn't know you were waiting to be asked.'

Suddenly coy, she poured more wine and waited.

Manson said, 'I don't know what I was waiting for. To feel ... different, I suppose.'

She said eagerly, 'And now you do?'

He wanted to be honest. 'I feel I've been away too long. It's odd to be a guest in your own house.'

'This is still your home.'

'Is it?'

'I mean if you want it to be.'

A perilous moment. He said, 'What do *you* want, Cass?' Silence. He made a great effort. 'It's an odd thing about living alone. You get used to it. What starts off by being difficult becomes ... so terrifyingly easy.'

Cassie said, 'Yes, I know.'

He felt aggrieved. 'But you're not really alone.'

'Well, I have Eve, but she doesn't say very much.'

'But he visits her, doesn't he?'

'Gavin? Yes, every week-end.' She seemed to shift uncomfortably in her chair. 'He's very conscientious.'

Manson said, 'He's still living in the flat, I notice.'

'But he's paying you rent, isn't he?'

'Mm.'

Cassie said defensively, 'It's all he can afford.'

'After all his boasting that he was going to move out.'

'I don't think he can bear to ... leave the memories.'

Silence. Manson got up and wandered about the room. 'It's not been easy for any of us.'

'No.'

'Does he try to interfere?'

'What?' She sounded startled.

'With the baby.'

'No. No, he doesn't.'

'I should hope not. He ought to be grateful – having you to do everything for him – look after her – take on all that responsibility and let him walk away ...'

'He does all he can.'

'But you're here alone with her.'

'Yes.' She paused. 'I do feel that very much sometimes. If anything went wrong with her and I'm the only person here.' He had never seen her so nervous. 'It's odd. At first you resent all that, and then – in self-defence probably – you get to like it.' She looked embarrassed. 'And finally you don't even want to share any more because you haven't been allowed to for so long. You become self-sufficient.'

Manson said, 'Have you?'

She seemed to hesitate. 'Not yet.'

He said, 'I think that's what I've been afraid of. If I go on like this much longer, I won't need anyone. Sometimes I stay in the flat for days. I don't talk to anyone. I need to be alone. And yet it frightens me.' Memories of what he was describing rose up to remind him. 'When I come out, it's such an effort even to speak.'

She watched, she listened with concern. His heart warmed to her.

He said, 'I can't say I've missed you or I've been lonely. I can't say the right things at all.' There was an uncomfortable pause. 'This is all very difficult.'

She said with the generosity he remembered, 'D'you want to come back?'

He said, honest but unflattering, exposing his need without helping her, 'I want to live with you again before I forget how to live with anyone.'

*

They were having a final drink that neither of them wanted because they could not think what else to do, did not know how to prolong the evening nor how to end it, nor even which alternative they preferred. He looked at his watch.

'If I don't make a move I'll miss the last train.'

'You haven't got the car?' She was surprised.

'I don't drive much these days. I found I was getting very absent-minded and I thought I might have an accident.' He looked apologetic. 'Silly, really.'

'You worry me when you talk like that.'

'Nothing to worry about. I simply take the train.' There was a pause: she ached for the right thing to say. He looked at his watch again as if expecting a miracle. 'Well, I'd better be going.'

She said abruptly, 'Do you really want to come home, Peter?' It was not what she had meant to say and she was sure it was not tactful. But she suddenly had to ask.

Silence.

He said unconvincingly, 'Yes. Yes, I do. I've thought about it a lot. It's just that now I'm here ... it all feels ... unreal.' He paused. She could see him struggling for the right words. 'I think we'll have to take it gradually.'

'Yes?'

'If I came ... just for week-ends at first – would that be all right?'

'Of course.' He was so hesitant. How could she be offended?

'I think it might be easier.' He seemed relieved. 'To begin with.'

'Yes, it will take us time.' Perhaps he was right.

He said gratefully, 'You're being very good.'

Another long silence. She studied him and felt the familiar ache of pity. She said, 'You look tired. Don't go back to town tonight.'

He said, surprising her, 'I'd like to stay.'

Vicky said, long after Gavin thought she was asleep, 'It *was* a good dinner.' She sounded as if she was continuing an argument and determined to have the last word.

'Okay, it was, it was. Now shut up and go to sleep.'

They kissed. He turned over and she curled round him, thinking it was, after all, one of their better days. She even began to doze off. Then Gavin moved. Started to get up. She could not believe it.

'Where are you going?'

'Work.'

'Now?' She hated to sound plaintive but she knew she did. 'It's the best time.'

He pulled on a robe and went out. She lay and watched the light go on in the other room. It showed up her luggage on the floor, still not unpacked.

Cassie said, 'I've put Eve in the boys' room. I hope you'll be comfortable in here.'

'I'm sure I will.'

'I've put the blanket on.'

'There's no need.'

'Just to air the bed.' She drew the curtains, switched on the fire. The spare room. He actually wanted to sleep in the spare room. She wasn't sure if she felt relieved or insulted. 'Will you be warm enough?'

He said awkwardly, 'Cass, you mustn't feel I don't ...'

'I know.'

She saw him looking at the twin beds where Prue and Gavin had slept.

'It will be all right,' he said. 'Just give me time.'

'Yes.' She kissed him on the cheek and he embraced her. She felt foolish. 'Sleep well. Can I get you anything? A drink? Another blanket?' Suddenly she found she was very embarrassed and wanted to keep talking.

'No, no, I'll be fine.'

'Well. I'll say good night then.' But she paused at the door, suddenly curious, even angry. 'What made you pick today?'

'What?'

'To come home.'

Was she hoping for some last-ditch compliment? It didn't work. He said bluntly, 'I think I was suddenly afraid if I didn't do it now, I never would.'

It was always a waste of time making breakfast for Gavin, so why did she continue to do it? Vicky sat drinking her coffee and watched Gavin scurry through the meal so lovingly prepared, leaving most of it. Annoyance made her tactless.

'You won't be back late tonight, will you?'

Promptly as ever, he rose to the challenge. 'I might stay over.'

Her heart thumped painfully. 'Whatever for?'

'I see little enough of Eve as it is.'

'She's not going to sit up all night just because you're there.'

'No, but she's going to wake up early as usual and I'd like to be around when she does.'

'Does she really know who you are?'

'Of course she does.'

She tried to make it sound like a joke. 'Well, who are you?' But he didn't respond; he went on collecting books and papers. More feebly she added, 'Shall I see you in the canteen for lunch?' but she already knew she had lost that round.

On his way through the door he said, 'No, I'm going to the library.'

Cassie stood and watched him. All her resentment had gone: he looked so vulnerable. Then she felt guilty for spying on his sleep. She put down the cup loudly enough to wake him.

Manson stirred. 'Oh ... Cass.'

She said, 'Did you sleep all right?'

'Yes, I think so ... I suppose I must have done. It's odd being in here.'

'I brought you some tea.'

'Thank you.'

They were both awkward.

She said, 'The perfect hostess is supposed to try her spare room every now and then, just to make sure it's comfortable. I can't believe anyone really does.'

He smiled politely, like a stranger. Like a guest. 'Well, I've tried it for you and it's perfectly comfortable.'

Another silence. She said desperately, 'D'you want some breakfast? I'll be finished with Eve in a minute – I could bring you up a tray.'

'I'll just have this.' He sipped his tea. 'You didn't ... mind about last night?'

'No, I think you were right.' She heard herself being brave. 'We ought to take it slowly. I only thought ... it might be comforting to be together.'

'We will be.'

She tried harder. 'I think – I've been lonely without realizing it.'

'Don't worry. It'll be all right.'

Did he mean it? 'Yes, of course.'

'I need time to adjust, that's all. I have to be alone some of the time, you see.'

She said, 'Me too. So there's no problem.'

Sarah paid off her taxi and went up the steps of the doctor's house. The equivalent of Harley Street in Frankfurt, she presumed; it certainly cost enough. She was a little cross: it seemed so easy to renew a prescription. Why did he insist on seeing her? Sheer greed – or was there something to worry about? She rang the bell and waited.

The door opened and the receptionist smiled at her, charming, insincere. Sarah said in her carefully practised German, *'Guten tag, mein name ist Frau Roberts. Ich habe ein verabredung mit Doktor Zimmermann.'*

Of course he did stay to breakfast, and talk, and play with Eve, so that he was late for work and Cassie had to run him to the station. Getting into the car, he said, 'Well, I'll see you at the week-end then,' as if it was settled.

Cassie said, 'Friday or Saturday?'

'I'm not sure. I'll ring you.'

Resentment boiled up. He was taking her for granted already. She said, 'Peter, you will try to be nice to him, won't you?'

Manson appeared to be genuinely startled and dismayed. 'Oh God, will *he* be here?'

'He always is at week-ends. Had you forgotten?' She was shaking.

He said with irritation, as if it were nothing, like changing a dental appointment, 'Can't you get him to call in another time?'

Vicky washed up the breakfast things slowly, day-dreaming,

reviewing the past and rehearsing the future. The phone startled her and she let it ring for some time. She had never answered the phone in Gavin's flat before. But after all, why not? She was living here now, even if her cases weren't unpacked yet.

'Hello?'

Cassie said sharply, 'Is that three four nine one?'

'Yes.'

'I wanted to speak to Gavin.'

Vicky tried to gather her wits. Who was this strange woman? She made her voice light. 'Sorry, you just missed him. Can I give him a message?' She liked the proprietary sound of the words.

There was a pause. Then: 'Would you ask him to ring me ... Cassie?'

Relief. 'Cassie. Oh – you must be his mother-in-law.'

The voice said yes. But it didn't sound comfortable. Vicky felt better and better. 'I'll tell him you rang.' But after she put the phone down it didn't seem important. A trivial message. It could wait.

Cassie sought refuge in the garden, but it failed to soothe her. In fact it made things worse. A fine spring day, plants growing, Eve playing on the rug nearby ... and she was filled with hatred. By afternoon her throat was so constricted with tension she had to keep swallowing, but nothing seemed to ease it.

'Hi.' Gavin's face, cheerful, innocent, appeared over the gate. She said, 'What are you doing here on a Wednesday?'

He came into the garden. 'Was it something I said?'

She turned her back on him. 'Everyone always assumes I'm in.'

'Who's everyone?'

She didn't answer. He picked up Eve and cuddled her. 'Shall I go away and come back?'

Cassie glanced at him. 'Why come back? You've got what you came for.'

He walked up and down with Eve, looking at Cassie. 'Cassandra, what is all this?'

'Didn't you get my message?'

'What message?'

She flung the trowel into the hedge, wishing she could plunge it into him.

He said equably, 'Maybe we should start over.' He sat on a garden chair with Eve in his arms. 'I did call you.'

Cassie kept her back turned. 'When?'

'This morning. You were engaged.'

She said bitterly, 'That's impossible.'

'Well ... I called. Then I just ... came on down.' His tone softened. 'Cassandra. What's happened?'

Cassie turned round. 'Peter. He just turned up, like you. Yesterday. Oh, he came to see her, not me. We talked. He wants to come back.'

The silence seemed much too long. Eventually Gavin said, 'Are you glad?'

She thought about it; she tried to be honest. 'Yes, in a way. I'm sure he *needs* to be here. He was very odd – as if he'd forgotten how to talk. I'd like to help him – if he'll let me.'

'Why shouldn't he?' Gavin seemed unconcerned.

'He was very distant. I couldn't get close to him. He made me feel ... I had to be careful what I said ...'

'How d'you mean?'

She resented feeling that she and Gavin were like two doctors discussing a patient: it was necessary. She said, 'Careful not to upset him. And I was. Very careful. Yet at the same time I was so angry with him for staying away I wanted to punish him. You see, I don't know how to behave. That's why I rang you. I wanted to talk about it.' I needed you, she meant. A reproach.

'Here I am.'

How calm he was. Did he understand at all? She said, 'I want to do the right thing but it's going to make it harder for us ... And he scares me. I'm not sure I can live with him again.'

'You'll have to try, though, won't you.'

Rage flared up. 'Yes, it will suit you very well. Look, she answered the phone.'

'Oh, you're not going to start all that again.' He actually made it sound as if she were in the wrong.

'I'm not starting anything. Is she the one I saw you with before Christmas? The one on the college steps?'

'No.' His sulky look.

'You're certainly getting through them.' It came out more sharply than she intended.

He said sullenly, 'I didn't know two girls in six months was some kind of record.' Then he softened. 'I'm sorry. I didn't want to hurt you. That's the last thing I wanted.'

She was surprised how strong the pain was. 'I've tried so hard not to be jealous. It's so unattractive. I know I've got no right to be possessive about you but I can't help it –'

'It's not a question of rights.' He sounded gentle again.

'I wouldn't mind sharing you – really – I've trained myself – it's having nothing that's so ...' Was she telling the truth?

He seemed to believe her. He put Eve down, went across to Cassie, hugged her. 'I know. I'm sorry.'

'It's so humiliating.' But already it wasn't any more, now they were touching.

'Don't.'

'Can you stay?' She couldn't stop herself asking.

He hesitated. 'No, I better not.'

'Oh.' She pulled away, ashamed. 'My God, I'm behaving badly. I ought to have more sense at my age, oughtn't I?'

Gavin said, 'Don't be bitter. It's nothing to do with that.'

'Is she important? Do you love her?' She lit a cigarette.

'No. I love you. But it's no good with us any more. I've been meaning to tell you but I couldn't. I knew you'd be hurt.'

So much consideration. 'I'd rather you told me. Waiting and hoping and being disappointed is so much worse.'

He said, 'Cassandra, I'm sorry. I meant all I said. But since Prue died ... it's never been the same. You remind me of her, I guess. Your skin smells the same. It's kind of spooky. Like being in bed with a ghost.'

How did one bear so much pain? And she had asked for it. She closed her eyes. What did he mean? Never to make love – ever again?

She said, 'So she still wins.'

'What?'

'She's coming between us.'

He shook his head. 'No. It's just ... you remind me of her so much I can't bear it. After she died I just wanted and wanted her till I thought I'd go crazy.'

Silence. Cassie tried to calm herself. Why was Prue so powerful, even in death? 'Who is the girl?'

'She's nobody. She's okay.'

'Isn't that a little hard on her?' She was so glad to hear it.

'I told her when we started – I don't have any feelings left. It she wants to be around, that's up to her.'

Another victim. 'She must be in love with you.'

He said irritably, 'Stop bugging me, Cassandra, will you? All I know is – she doesn't remind me of Prue.'

Vicky, suddenly brave, was arranging her clothes in Prue's wardrobe and putting Prue's clothes into a large cardboard box. Occasionally sheer envy made her stop and hold a particular dress up against herself in front of the mirror, before she flung it in the box with the others. Her own clothes she hung up very carefully. She hoped they'd be there a long time.

Over dinner Cassie felt collected enough to tell Gavin what had happened. 'When I looked out of the window and saw she'd gone I nearly went out of my mind. When you're not here I have this dreadful feeling something might happen to Eve.'

'Christ – don't.'

She went on swiftly, 'Only I don't think of you then. It's always Prue I imagine having to tell. I actually dream about it.' She wanted him to understand how much these dreams oppressed her. 'I have to tell Prue something's happened to her baby and she always says the same thing: "But Mummy, I trusted you." '

Gavin said, 'Did you tell him all that?'

She sighed. 'I couldn't tell him anything. He was trying so hard to be cheerful, like somebody let out of hospital who thinks they're cured. How could I spoil that?'

'Maybe he'll loosen up later.'

'The thing that really struck me was – he never mentioned Prue at all. He made a huge fuss of Eve and he was ... polite to me and sort of ... conciliatory, but he never said Prue's name once.' She paused. Gavin stopped eating and watched her. 'And the odd thing was – he somehow made me feel I couldn't mention her either.'

Vicky put her empty suitcase on top of the wardrobe and hid the cardboard box beside it. She took her books into the sitting-room and began exchanging them for Prue's books on the shelves of the bookcase. She was content. She felt she had achieved a lot in the last twenty-four hours.

Cassie said, 'Do you really have to go?'
He looked evasive. 'I think maybe I should.'
'Because she's expecting you?'
'No. I told her I might stay over.' Always truthful.
'Well, then. Just to sleep.' She heard herself beginning to plead.
'You'll only get upset.' He looked around for a less emotive subject. 'When's he moving back?'
'At the week-end.'
'Isn't that kinda soon?'
'There's no reason to wait.'
He said abruptly, 'Did you sleep with him?'
'No. We didn't feel ready. But we will.' A sudden wild hope. 'Don't tell me you're jealous.'
He ignored that. 'Is he going to get all heavy about Eve, d'you think?'
'Yes, I think he probably is.'
'Hell. Just when I won't be here.'
'What?'
'I thought maybe I'd skip this week-end.'
'Oh, yes? I see.'
He looked shamefaced. 'It's not that I want to.'
Cassie said, 'Isn't it?'

Vicky, reading in bed, was surprised to hear the front door slam. Gavin came in.
'I thought you were staying there,' she said, hiding her pleasure. She could see he was not in a good mood.
'I only said I might.' He paced about. 'If you're going to answer the phone when I'm out, you might as least give me the message.'
'You weren't around,' she said defensively.
'You knew where I was. It's not far to come.'
'Was it important?'
'Yes, it was.'

31

'I'm sorry. I thought as you were going there anyway . . .'

There was a pause. She was amazed to see him actually look embarrassed.

'Look, about the week-end . . .'

'Oh, *no* . . .'

'I can't help it. He's going to be there.'

'Have they made it up?'

'Something like that.'

'But why does that mean you've got to go? I thought you were trying to avoid each other.'

'Don't you understand anything? He might try to muscle in on Eve. I told you what he was like with Prue.'

She really didn't understand. 'But what can he do with a baby?'

Cassie stood in the spare room watching Eve, envying her sleep. She herself was exhausted but she couldn't imagine not being awake. She felt threatened. So she was not going to be alone any more. But in retrospect the loneliness she had complained of looked like peace. She sensed trouble ahead and she felt too tired to cope with it.

With a sudden movement she pulled the sheets off Manson's bed.

It had all gone wrong. He had found out and flown into one of his rages. Now he was systematically removing her clothes from the wardrobe and throwing them on the floor. She watched helplessly, trying not to panic.

He said savagely, 'If it's closet space you wanted, you should have stayed at home.'

She tried to be brave. 'Gavin, I can't live out of a suitcase indefinitely.'

'Who says you're going to be here indefinitely? Now put her things back.'

'Why? She's not going to wear them again.' She could see he wanted to hit her, maybe even kill her, but she had to take the ultimate risk. She had been longing to say the forbidden words and now she did. 'Gavin, she's dead.'

32

He said slowly, meaning it, 'Why aren't *you* dead instead of her?'

It was too much. He had defeated her. She got out of bed, crying, and began re-arranging Prue's clothes in the wardrobe.

*

Saturday morning in Frankfurt. Sarah usually looked forward to it (late breakfast and lazy shopping) but today it was all spoilt. She had things on her mind and Geoff was determined to nag her.

'What was the matter with you last night?'

'I'm sorry.' She knew she was in the wrong.

'You hardly said a word and you didn't even seem to be listening half the time –' He was really angry.

'Yes, I know.'

'You *knew* it was important. I need that man's money. I *told* you.'

'I don't suppose his decision depends on my charm – or my conversation. You're either a good risk or you're not.'

'Look, I've got to make a success of this job. My father really trusts me for the first time.'

'You want to impress him.' She envied him for having such a father, so unlike her own.

'What's wrong with that?'

'I'm sorry I let you down.'

'For God's sake stop apologizing, and tell me what's wrong. You stupid cow, I'm worried about you.'

He sounded really concerned: she was touched.

'I went to the doctor yesterday. I ran out of pills.'

'And?'

'And he wouldn't prescribe any more.' The sense of panic she had felt in the surgery was still with her.

'Why not?'

'He says I've got to come off it for six months. But I feel perfectly fine.'

'He must know what he's talking about.'

Anxiety made her furious. 'Why? I bet if I shopped around I could find another doctor to say it's all right. He's just being old-fashioned. He wants my system to get back to normal, he says. But the Pill *is* normal for me, I told him. I've been on it since I was seventeen.' The good old days, she thought.

Geoff said, 'Maybe you need a rest.'

'I'm going to get a second opinion.'

'No. We're not taking any risks with your health.'

'*We?*' She was outraged.

'Is that all you were depressed about?'

'Isn't that enough*?*'

'Well, it's annoying but there's other methods you can use.'

'Not as safe as the Pill.' Why didn't he understand?

'Very nearly.'

She said sharply, 'You're either pregnant or you're not.'

'Would it matter so much if you were? We're going to have kids sooner or later; why not sooner? We can afford it.'

She was startled. 'I didn't know you wanted children. You never said.'

'No, I just ... took it for granted, I suppose. Are you saying you don't want them?'

'I don't know. Certainly not yet.'

'Weren't you taking a lot for granted too?'

Sarah panicked. Suddenly they were having a serious talk and it wasn't going well.

'When we got married you promised me nothing would change. We'd go on just the same, just as if we weren't married.'

He said lightly, 'I had to say something. You were so anti-marriage.'

'Then you were lying? It was just a trick, to get me to marry you.'

'No.'

'But you didn't mean it.'

'I did at the time. I just wanted us to be married. I didn't think very far ahead. But you do feel different after a while – don't you?' He looked desperate, cornered.

'Do you?'

'I can't help it – it's *not* the same as living together – of course I want children eventually – you're my wife.'

'That doesn't mean you own me.'

'No, of course not.'

'That's how it sounds – and I don't like it. That's not my idea of marriage.' She was appalled at what they had uncovered.

He looked at his watch. 'Christ ! It's eleven o'clock.'

Manson was still living in the flat he had rented for Sarah. In the beginning he had meant to move out, to find somewhere smaller and cheaper, but inertia had overtaken him. It was so much easier to stay there. He had made no changes, merely covered the wall behind the bed with photographs of Prue at all ages. They might have startled a visitor, but he had no visitors. To him, the pictures were part of his normal surroundings, like statues in a shrine, and he slept peacefully beneath them. Now he selected his favourite to put in his suitcase before he picked up the phone.

Cassie answered at once. 'Hullo?'

He said, 'Hullo, Cass.'

Her tone changed at once to anxiety. Was that how he affected her now?

'What's happened?'

'Nothing. I'm on my way. How are you?'

'Fine.'

'Good.' What else could he say to her? 'I'll be on the five o'clock.'

'Shall I meet you?'

'No, I'll get a cab.' He hesitated. 'How's Eve?'

'Bored – she's yelling her head off in the garden.'

'Hadn't you better go to her?'

Cassie said smugly, 'I know a bored sound when I hear one.'

He persisted. 'I'll hang on.'

'All right.' She sounded amused, annoyed. 'Just to please you.' She put down the phone.

In the garden Eve was lying in her pram, crying. Cassie went up to her and rocked the pram.

'Hey – what's all this?' she said. 'You're upsetting your grand-father. And he's coming to see you today, so you'll have plenty of attention later on. You'll like that, won't you?'

The yelling went on. Cassie gave in and picked up Eve, who was instantly quiet.

'All right,' Cassie said, 'you win.' She cuddled the baby. 'And who do you remind me of, then? Mm?'

She carried Eve into the house. When she picked up the phone again Manson said instantly, 'Is she all right?'

'She's perfectly fine. I've got her right here. She's just playing me up and you're encouraging her. Look, I'll have to go.' She felt stronger with the child in her arms.

'I'll see you later then.'

'Yes.'

'Oh – Cass?'

'Yes?'

'Is *he* going to be there?'

Instant deflation.

'No. Not this week-end.'

'You put him off.'

The ambiguity hurt.

'Yes.'

As Gavin made a move, Vicky clung to him. 'Don't get up yet.' She was still peaceful and drowsy after making love.

'I'll miss the train.'

'You can catch the next one. It's the only place we're really happy.'

'The train?'

She kicked him lovingly. 'Bed. This week-end's going to be murder, isn't it?'

'Probably. What's left of it.'

'Well, don't let him bully you. Tell him you can pay double the rent now, that ought to shut him up.'

He didn't move. His reluctance to go pleased her so much, she made a quick decision to gamble on their future together.

'Course, there's only one solution really, isn't there, now he's back. We'll have to have the baby here.'

He said, amazed, 'But you don't want that.'

'I never said I didn't want to. I just don't know anything about babies. I feel stupid with them.'

'She's a very good baby.' His voice was full of pride.

'Well – you'd have to tell me what to do. I haven't a clue about feeding them or anything.'

36

'Oh, no, no, I'll do all that.'

He was delighted with her, just as she had hoped he would be.

'All right, you tell them we'll have her at week-ends. Then you won't have to go there any more.'

Sarah, seated outside the café in Frankfurt, almost enjoyed working herself up into a rage. She felt so much in the right. By the time Geoff came back she was seething with anger and self-justification.

'It just isn't good enough,' she said instantly. 'You can't run away to the office every time we start talking properly.'

'No.' He sat down opposite her.

'All right, I know you had to go there today, even though it is Saturday – but we've got to talk about this, you can't just avoid it, it's important.' Getting no response, she stopped. 'You're not listening.'

'What?' He sounded dazed and she was suddenly anxious. 'Are you all right?'

Geoff said, 'There was a message. My father's had a heart attack.'

On the aircraft, remembering his fear, she held his hand. But he didn't seem to notice.

Cassie watched the taxi arrive. She was on her way to the door when the phone rang. Pips. She felt alerted to some emergency. Then Gavin's voice, alarmed.

'Cassandra. Is it okay if I come after all?'

'What? But he's just arriving. I told him you weren't coming.'

The door bell rang. She ignored it, but it distracted her all the same.

Gavin said, 'I know, I'm sorry. But I think I ought to be there. Okay?'

She knew it wasn't okay at all and she ought to refuse, but in some way she was relieved.

'All right,' she said, and hung up. She got to the door just as Manson had found his key.

'Hullo,' he said.

'Hullo, Peter.'

He indicated the key in his hand. 'I wasn't sure if I should use this or not.'

Cassie said, 'I'm sorry. I was on the phone. Come and have a drink.'

He came in and put down his suitcase. He said predictably, 'Where's Eve?'

'I've just fed her and she's asleep, I hope. Sherry?'

'Please.' He looked around, sat down. He seemed pleased with himself. 'Well, this really feels like a homecoming.'

Cassie said, 'Good.'

'It didn't the other day, I was actually nervous. Wasn't that absurd?' She gave him his drink. 'Thanks.'

'Welcome home.'

They drank. He said warmly, 'Oh, Cass, this feels good. I can really relax. I don't know when last I did that. Just you and me and the baby for a whole week-end.'

'Peter.' She felt apprehensive and there was a perverse satisfaction in puncturing his mood of wellbeing. She was shocked at herself.

'Mm?'

'I'm sorry, I've got to tell you now, we've only got an hour. Gavin's coming.'

'You said he wasn't.'

'He changed his mind.'

When Geoff and Sarah got out of the taxi, Freddy was waiting for them. He and Geoff shook hands and then they embraced.

'Good to see you, Geoff.'

'Freddy.'

Sarah watched them, detached and full of pity. Freddy turned to her.

'Sarah.'

She said, 'I'm so sorry.'

Freddy kissed her on the cheek. He seemed nervous: the strain of it all, no doubt; coping alone. She had to remind herself how young he was.

'Come in,' he said. 'Sorry I couldn't meet you. I only just got back from the undertaker's.'

Sarah looked at the house in horror. She had forgotten what coming home meant.

'All set for Monday. Come and have a drink. I'm sure you need one. I've got to pop out for an hour, there are one or two problems at the factory ...'

They went in. The front door shut heavily behind them.

In the end there was nothing else for it. She had to bring Eve downstairs.

'I don't know why she's so wide awake,' she said apologetically.

Manson took Eve from her. 'She doesn't want to miss anything – do you, my lovely?'

He cuddled the baby. Cassie watched resentfully, blaming herself for being resentful.

'Another drink?' she asked.

'Thanks.' She poured the drinks. He went on playing with Eve. He said abruptly, 'We're bringing out a book about changing direction in middle age – new jobs, new hopes. People who sell up and sail round the world or start a totally new career when other people are thinking of retirement. That kind of thing.'

'Oh yes? Should be popular.' She wasn't really listening.

'It could apply to us.'

'How d'you mean?'

'Well ... there's nothing to keep us here. This house is too big, it's a lot of work for you. The boys could come to us wherever we were. We could live anywhere.'

She was shocked. 'You want us to move?'

'Why not?'

'What about the business?'

'I think Rupert would buy me out. In fact, I'm damn sure he would.'

'But what would you do for a living?'

'Something else. That's the whole point. If we sold the house and the business, we'd be free.'

'Free to do what?'

'Anything we like. We could ... live in Scotland. Try our hands at farming. Remember on our honeymoon you said you'd like to live there? Or Cambridge. We could go back there. Open a book-shop. Anything at all.'

'Are you serious?' She studied him.

'Don't you like the idea?'

'I don't know. Have you been thinking about it for long?'

He said cheerfully, 'No, it's only just occurred to me.'

And at that moment Gavin arrived.

'Hi, Cassandra.'

'Hullo, Gavin.'

He came into the sitting-room, looked at Manson.

'Hullo, sir.'

Manson looked back at him. Six months since they met. He didn't speak.

They were having drinks on the terrace. Already Sarah felt oppressed, imprisoned.

'Poor Freddy. He's had the worst of it.'

'Yes.' She stared at the house, the garden. Heavy, ornate, inhospitable, all of it. Not for her.

'How long do we have to stay here?' Geoff looked puzzled. 'I mean after the funeral. How soon can we go back to the flat?'

He said, as if she was stupid not to know, 'This is our home now.'

While they were eating, Gavin said, 'What do you think of your granddaughter, sir?'

'She's wonderful.'

'Yeah, she is pretty good, isn't she?'

They had quickly exhausted the only topic on which they agreed. Cassie tried to dream up an innocent diversion but she wasn't quick enough.

Manson said, 'And what are you doing with yourself these days?'

'I'm still at college, sir.'

'Still there, are you? My word, I'd forgotten how long it can last.'

'One more year, sir.'

The hatred between them frightened her.

'You mean after this year?'

'One term and one year.'

'And what will you be then?'

'A Ph.D., sir. All being well.'

'Won't that be nice? You might actually start earning money.'

'I can pay you extra rent right now.'

'Oh really? Your grant been increased, has it?'

'I've – got a part-time job.'

'Won't that interfere with your studies?'

She said sharply, 'If you two would stop bickering and finish eating, I could clear the table.'

In another room Eve cried. Manson sprang to his feet.

'I'll go.' Gavin got up.

She wanted to scream. She said quietly, 'Why don't you both carry on eating and I'll go. When I think it's necessary. After all, that's what I'm here for.'

They both sat down. The crying went on. Cassie waited. 'It's not good for her to get her own way all the time.'

They tried to finish eating but they couldn't. She took away the plates and went out. After a moment Manson said, 'My wife tells me you come here every week-end.'

'Yes.'

'That's very dutiful of you.'

'It's a pleasure, not a duty, sir.'

Manson said smoothly, 'Will you be able to manage it when we go to live in Scotland?' Gavin's startled look was all the reward he wanted. 'Well, there's nothing to keep us here, so we thought we might get right away ... from it all ...'

Gavin said, 'You can't take Eve to Scotland.'

'I thought you needed my wife to look after her while you finished your . . . Ph.D.'

'I do.' He was barely audible.

'Then Eve's place is with my wife and my wife's place is with me – wherever I choose to live. You would of course be welcome to visit us whenever you could afford the fare.'

The sheer pleasure of it all made him feel dizzy.

'She's fine,' said Cassie, returning. 'She was just trying it on. Now, who's for pudding?'

41

She saw their faces, heard the silence.

Gavin said, 'Cassandra, you didn't tell me you were moving house.'

She looked from him to Manson.

'I've just been telling him our plans.' Manson doing his best to look innocent. She could see Gavin gathering himself for the counter-attack.

'It's kinda funny. I've been making plans too. That's what I came down to tell you. I'm ready to have Eve for week-ends now.'

She was shocked; she could not speak.

'How will you manage that all by yourself?' Manson asked, disbelieving.

Gavin said, 'I've made arrangements.'

Alone with Freddy on the terrace, Sarah said, 'Have they really all gone? Are you sure I shouldn't be *doing* something?'

'I think Geoff's seeing the last ones off now. Tired?'

'Exhausted.' She flopped in a chair. It was her first funeral and had set up all kinds of agitation she did not understand. She wanted to bathe and change her clothes.

'You've done very well,' said Freddy sympathetically.

'I'd no idea there'd be so many people.' She didn't know how to describe what she felt.

'Well ...' He was proud of his father's status, the numerous mourners.

'All clear,' said Geoff, returning. 'Thank God that's over.' He sat down. Sarah got up and poured him a drink. He said to Freddy, 'It's up to us now.'

Freddy said, 'Yes. I'm assuming you want me to take over in Frankfurt.'

'I'm counting on you. I'll have my hands full here.'

'When I think how the old man slaved away for years and now – just when he could afford to ease up a bit and enjoy life ...'

'Yes.'

They were both totally absorbed in grief and plans, ignoring Sarah. She could hardly believe it. They even turned their backs on her.

'What about the flat?' Freddy asked.

'In Frankfurt? You may as well take that over too. If you like it.'

Sarah said, 'What about our things?'

'I could pack them up for you and have them sent on. Save you a trip. Unless you specially want to go over.' Helpful Freddy. Her whole life being taken over, just like that.

The telephone rang.

'Oh, God,' Geoff said, 'not again. I'll go.' He went into the house.

Sarah said slowly, 'I don't think I've really taken it in yet – how different everything's going to be.'

'No, it's been a big shock for us all.'

What could they talk about to make this panic feeling go away?

'D'you know the first thing Barbara said to me?'

'Barbara?'

'My sister.'

'Oh yes, of course.'

'"Isn't it lucky black suits you?" How's that for a bloody insensitive tactless remark at a funeral? Typical Barbara, though.'

'I didn't see much of her.'

'No. She was too busy eating and drinking as much as she could. And telling me how lucky I am to have a big house and lots of money and what a good thing I came to my senses and got married – as if I didn't have any feelings.'

'I take it you don't get on.'

Help me, Barbara, she thought. Hang on to me. You're part of my past, you're real. Don't let me slip into their world without leaving a trace, like something disappearing under water.

She said, 'We never have. But there's a sort of gruesome fascination that makes us keep in touch. That's why I've always envied you and Geoff getting on so well.'

'Anyone'd get on with Geoff, he's so easy-going. God, I was so relieved when you two got married. If you'd seen some of the people he went around with in the old days ...'

Now what was coming? 'That's what Barbara says about me.'

'Oh – some of them really took him for a ride.'

'Yes.'

'Well, you know ... He needs someone to *lean* on – the right

43

sort of person. Dad often said so. He really liked you. Now this has happened – it's going to make all the difference to Geoff, being married to you.'

So the old man she'd hardly known had given his seal of approval too. She felt weighed down with responsibility.

'I'm not sure about that. When you two get together you seem pretty self-sufficient to me.'

'Don't you believe it. That's just shorthand. Anyway, if Geoff is more confident, it's all due to you.'

'I don't see why.'

'It's obvious – isn't it? Having someone like you to depend on, make a home for him . . . Just knowing you're there.'

Panic. 'That makes me sound awfully passive. As if I haven't got a life of my own.'

'How d'you mean?'

'Don't I have any identity at all?'

'You're Geoff's wife.'

'But I'm me as well.'

He stared at her with utter incomprehension. Geoff came out of the house. He looked weary.

'That bastard Samuels after his pound of flesh, of course. Today of all days, he has to rake up the past.'

She had not meant to do it. Until the day of the funeral it had not entered her head. But after that it seemed inevitable. She did not even bother to analyse her reasons.

Manson, crossing the road to the park, suddenly saw her on the bench where she had been sitting, knowing it was only a matter of time. His surprise made her smile as she stood up to greet him.

2

TENSIONS

VICKY watched Gavin make a shopping list for Eve. It seemed to go on for ever.

'Twelve tins baby food, six packets of milk formula, two dozen disposable diapers. I wonder if that'll be enough.'

'I've no idea.' As the week-end came nearer, she grew more apprehensive. He had already stopped appreciating what a huge gesture she had made.

'Maybe I'd better get three dozen of everything.'

'Gavin! For a week-end?'

'There are all the other week-ends to look forward to. And it's cheaper to buy in bulk.' He scribbled enthusiastically. 'Baby powder, vaseline, bottles, teats and a comforter.'

'Whatever's that?'

'Dummy to you.'

Visions of babies in prams, sucking, dribbling, stuffed with rubber.

'Oh, she *doesn't* have one of those, does she?'

'Why not? She's got to have oral satisfaction – it's like sex to her.'

'Maybe, I should get one.'

He ignored that. 'I wonder if I've forgotten anything.'

'Doesn't sound like it,' she said bitterly.

'Yeah – stuff to sterilize the bottles. And zinc ointment, in case she gets a rash.'

She couldn't understand the fuss. 'Won't your mother-in-law bring all that stuff?'

'She's done enough. I told her I could cope and I'm not going to ask any more favours.'

'It's going to cost a fortune.'

'Yeah, babies are expensive.'

He sounded amused, tolerant. She tried to laugh. 'Just as well it's only two days.'

'Didn't I tell you? Cassandra's going to bring her on Friday afternoon. Isn't that great? And *he*'ll pick her up on Monday.'

Silence. He avoided her eyes.

'That's a long week-end,' she said accusingly.

'Yeah, we're in luck.'

Lunch in the restaurant where they used to meet. Everything looked exactly the same, making Sarah feel she had stepped back into last year. Frankfurt was a dream, no more.

Manson said, 'Well ... here's to married life.'

'Cheers!'

They sipped their drinks. Sarah looked round. 'It hasn't changed a bit,' she said.

'Neither have you.'

'It's nice to be back.'

They stared at each other greedily.

'That's a very large diamond.'

'Yes. It is rather ostentatious.'

'Diamonds ought to be.' He smiled approvingly.

'It was Geoff's choice, not mine. It belonged to his mother. We had it re-set.'

'It's beautiful.'

'He spoils me, I'm afraid.'

'Don't you deserve it?'

'You'll have to ask him.'

What was the matter with her? Why did she want to flirt and show off? Couldn't she risk being real?

'You're looking well,' she said, wishing it were true. She was worried about him. Had he been ill?

'Yes, I'm fine.'

'I thought about you a lot.'

'Oh, I went through a bad patch for a few months but now I'm home ... well, it makes all the difference.'

'Yes, of course.'

So now they were both pretending.

'I stayed in the flat for a while.'

'Oh yes?'

'In fact I've still got it.'

'That's nice.' She liked to think of him there.

'Where are you living?'

'Hampstead. We've inherited the family house. It's much too big for us – and there's a huge garden, and a swimming-pool – just like the movies.'

'It sounds delightful.'

'I only wish we hadn't got it . . . through Geoff's father dying.'

Their first course arrived.

She went on, 'It was such a shock. He was really fond of his father.'

Manson said, 'Yes, it must have been terrible for you.'

They began to eat.

'If that hadn't happened,' Sarah said thoughtfully, 'we'd still be in Frankfurt.'

'How was Frankfurt?'

'Lovely. I gave lots of dinner parties and actually learnt some German.'

'You always said you wanted to travel.'

'Yes.' She hesitated. 'Geoff'll have to go back from time to time, of course.'

'Won't you go with him?'

'Sometimes. If it's convenient.'

'I suppose you have a lot to do at home.'

'I certainly want to make a few changes in the house. And we'll have to entertain quite often.'

'I expect you're very good at that.'

'It's hard work – but I enjoy it.' They were still fencing and she didn't know how to break the pattern. 'How are things at the office?'

'Running smoothly.'

'Have you got a good secretary?'

'Yes, I have.' He paused, teasing her. 'Monica. She came back.'

'Oh !'

'Her marriage broke up.'

'I'm sorry – it's lucky for you though. Is Rupert still with you?' Strange how idyllic it all looked from a distance, how fond she felt of them all.

'Oh yes, I couldn't do without him. He practically runs the place now.'

'It's funny to think of it all going on without me.' She felt lost, in exile.

'It's not the same, of course.'

She smiled. 'It feels very strange not to have a job.'

He said, 'Count yourself lucky. I'm thinking of giving the whole thing up. Retiring early. Moving house.'

'Not seriously?'

'Oh yes, quite seriously. The only snag is, I'm having a bit of trouble persuading my wife.' He paused. This was important. 'Life's so short. We don't make the most of it, fretting about work and things that don't matter.'

'No, that's true. But it's not always easy to tell what's important ... till it's too late.'

'We can always learn from our mistakes, don't you think?'

'If we get the chance.'

She felt they were both on the verge of something vital but the waiter, discreetly refilling their glasses, broke the mood. She remembered there was something she had forgotten to ask.

'How's the baby?'

'Extremely beautiful and growing fast.'

'Do you see a lot of her?'

'Oh yes, she lives with us. He's quite incapable of looking after her but he visits her now and then.'

'That must keep your wife very busy.'

'Yes, she's got her hands full. And the boys are due back any minute.'

They gazed at each other.

'Just like old times,' she said.

'Not quite.'

'No.'

Cassie wheeled Eve into the garden and settled her down. How nice, she thought, to be a baby and have nothing to do but eat, sleep and be cuddled. And what a poor preparation for adult life.

Finishing her main course, Sarah found Manson watching her indulgently.

'That was good,' she said.

'I'm glad to see you haven't lost your appetite.'

'No, I certainly haven't.'

They both looked at her empty plate.

Manson said, 'If you're ever at a loose end ... when your husband's on one of his trips ... I stay up in town part of the week and I'd be delighted to give you dinner.'

'I'd like that.'

'Can I ring you at home?'

She hesitated. 'Yes, or perhaps I could ring you at the office.'

'Of course.'

'That might be simpler.'

They smiled at each other. Conspirators again.

Cassie didn't want to get up. She had been apprehensive about their first night together but it had gone better than she dared hope. Just like the early days, she remembered, when mornings had always been good.

'We'll have to get up soon,' she said reluctantly.

'She hasn't made a sound yet.'

'We've got to meet the boys.'

'I know.'

She teased him. 'Is that why you're so cheerful?'

'I'm just cheerful.'

'I noticed.' All her confidence was returning.

'Do I have to have a reason?'

'No.' They kissed.

'You're cheerful too. Do you have a reason?'

'Yes, I do. Everything's getting back to normal.'

Very alone in his head, he thought of Sarah, who had made it all possible.

The twins saw them first. They waved and raced to the barrier.

'Dad, Dad,' they shouted, hurling themselves at Manson. 'Dad, you're back.'

'Yes, I'm back.' Manson lifted them, hugged them.

'Why didn't you come back before?'

'Never mind,' Cassie said. 'He's here now.'

'Hullo, Mum.' Belatedly, they hugged her too.

'Dad, are you better?'

'Yes, I'm fine.'

'Honestly?'

Together again they walked out of the station like an ordinary family. Andrew looked at the carry-cot.

'Why've you brought *her*?' he asked Cassie.

'We're taking her to stay with Gavin.'

'Oh, good.'

David looked anxious. 'Does that mean we won't see her?'

'No, she'll be back on Monday.'

'That's all right then.'

The door slammed. Vicky looked up from making the bed and Gavin came in with a heap of scrap metal in his arms.

'Look what I got for a fiver,' he said triumphantly.

'Whatever's that?'

'A cot. What does it look like?'

'That wasn't on the list.'

'Well, it was obvious.' He started trying to assemble it. 'She's got to have somewhere to sleep.'

'Won't your mother-in-law bring her in something?'

'Yeah, a carry-cot. She can't sleep in that.'

'Why ever not, if she can travel in it?'

'How would you like to sleep in a bus? Look, give me a hand with this, can't you? It's all over the place.'

'Okay.' She examined it more closely. 'It looks awfully tatty. Will it be all right?'

'It only needs a coat of paint. You've no idea what they cost new.'

They struggled to put it up. One end fell on Vicky's fingers.

'Christ.'

'Watch out.'

'Thanks a lot.'

'Look – if you can just hang on to that bit – this bit slots in. The main thing is not to let go.'

'So I noticed.' Was this what her life was going to be like from now on?

The boys, still excited, bounced around in Manson's car.

'Dad, can we play cricket and go swimming?'

'I expect so.'

'Will you come with us? Oh, go on, promise.'

'Course I will.'

How could he refuse? Everything was going to be all right.

The cot was finally assembled to look like a cot. They both slumped over it, saying in unison, 'There. Not so difficult, was it?'

'My God, I'd no idea they were so complicated.'

They laughed. It was a new, easy feeling of closeness. She was surprised.

'Come here.' He held out his arms.

'Oh, what a mess. I'm useless.' She rushed to him.

'You're not doing so badly.' He kissed her. 'Now – give me a hand with the shopping. It's all over the kitchen.'

'Hadn't we better move this first?'

'Move it?' He looked at her blankly.

'The cot.'

'Why?'

'Well, we can't leave it here. The sooner we get it in the living-room, the better.'

There was a terrible silence. She said, 'That *is* where it is going, isn't it?'

'No.'

'Oh Gavin, not in here.' The awful truth.

'Why not?'

'Not in our bedroom.'

'There's nowhere else.'

'There's the living-room.'

'Too far away.'

'It's only next door.'

'I know, I know. Look, this is only temporary, but she's bound to be upset, it's a big upheaval for her, if she wakes up and she's all alone, she'll be scared.'

She tried to be logical. 'Do you mean to tell me your mother-in-law has her in her bedroom?'

'No, but she's been there all her life. This is different.'

'Gavin, you really should have told me.'

'Why? Would it have made a difference?'

The doorbell rang.

'Oh Christ, not yet!'

She went to the window, reported unhappily, 'There's a car outside – and kids and a man – it must be them.'

'Oh God, they're early.'

'You'd better let them in, hadn't you?'

He opened the door and there was Cassie with Eve in her carry-cot, plus a holdall of essentials.

'Hi, Cassandra.'

'Hullo, Gavin.'

They were both embarrassed.

'This is very good of you.'

'Not at all. Can you just take her? I don't want to hang about.'

Suddenly Vicky appeared beside him. 'Oh, Mrs Manson, do please come in. I'm Vicky.' She held out her hand.

He could see Cassie assessing her rival.

'Thank you, Vicky. I've brought a few things I thought you might need.'

'That's very kind of you.'

Gavin said, 'I think we've got everything.'

Silence. They all looked at each other.

Cassie said, 'Well, here you are.' She put the holdall down and handed the carry-cot to Gavin.

'Hi, beautiful.' He cuddled Eve, glad of the distraction.

Vicky said gushingly, 'Would you like some tea?'

'No, thank you.'

'Or a drink?'

'No, really.' Cassie was icily polite.

'Are those your boys in the car?'

'Yes.'

'Wouldn't they like some orange squash or something?'

'No, I don't think so.'

'I meant if you and your husband would like to come up . . . ?'

'I think we'd all rather get home, if you don't mind. We've got a long drive.'

Gavin was desperate to put an end to the meeting. 'Okay, Cassandra, I'll see you on Monday.'

He was ashamed of the pain he had caused her: he admired her dignity, her courage.

'No, you'll see Peter,' she said.

'Of course, that's what I meant.'

'Yes, same thing, really, isn't it?'

He watched her leave.

Vicky sensed something was wrong but she couldn't identify it. Gavin sat on the sofa with Eve and she stared at them both thoughtfully.

'Isn't she beautiful?' Gavin said, looking at the baby.

'She's ... very nice.' What else could she say?

'Oh, come on. I've heard of British understatement but that's ridiculous.'

'I can't help it. Babies all look alike to me. Perhaps when I get to know her ...' Bald and cheerful, the baby stared at her blankly.

'Well. I know you're beautiful,' Gavin said to Eve, 'and you know you're beautiful and that's all that matters, isn't it?'

'Gavin.' She had to ask him.

'Uh-huh?'

'I didn't say anything to upset your mother-in-law, did I?'

'No. What d'you mean?'

Was he really listening?

'Only that she seemed a bit ... offhand.'

'She's probably fed up coping with his moods. He's a surly bastard at the best of times and he won't have liked handing Eve over one bit.' He addressed the baby. 'But you'd rather be here, wouldn't you, my beautiful?'

Vicky still couldn't shake off her disquiet.

'She was quite attractive.'

'Mm?'

'Your mother-in-law. I was surprised. I mean she must be over forty.'

'I guess so. I never gave it much thought.' His tone was suddenly brisk.

'She looks younger than my mother. I mean when you say mother-in-law ... you picture a sort of granny. Especially with a baby around.'

He got up. 'Yeah, well, talking of babies, I better get this one fed. It's nearly time.'

'Can't I do it?' She badly wanted to help.

'No, you don't know what to do.'

'I can learn. Doesn't it say on the packet?'

'Yeah, but ... oh, it'll be quicker if I do it. And she yells if she has to wait. Don't you? You've got a very loud voice.'

The baby laughed at him. He put her down on the sofa, said to Vicky, 'You keep her amused while I'm gone. It's about time you two got acquainted.'

Alone with Eve for the first time, Vicky approached her warily, sat beside her and tickled her with a finger as she had seen other people do. Nothing happened. Eve didn't seem to mind. Encouraged, Vicky picked her up. She found her heavier and more solid than she had expected, tried to settle her and hold her properly, made soothing sounds, felt a fool. The baby stared at her for a long moment, sensed her uncertainty, and decided to cry.

*

When the crying stopped it was awe-inspiring. They lay side by side in the dark, listening to the silence.

'I can't believe it.'

'Ssh.'

'She's actually stopped. God, I'd forgotten how beautiful silence is.'

'Don't exaggerate. She hasn't been that bad.'

They were both whispering.

'Come off it. She's aiming at the title. The next Olympic Games, she'll get a gold medal.'

'It's bound to take her a while to settle down.'

'Like all week-end?'

'She can't help it. She's in unfamiliar surroundings. Next week-end will be better.'

'I know. It's all right.' She cuddled up and began stroking him. He didn't respond.

'I really am tired.'

'You've been tired ever since she came.'

As if on cue, Eve started crying again.

'Oh, God,' Vicky said.

'It's okay, I'll see to her.' He seemed eager to get out of bed.

'Gavin – ' She held him back.

'What?'

'Maybe – don't you think perhaps if you didn't keep jumping up every time she cries – she might give up sooner?'

'She may need something.'

'But don't the books say it's bad for them to be picked up every time they cry?'

'What have books got to do with it?' He put on the light and got up, took Eve in his arms. 'No wonder she was crying. She's soaking wet. You see? There's always a reason.'

To Vicky's amazement and horror he began changing the baby's nappy.

'Oh, you're not going to do that in here ...'

'Why not?'

'Well ...' If he didn't know, how could she tell him?

'Okay.'

He didn't sound pleased but at least he took Eve into the bathroom. Vicky looked at the clock and sighed. She tried to think what she could say that Gavin would find reasonable and persuasive.

He came back, saying pointedly to Eve as he put her back in the cot, 'Now you go to sleep or you won't be popular.'

He got into bed, switched off the light, turned his back on Vicky.

'Gavin.' She had to try.

'What now?'

'Has it occurred to you that maybe *we're* disturbing her. If she wasn't in here with us she might not wake up so much. I know what you said about unfamiliar surroundings but after all she's *used* to a room of her own. It's having *us* here that's unfamiliar.'

She waited apprehensively, but he didn't answer. Presently Eve started crying again.

Monday afternoon. The week-end seemed like a lifetime of broken nights. Numb with fatigue, alone with Eve, Vicky poured the feed into the bottle. A saucepan of warm water was waiting to heat the bottle, but the teat kept slipping; she couldn't get it on. In the next room Eve screamed: hard persistent screams of rage and hunger.

Vicky shouted, 'All right, all right. I'm doing the best I can.'

The doorbell rang. Startled, she let the bottle slip. It fell on the floor and spilled. She began to cry with rage. Eve screamed louder than ever. The door-bell rang again.

Manson could hear the screams from the doorstep: he was alarmed. A tearful, dishelleved young woman with long red curly hair opened the door.

'Oh. Hullo.'

He said, 'I've ... come to collect my granddaughter. I'm Peter Manson. I'm afraid I'm a bit early.' They both listened to the yells. 'Is she all right?'

The young woman said, 'She's hungry – I was just doing her bottle and I dropped it – oh, please come in.' She seemed desperate.

'Well, I'd rather just ... all right.' He had been hoping to go straight home, but how could he refuse?

She seized his hand. 'I'm Vicky Lewis. It's nice to meet you.' And led him into the flat. Prue's flat. He was speechless with memories. All he had wanted to avoid – and longed for – was here.

Vicky said, 'I'm sorry she's not ready for you. If you could just wait while I feed her ...'

She showed him into the living-room. Eve in her carry-cot was still yelling. Her things were all over the place and the room was a mess. Manson picked her up and she stopped crying instantly.

Vicky said, 'Oh – it's like magic. She'll stop for you and Gavin – but she won't stop for me. I tried.'

He felt suddenly in command of the situation. 'Let's see about that feed.'

In the kitchen he saw at once the chaos she was in. He said,

56

'You make the bottle and I'll hold her. It's easier if she can see you – keeps her mind off her tummy. Leave her alone and she cries out of sheer boredom.'

Vicky was impressed. 'Yes, of course.'

'Have you been here long?' Her admiration relaxed him.

'Only a few weeks. I hope you don't mind. And I don't know a thing about babies.'

He wanted to be kind. 'She'll get used to you.'

Suddenly, without malice, she dealt him a death-blow. 'Mr Manson – I was awfully sorry about Prue.'

Geoff was packing. Furious, silent, sulky. Sarah didn't know how to deal with this mood and she longed for him to be gone.

'I thought you liked Frankfurt,' he said reproachfully.

'Darling. It's only for a couple of nights and I've got so much to do. 'She heard in her own voice the wheedling note she despised.

'You only call me darling when you're saying no – like when you're too tired to make love.'

'That isn't very often,' she said defensively.

'Often enough. And why have you got so much to do? There's a daily help. There's a gardener. What do you do all day?'

'I run your house.'

'You cook dinner.' They were both shouting. 'I'm sorry.'

'It's all right.'

'It's just ...'

'I know.'

She hugged him. He kissed her. Guilt, remorse, resentment. She said, 'Ring me as soon as you get there. If I'm not in, I'm either with Barbara putting my feet up, or somewhere buying curtain material.'

'Don't make too many changes.'

'Why not?'

'I like it the way it is.'

Cassie watched from the kitchen window. Manson was taking pictures of Eve and the twins were playing nearby. She felt pleased, yet strangely excluded. He came in, ebullient, unfamiliar.

'I think I got some good ones. She's very photogenic. What time's supper? Only I promised the boys I'd have a game with them. They drew the line at having their pictures taken.'

She said, 'You've got half an hour. Then I must put her to bed.'

'Fine.'

She said sharply, 'Bit of luck for the boys, having you here in the week. I hope they're grateful to Eve.'

'Well ... she's not here at week-ends any more.'

'I thought you wanted to be alone during the week.'

'There's still Wednesday and Thursday.'

'Yes. Is that enough?'

'It seems to be.' He finally got the point. 'Don't nag, Cass. It's not like you.'

'Pay no attention. I'm only jealous. She can work miracles and I can't.'

He with an air of innocence, 'I love being with you all.'

'I know.'

She watched him go back in the garden to play Pig-in-the-Middle with the boys. The game reminded her of how she felt.

Over supper Manson said to the twins, without any warning, 'How would you like to live in Scotland?'

'What – leave here?'

'Yes – sell up and buy a new house in Scotland.'

David was keen. 'Oh, yes. Let's.'

Andrew was doubtful. 'I don't know. I like it here.'

They always disagreed. She had seen it so often.

'You could have lots of animals in Scotland – chickens, sheep, pigs – maybe even a pony.' Manson at his most persuasive.

'I'd like a pony.'

'We wouldn't have to leave school, would we?'

'No, you'd stay at the same school if you wanted to, but in the holidays you'd come to Scotland instead of coming here.'

'I think it's a smashing idea. Scotland's all lochs and mountains. isn't it?'

She had been mesmerized by the performance; suddenly she snapped, 'Peter, what's the point of getting them all excited?

We *haven't* decided anything and it's no good pretending we have.'

'It seems to be three to one.' He was pleased with himself.

'That's unfair.'

'Your mother doesn't want to come,' he said to the boys, posing as the indulgent parent.

They started on her. 'Oh, Mum, why not?'

'I didn't say that. But we'd have to talk a lot more first. We can't take Eve away from Gavin just like that.'

'Oh, we wouldn't have to take her with us, would we?'

'Course we would. She's only little. She can't manage by herself.'

'She wouldn't be by herself, you twit. She'd be with Gavin. He's her father.'

'I'd rather she was with us. I like her.'

'I don't like her. She made Prue die.'

The silence hurt.

Manson said, 'Come on, you two, time for bed.'

'Oh, Dad, it isn't ... '

'Not yet.'

'You've finished your supper. Off you go.'

'Peter, it's still early.'

They all looked at each other, evaluated the situation. Open. Exposed. She was frightened.

'Oh, all right. But it's not fair.' David trying to cling to the remnants of justice.

Cassie said, 'I'll be up presently. Why don't you two have a bath? I'm sure you need one.'

Andrew said, 'Oh, *Mum*.'

'Go on.' Cassie wanted to be on their side but she also needed them out of the room as quickly as possible. When they had gone she said, 'Don't take it out on them, Peter. We must talk about it eventually.'

'There's nothing to talk about.' He was remote again.

'You've got to face facts sometime – you can't go on living in the past.'

'Isn't it you who's doing that? I rather thought I was trying to live in the present – and not doing too badly.'

'But no one's allowed to mention her name. You're behaving

59

as if she never existed. Peter, she lived and she died. I know it's terrible but you've got to face it. There are things to discuss, like the gravestone and the inscription. We can't go on pretending we never had a daughter –'

She was only saying what she thought had to be said, but he got up abruptly and went out of the room. She stayed at the table, slumped, her face in her hands. Defeated.

Vicky thought about him. Grey-haired, good-looking, gentle. Like a proper father. She said, 'You know, he wasn't a bit how I'd imagined him.'

'Huh?'

'You always make him sound such an ogre. But he was really quite nice.'

Gavin was silent, working. Ostentatiously ignoring her.

'I thought he might object to my being here – you know, because of Prue – but he didn't seem to mind. And he was ever so good with Eve. He made her stop crying and helped me with her bottle and everything.'

'Great.'

'It's true.'

'Look, you can fall in love with the guy if you want, it's all the same to me, but I have to get these notes finished – okay?'

'That means shut up.'

'Right.'

She tried to shut up.

'I only wanted to be fair to him,' she said.

Freddy dropped Geoff at Frankfurt airport.

'Thanks for speeding it all up.'

'Delighted to get rid of you a day early. Shall I ring Sarah for you?'

'No, I want to see her face when I walk in.' He showed Freddy the gift-wrapped parcel he was carrying. Freddy thought of the surprise, the welcome, the love-making. He envied Geoff.

Over coffee and brandy Manson said, 'I'm so glad I didn't ... spoil everything for you last year. I mean it's right you should get married and be happy.'

'I don't know why we bothered,' Sarah said. 'We could just have gone on living together.'

'It's not the same.'

'No, it isn't. Geoff said it would be but it isn't.' She paused and looked at him very directly. 'I think I only did it to prove I'd got over you.'

'And here we are.'

'Yes.'

There was a long silence.

Manson said, 'I'd like to think . . . if you ever had any problems . . . you could talk to me about them. After all, there's no reason why we shouldn't be friends, is there?'

'None at all.' She trembled with delight. On the edge of something dangerous, she began to feel safe again, restored to herself. Free.

Vicky had had the idea in the back of her head for some time, not looking at it. They were such pretty clothes. They were her size. She knew she would do it eventually but she did not plan exactly when. At first she just held the dresses up against herself, but the colours excited her and presently she took off her shirt and jeans and began trying things on properly. The front door slammed, making her heart thump with terror. She had not expected Gavin home for hours.

'What the hell d'you think you're doing?' He was suddenly beside her.

'I'm sorry.'

She expected rage, rejection; she hardly dared look at him. But to her amazement he reached for her.

'No.' He kissed her. She could feel his excitement and she was astonished by her own good fortune.

In the flat Sarah walked up and down, unable to settle. It all looked exactly the same. She was enchanted. Here was her past, her freedom.

'It still feels like home,' she said tenderly, touching things.

He gave her a drink. 'Here you are.'

'Thanks.'

'To last year.'

They both sipped brandy, although they had already had enough.

'We were very happy here,' she said.

'Yes.' He watched her steadily, making her feel warm and wanted.

'No, that's a lie. We had screaming rows. I remember.'

'That's right.'

'But we were very happy as well.'

'Yes.'

She thought about it.

'We didn't have much time, though, did we?'

Vicky had been so happy. But now Gavin was beginning to hurt her. She didn't know what to do. She tried to respond, but it was too painful.

Sarah curled up in the big armchair. 'You must have had to renew the lease after I'd gone.'

'Yes, I did.'

She looked round lovingly at the room. 'I'm glad you kept it. As soon as I got back to London, I went round some of my old haunts and d'you know, they'd actually knocked down one of the houses I'd lived in.'

She remembered the dreadful feeling of walking down the street and seeing bricks and emptiness and dust, where she had once been happy.

'They're doing that all the time. It's terrible.'

'It gave me a weird feeling – like seeing part of my life destroyed.'

They smiled at each other, relaxed, united in a perfect understanding.

The pain got to be too much but Vicky couldn't stop him. It was too late. He seemed like another person, savage, unfamiliar, frightening, and she was someone else. She began to cry.

Sarah said, 'I always felt we were cheated out of something. Our fair share of happiness.'

'If there is such a thing.'

She was sitting with her legs over the arm of the chair. He watched her legs.

'Yes. I probably mean our fair share of misery. Remember how I said no one would get hurt.'

'I remember.'

She felt so comfortable with him. So much at home.

'And in the end everyone got hurt. Including me.'

'Especially you.'

'No. I just shouted loudest. I was always good at making a fuss.'

Vicky screamed at the end. Partly from pain and partly from relief that it was over. But most of all from the knowledge that she was no longer a person to him, merely an object.

Sarah came over to him. 'I've missed you.'

'I've missed you too.' He put his arms round her, unable to believe his luck.

'I felt safe with you.'

'But you weren't.'

She held him close. 'Doesn't matter. I felt I was. And now I'm trapped.'

'Sarah.'

He could feel time receding. It was last year and Prue was alive. They were happy.

Sarah kissed him.

Now that it was over, Gavin was more shaken than Vicky. 'Stop crying,' he kept saying, 'stop crying, for God's sake. Please stop crying.'

'You hurt me,' she said truthfully, but making the most of it all the same.

'I'm sorry, baby, I'm sorry.' He was ashamed: he turned away.

'No. Don't be sorry, please. It's all right. Really.' She was surprised at her own sudden surge of strength. 'Was it like that with her?'

'Let's go to sleep.' He would not look at her. All he could think of was Prue but he did not want to share that.

'I don't mind what you do. I don't mind anything. Only please love me.' As she said the words, she found they were true.

Sarah made love to Manson slowly and gently. They were both so relaxed, so cheerful, so drunk, they did not feel part of the real world at all.

*

On her way home she didn't feel guilty, merely light-hearted and free. She parked the car carefully in the drive, mindful of excess brandy. It was a shock to see lights on in the house: they took her out of her dream.

'Geoff?' She called as she went in. 'Is that you?'

She ran up the stairs calling him. He was in bed, wide awake.

'Darling,' she said, 'what a nice surprise. Why didn't you answer? I was scared you were a burglar.'

She felt herself talking too much from nerves and she went to kiss him. He drew back, then turned round, furious.

'Where the hell have you been till this hour?'

'What on earth d'you mean?'

'It's half past three.'

'Yes, I know what the time is, I've got a watch.' She already felt innocent; under attack, she was suddenly furious as well.

'I'd like an explanation. If it's not too much trouble.' He was always pompous when angry: it was something she disliked very much.

She said, 'What's the matter with you? You weren't due home till tomorrow so I went to see Barbara. I told you I might.'

'Till half past three?'

'Well, I didn't like leaving early and she offered me a bed for the night, but I said no, I had to get home, because you'd be back first thing in the morning. I wish I'd stayed now. If I'd known you'd turn up in this mood, I would have done.'

'She's not on the phone, is she?'

'No, she isn't. She can't afford it.'

'Perfect.'

'What's that supposed to mean?'

She felt so justified she knew she would win. As if conceding defeat, he suddenly changed tactics.

'Don't you understand, I was worried about you. You might have been anywhere.'

'And you couldn't check up – is that what you mean?'

'You stupid cow, you might have had an accident.'

He was right, of course. 'Why? You always used to tell me what a good driver I am.'

'You might have gone for one of your burn-ups – like you did last year.'

Last year was a subject to be avoided. 'Well, I didn't.'

'How was I to know? Anyway, there are so many fools on the roads – anything might have happened to you.'

'Well, it didn't, I'm here, you're back and it's late, as you pointed out, so let's get some sleep, shall we?'

Was that the end of it? She slipped out of her dress with her back turned and tried to get quickly into her dressing-gown. He never stopped watching her.

'You're so beautiful,' he said, his voice changing. 'I have missed you.'

'I've missed you too.' Forced to say it again, she heard the echo.

He held out his arms to her and she kissed him reluctantly. She could not understand his hunger for her now that she was so familiar. Did he sense what she had been doing?

'You taste of brandy,' he said.

'Yes, I took a bottle to Barbara. It's the only thing that cheers her up.' The lies sprang so naturally to her lips, they seemed like the truth. Geoff went on being affectionate till she could bear it no longer. She wriggled away. 'Darling, I really must have a shower – Barbara's kids were crawling over me all day and you know how yukky they are.'

Next week-end Gavin was ready early and watching for Cassie's car. He ran out on the pavement to meet her.

'I won't come in,' she said, passing him the carry-cot with Eve in it.

'No. All right.' They stared at each other with painful concern. 'How's everything?'

'Oh – not too good.'

'Is he still on about Scotland?'

65

'Yes, I'm afraid he is.'

'Can't you talk him out of it.'

'I can try.'

'It's bad for me if you go.'

'Yes, I know.' She gathered her courage to ask, 'Is everything all right here?'

'I guess so.'

'What does that mean?'

'Not really. She can't cope with Eve and we fight a lot. It's not her fault. I'm hell to live with.'

He felt he had given her something and she was pleased.

'Well – I must be going,' she said. 'Peter will be waiting.'

'Take care, Cassandra.'

'Yes. You too.'

He watched her get into the car and drive away. Already he had a sense of loss.

Vicky made supper later than usual but Eve was still crying when they sat down. It put him off his food, though he tried not to let it.

'It's no good, I'll have to go to her,' he said, getting up.

Vicky said firmly, 'If you'd just wait long enough, she's bound to stop. Finish your supper.'

'I can't. If she was your own, you'd understand.' He went to Eve with a sense of relief. It was more peaceful in the bedroom with the screaming baby than at the table with Vicky. And he felt more adequate: he could give what was needed.

Manson was actually drying up for Cassie while she washed: a symbol, she supposed, of their new life together. She wondered how long it would last.

'You didn't tell me he had a girl living with him.' He spoke abruptly, as if he had been working himself up to it.

'It's very recent. I thought you might be upset.'

'Why? It's only what I'd expect from him.'

She said, 'I suppose he was lonely.'

'Well, he's not the type to wait very long, is he?'

When Gavin got back to the table Vicky had finished eating.

'Did she want changing?' she asked.

'No. Just a cuddle.' He sat down again and tried to eat.

'I know the feeling. What's more, when she wants one, she gets one.'

'She's only little.'

'If I could shrink?'

He pushed away his plate. 'I think I've had enough.'

'I haven't,' Vicky said, touching him hopefully.

'I know – I'm sorry – I'm just not in the mood.'

'You never are when she's here.'

Safer to ignore that.

'Cassandra said he's still talking about moving to Scotland.'

'She doesn't like me, does she? I wonder why. Because of Prue, I suppose.'

'She doesn't even know you . . .' he said, inadequate.

'That's why she wouldn't come in.'

'You can see what he's trying to do, can't you? Take Eve away from me. He knows I can't afford train fares to Scotland.'

As if on cue Eve started to cry again. He sprang up instantly. Reflex.

Vicky said, 'No. Let me go this time. She's got to get used to me.'

In the bedroom she rocked the cot as best she could with one hand, undressing rapidly with the other. It had worked before; it might work again. The memory of pain had faded: at least she had had his undivided attention. When the crying stopped she shoved a dummy in Eve's mouth and took the red dress out of the wardrobe.

Gavin was in the sitting-room, reading. She came in quietly, suddenly shy, although she was trying hard to be seductive. She said softly, 'Are you sure you're not in the mood?'

He looked up. 'Take it off.'

'But the other night . . .'

'I'm ashamed of the other night.' His face darkened.

'I'm not. I don't mind pretending. I'll do anything you want.'

'Then take it off.'

'But you liked it, you know you did.'

'I don't want you to wear her clothes ever again. It's over, it's

67

private and she's dead. No amount of pretending will change that. And playing games is cheap.'

Vicky began to undress, crying silently. 'It wasn't a game. I was only trying to please you.'

'I know. And all I did was hurt you. I'm sorry.'

'I told you I didn't mind. It was so much better than nothing.'

'That's not really the point. If we're down to that, we should quit.'

'Oh, don't. Please don't say that.'

She stood in front of him, naked. He was embarrassed by her vulnerability.

'I'm here,' she said. 'Just me. Just like at the very beginning. Won't I do?'

'I wish I could say yes.'

'Oh, God.' She was suddenly frightened.

'I'm sorry.'

'Please.'

'Don't be so humble.' He sounded angry with her.

'It's since *she* came, isn't it? I mean, I know how much you loved Prue. I know I'm just a substitute, but at least you used to fancy me. Now you don't even do that.'

Silence. It was almost a relief when Eve started to cry. Gavin got up and went to her. Vicky didn't try to stop him.

Getting ready for bed, Cassie said, 'Look, I simply don't think we have the right to separate him from his child. He loves her very much. Whatever you think of him, you must admit that.'

'Yes, I know he does.'

'Well – can't we give him a year of peace? He's got so much work to do. Once he's qualified and got a job, it'll be different. He'll be able to afford to pay someone to look after her. He may want her with him all the time.'

'Why should he pay someone when he's got that poor girl doing it for nothing?'

The sympathetic tone was infuriating. 'Because she hasn't a clue.'

'She can learn. She seemed very eager to please.'

'No doubt she is. But he has to supervise her all the time.'

'Funny. He wasn't even there when I called.' He got into bed.

'He has a tutorial on Mondays. Anyway, she's studying too. And it may not last. We can't depend on her.'

'What you're really saying is, you don't want to go to Scotland.'

She got into bed beside him. 'No. I'm not saying that. I just don't want to go in a hurry. All this talk of selling and moving – it's too sudden. It worries me. I'm not sure we can afford it. And I do wish you hadn't got the boys all excited about it before we'd really made up our minds.'

'I thought the idea of a totally new life might appeal to you.'

'Well ... in a way it does, of course, but ...' She didn't know what more she could say.

'But not yet. All right, I can wait.'

'Really?'

'Yes, of course. Why not?'

'But you made it sound so urgent.' The sudden reversal amazed her. She felt stupid, as if she had been arguing something that was already settled.

'Well, you've talked me out of it.'

She considered. 'I don't think I have. I think you've just changed your mind. You're very unpredictable these days. I can't keep up with you.'

Sunday morning in the park. Everything seemed suddenly better, humiliation forgotten, the sun shining. They were both pretending Friday night had never happened: Gavin pushed the pram and Vicky walked beside him.

'Anybody watching us would think we're a real family,' she said happily.

'Yeah, but you couldn't stand it, could you – if we had her with us all the time?'

'How would I ever get to college?'

'Yeah. I know.'

There was a pause. She wanted to prolong the conciliatory mood and searched for a compliment. 'She's really very sweet when ...'

'When she's asleep.'

69

'When she's cheerful, I was going to say. But she hasn't exactly taken to me, has she? Every week-end I hope it will be better but it never is.'

'You don't have much to do with her.'

'I would if you'd let me. But you seem to want to do everything for her yourself.'

'Well, it's quicker and easier. I know what to do.'

'What makes you such an expert?'

'Cassandra taught me. She's marvellous with Eve.'

'Well, she's had a lot of practice, hasn't she?'

'I guess so.'

Afterwards she could not remember how the conversation had escalated so quickly from harmless to lethal.

'Must be weird to have a name like that.'

'I think it's a beautiful name.'

'Yes – it's nice – but it's a bit creepy. Anyway, even *Cassandra* must have had to start somewhere. How am I ever supposed to be a perfect mother-substitute if I don't get any practice?'

'It's unsettling for Eve to have too many people handling her.'

'You don't mind Cassandra handling her.'

'She does it properly. And do stop using her name.'

'Why?'

'It's kinda private.'

'How can a name be private? You mean I should call her Mrs Manson? I did, to her face. The only time I saw her face, that is.' She still resented that cold meeting.

'I meant most people call her Cassie.'

'Why do you have to be different?'

'Oh – it started when Prue was in hospital.'

'What started?'

'Our friendship.'

'You talk about her so fondly.'

'She's had a tough time.'

'I don't see why. You've all lost Prue – why is it worse for her? She's got two more children – and she's got her husband back – she doesn't have to worry about money or do a job ...'

'Leave it, Vicky.'

'What's so special about her?'

'I said leave it.'

70

'God, you're so protective – anyone would think you were in love with her.'

The words came out like a joke. But the silence reinforced everything she had feared without even knowing she was afraid.

She said, 'You're not, are you? I mean you can't be. She's so old.'

'The other day you were saying how young and attractive she is.'

'Gavin, tell me the truth.' She was shaking with fright.

'Since Prue died I'm not in love with anyone.' He seemed quite unruffled.

'But you fancy her. You do, don't you. Tell me.'

He said calmly. 'We had an affair. Yes.'

'Oh, no.' She felt sick.

'Why ask if you don't want to know?'

'But she's Prue's mother. How could you?'

'She's a wonderful person, I'm very fond of her, we had an affair and it's over. Now are you satisfied?' He sounded proud and irritable.

'So that's why she hates me. Of course. She's jealous. I knew there was something. I knew it.'

'Congratulations.'

'When was it? Long ago? Before we started?'

'Yeah, ages ago.'

She felt small, like a child. He was boasting that he was grown up.

'Not while Prue was alive.' she said. Surely something was sacred?

'Yes. And a bit after. Not for long.'

'Oh, God. Did Prue know?'

'No, of course she didn't. Nobody knew.'

'Didn't it feel wrong?'

'Why should it?'

'Well – it's like incest.' Why didn't he understand?

'Come on – we're not related.'

'Didn't you feel guilty at all?'

'Oh, do shut up about it. You're making such a fuss.'

He was pushing the pram faster and faster. She had to hurry to keep up with him.

'God – it changes everything.'

'I don't see why.'

'Is it because of her you don't fancy me?'

'I do fancy you. Just ... not all the time. And anyway, it's all over with her. I told you.'

She said, 'I don't believe you.'

Sarah disentangled herself from Geoff and turned over in bed. All she wanted was to be allowed to go to sleep, but Geoff, she knew, would insist on a post mortem. She braced herself for it.

'What's the matter, love?'

'Wasn't it obvious?' His heavy, serious voice made her irritable.

'Sorry.'

'Not your fault. I just wasn't in the mood.'

'No. I noticed.'

'Didn't put you off though, did it?' she said sharply.

'Sometimes when you're not in the mood you change your mind half-way.'

That was true. She had to grant him that. 'Yes, I know. Sorry I didn't this time.'

'Can't win 'em all,' he said, falsely jocular. 'You haven't really been yourself since we came back.'

'No. Right little raver I used to be.' She thought of her past exploits with nostalgia. They seemed part of another life, someone else's.

'I didn't mean that.'

'Well, I was. Don't say you've forgotten.'

'Is it anything special?'

'What?'

'Putting you off.'

'You're not doing anything wrong, if that's what you mean. Just as talented as ever. Full marks.' She had read in magazines that you had to reassure men all the time but she sounded bitter all the same.

'I feel a bit embarrassed actually,' he said, to her surprise.

'Why?'

'I thought ... Dad dying would really turn me off. But it

hasn't. In fact there seems to be something about death that makes me awfully randy.'

His honesty touched her, but she couldn't cope with it. 'That's all right,' she said. 'There's probably some terribly sound psychological reason.'

'You're being very clinical.'

'Sorry.' He had misunderstood but she couldn't explain.

'Is there really nothing wrong?'

'Well, coming off the Pill doesn't help.'

'But that thing's safe, isn't it?'

'So they say.'

After a while he said, 'It wouldn't matter so much if we had a kid.'

'It would to me. I don't want one.'

'Not ever?'

'Not yet.' Why couldn't he accept that? Why this awful pressure? There was a long silence. She hoped without conviction that he had gone to sleep.

'D'you wish we were still in Frankfurt?' The question sounded abrupt in the darkness.

'No. Why?'

'You seemed happier there, that's all.'

'Oh – I don't know.'

'I thought you'd be glad to come home.'

'I was.' She wished she could explain but she couldn't.

'You don't like this house, do you?'

'I'm sorry.'

'You can make it look different. Whatever you want. Just buy it.'

'But we can't move?'

'Do you hate it that much?'

'It's just ... not me.'

'I know. It's not me either. But the old man worked so hard to get this far – it meant so much to him – living here is part of being his son – not letting him down.'

Suddenly she felt a great rush of pity for him, and understanding, and she knew she was trapped. She hugged him. 'Oh, Geoff, I'm sorry.'

By Monday the nightmare was confirmed. They could not take back what they had said. Eve cried, it seemed, all the time. Gavin went to college and Vicky was alone with her. Gavin and Cassandra. It went round in her head. She could not think clearly: the baby seemed to need endless feeding and changing. The crying got inside her mind till she hardly knew if it was Eve or herself making such a sound.

'Oh, do stop crying, can't you? Please stop crying.' She did not know how to speak to her: as an animal or another adult. 'Look, I know you don't like me, and I'm not mad about you, but we've got to get along.'

The crying went on and on. It seemed there had never been a time without it.

'Do you *have* to make that noise? I'm doing the best I can. It's nearly ready. I know you're hungry. Oh, do please stop.'

She put down the bottle she was preparing and picked up the baby.

'Oh God, you're wet. Is that what's wrong? Well, I can't do both.'

She put Eve down, to fetch a clean nappy. The saucepan, intended to warm the bottle, boiled over. She came back and looked at the mess.

'Oh God. Oh no.'

Eve yelled louder, as if on purpose. 'Oh *shut* up. For God's sake, can't you stop that row for a minute?'

She didn't know what to tackle first: the feed or the nappy or the mess on the floor. She began to cry, tears of rage and helplessness. Gavin and Cassie. It was true. He had said so. She shouted at the child with all her strength: 'It's all your fault.'

Gavin, coming in with peace-offering flowers, propped the front door open with books to give Vicky a surprise, heard the cries, approached the kitchen.

'You've got to stop,' Vicky was saying. 'You've got to.'

Eve didn't stop. Vicky shook her and screamed: '*Stop* it.'

And at that moment Gavin came in. Vicky put the baby down, backed away, terrified.

'I didn't hurt her. Really I didn't.'

She thought he might hit her, kill her, anything, but he only went to the child and took her in his arms as if there was no one else in the world.

'Get out.' He put Eve tenderly in the carry-cot.

Vicky heard herself jabbering: 'I really didn't hurt her. Oh please. I just couldn't stand it. I had to make her stop. But I didn't hurt her.'

'I don't want you here when I get back.' He went out with Eve. Vicky followed him, frantic.

'Where are you going?'

'Back to Cassandra, of course. Only for good this time. I could kill you. How dare you touch her?'

As he went through the door she screamed at him, 'Was that worse than you hitting Prue when she was pregnant?' He didn't turn or answer; he disappeared with the child. Vicky let herself go, lay on the floor, wept.

Gavin telephoned several times. Eve in her carry-cot lay at his feet in the call box, seemingly calm and cheerful, amazingly recovered, looking at him with sober curiosity. But there was no reply. He pictured the empty house, the phone ringing. How could she be out when he needed her so much?

Manson walked up the steps to the flat and, finding the door open, went in. He heard sobbing. There was a heap of suffering at his feet. That girl with her mass of frizzy red hair and her pale face huddled on the floor. In the middle of saying automatically that he'd come to collect Eve he stopped, feeling foolish and concerned, and asked instead what was wrong.

'She's not here.' The words were barely audible.

'Is she all right?' He was alarmed. 'What's happened? Where's he taken her?'

'Back to your bloody wife.'

She went on howling, out of control. He was overwhelmed by so much emotion; puzzled, angry. Had he heard her correctly? He asked if there was something he could do and she looked up at him with her ravaged face.

'Yes – make them stop it.'

3

ACCUSATIONS

MANSON had heard the words but he blocked them out. This creature on the floor was real and in need of help: the rest was a fantasy. He wanted above all to be practical.

'Come on now, you can't sit here all day. You'll soon feel better when you've washed your face and had a cup of tea.'

Vicky, still sobbing, allowed him to help her up. 'He told me to get out.'

Outside the house Gavin waited with Eve in her carry-cot. She was fractious now, but there was nothing he could do. In the supermarket Cassie shopped peacefully, mindlessly; came out, loaded groceries into the back of her car.

Manson got Vicky settled on the couch. He offered her a glass of water but she ignored it. He felt it was important to hang on to the ordinary everyday things. They made life seem more normal.

'Shall I make you some tea?'

'He was so angry. But I didn't mean it.'

'Do you want to tell me what happened?' He tried to sound soothing.

'Don't you care what they do? It's not fair, she's got everything and I've got nothing.' She seemed to be in a trance-like state: she went on saying things he did not want to hear. Impossible things.

Gavin was so relieved to see Cassie return, he could have kissed the car. 'Thank God you're back.'

'What are you doing here?'

'I had to bring Eve.'

'But Peter was bringing her – why didn't you wait?' She seemed more surprised than pleased to see him.

'I forgot all about him.'

'Are you all right? You look awful.' She began to take shopping briskly out of the car. He helped her, feeling foolish.

'Can we go in? I left in a hurry – she's a bit upset.'

Manson said, irresistibly drawn, against his better judgement, 'I think you'd better explain, don't you?'

She was still crying. She didn't try to control herself or be tactful. She simply said, 'I can't bear it. I've tried so hard. Please make them stop. You've got to. Please. Make her leave him alone.'

Then she lay down on the couch, no longer hysterical but settling herself comfortably for a long therapeutic session of tears. He stared at her, his worst fears confirmed. So casually she had put in the knife. And yet – he could not believe it. He left.

Gavin put the kettle on and Cassie came back from attending to Eve. He said anxiously, 'Is she all right?'

'She's nodding off. She just wanted changing. And I think her teeth are bothering her a bit.'

'It was awful on the train. There was nothing I could do for her.'

'Why did you leave in such a hurry?' She was so brisk: he couldn't understand her.

'It's all over with Vicky.'

'Oh, really? Why did that stop you changing Eve's nappy?'

'You're sure she's okay? Not ... hurt at all?'

'Gavin, what is this?' She went on putting away shopping. 'Is she really all right?'

'Yes, she's fine. Now *tell* me.'

'Vicky ... got rough with her. She went mad, I came in, she was shaking her, screaming – God, I was angry – and so frightened – I didn't know what to do – I just told her to go and I took Eve and ran. All I could think of was getting her back to you.' He expected a reaction: something to match what he felt.

Cassie said, 'Lucky I'm here.'

'But you weren't.'

'Well, you didn't have long to wait. Even *I* can't manage a twenty-four-hour service – though I suppose that *is* my role in life.'

He was astonished. 'What are you so angry about?'

'I feel rather taken for granted. Does that surprise you? If it suits you to take Eve away to your girlfriend, I have to let you. Not only that, I'm expected to deliver her by hand. When it suits you to bring her back, I'm supposed to be here, ready and waiting.'

'I did call you but –'

'But I was out – living it up in the supermarket.' She slammed her purchases into the cupboard.

'You don't seem very worried about Eve. She might have been injured.'

'You chose her nanny for her. Don't tell me you made a mistake.'

He said angrily, 'I don't like you in this mood.'

'No, I'm not very keen on it either.' Silence. They were both upset. 'Look, give the wretched girl her due – many's the time I've shaken Prue and the boys when they were little. It looks awful but it doesn't do any harm. I mean it's one of those things you can do yourself but other people shouldn't do it. She wasn't *hitting* her, was she?'

He didn't like the sound of that. 'No. Not as far as I know.'

'Well, she seems fine to me. So don't worry.'

The kettle boiled. She made tea, seemingly calm again. 'Babies are really quite tough, you know, or they wouldn't survive at all. And when you get back she'll be penitent and you'll make it up and everything will be fine.'

'No. It's over. I meant what I said. I couldn't – not after that.'

'You don't feel perhaps ... you ought to make allowances?'

'Not where Eve is concerned.'

She looked thoughtful, poured milk and sugar. Didn't she *care*?

He said, 'I better go.'

'Have some tea first.'

'No, thanks.'

'Because of my rotten mood?' She was suddenly penitent.

78

'Of course not. You're entitled. I don't want to run into *him*, that's all.' It was true but it was more than that.

'He won't be pleased at having a wasted journey. Let me see if I can catch him at the office.' She went into the hall to telephone and he listened, wondering how much of her he knew. 'Oh, hullo.' Her office voice. 'Is Mr Manson still there? It's his wife. Oh, I see. Thank you.'

She came back. 'He left at lunchtime.'

'Then he could be here any minute. I'm off.'

'It's not *that* bad.'

'No – I've just had enough hassle for one day.'

'I'll make your excuses.'

'You may as well tell him the truth. I'm sorry, Cassandra. I don't know how you put up with me.'

'Don't have much choice, do I?'

They hugged each other, sadly, in friendship.

Back in his flat, Manson walked up and down, Vicky's words echoing in his head. He stared at the pictures of Prue on the wall, singling out Gavin and Cassie at the wedding. It was impossible. And yet – it would explain everything. He had thought the worst had happened when Prue died, but now there was this new torture. On an impulse he looked up Roberts in the phone book and dialled. It rang for a long time. He was desperate, ready to give up, when she suddenly answered.

'Sarah.'

'Hello? Peter?' She had just come in; there were carpet samples all over the hall; and now this urgent voice on the phone.

'Thank God you're there,' he said fervently.

'What's the matter? I thought we agreed you wouldn't ring me at home.'

'I know – I'm sorry – I've got to talk to you.'

'Just a minute – let me shut the front door. I've only just got in.' She put down the phone and slammed the door. It was hard to reconcile her two lives, to move smoothly from one to the other. She would have liked transition time. 'What's happened? Are you all right? You sound very odd.'

Cassie brought Eve downstairs and held her while she rang Manson. 'What's happened to your grandfather, then? He's very late. D'you think we'd better ring him?' All she got was the engaged signal, which always seemed vaguely insulting. 'Well – he's there all right. Who's he talking to?' She hung up.

Manson said desperately, 'I can't tell you on the phone. Please come. I've got to talk to you.'

'But Geoff will be home in an hour and we've got people coming for drinks and we're going out to dinner ...' Why couldn't he understand what her life was like?

'I'll go mad if I don't talk to someone.'

'All right – but I can't stay long.'

Cassie re-dialled but the number was still engaged. She hung up and said to Eve, 'Well, he's got a lot to say to somebody.'

Vicky had cried herself to sleep on the sofa. The slam of the front door woke her.

Gavin said, 'I thought I told you to go.'

'I'm sorry – I felt awful – I meant to go but I cried so much I went to sleep.'

'I don't want any sob stuff, I just want you out.'

But not for ever; surely he couldn't mean that?

'Gavin, please – we've got to talk.'

'There's nothing to say.'

'But I didn't mean it – and I'm so sorry – I'll never do it again.'

'You won't get the chance.'

She struggled up. 'I didn't hurt her. Really I didn't. Please let me stay. Please. I'll make it up to you.'

'You've got five minutes to pack.'

'But I've nowhere to go.'

He said with final cruelty, 'You've got friends. You've even got parents. There are dozens of floors you can sleep on.'

Sarah sat on Manson's sofa and waited to be told whatever he couldn't say on the phone. But all he did was pace up and down, saying he didn't know how to tell her.

'You said you wanted to talk,' she reminded him, 'and we haven't much time.'

'It's so ugly.'

'What?' He didn't answer. 'Peter, please tell me. How can I help if you don't tell me?'

'I'm afraid to put it into words. It's Cassie and Gavin.'

'What about them?'

'You're not going to believe it, I didn't at first.'

He looked haunted, tormented. She didn't want to be callous, but time was passing. 'I can't stand much more of this,' she said.

He turned round, almost savage. 'An affair. Is that plain enough for you?'

'That's impossible.' She felt herself almost smiling, it was so ridiculous.

'That's what I thought – but it's true. That poor little girl told me – the one he's been living with. I went to collect the baby and she told me.'

'Just like that?' She subdued the smile, knowing it would offend him.

'She was in floods of tears, poor little thing – lying on the floor – sobbing her heart out. He wasn't there – he'd taken the baby and gone. "Back to your bloody wife," she said. She just went on crying. "Make them stop it," she said. God, it's revolting. My own wife. He's no good, I've always known that, but Cassie. Her own daughter's husband. How could she? A boy half her age. Even if she doesn't give a damn about me – well, it's obvious she doesn't – but Prue. How could she do such a thing to *Prue*?'

Even while he raged, Sarah's brain ticked over. 'Wait a minute.'

'Aren't you shocked? Don't you even care?'

'Yes, of *course*, if it's *true*, but I'm not sure it is. Is that all she said? "Back to your bloody wife" and "Make them stop it"? That could mean anything.'

'No, she said more than that.'

'Tell me everything she said.'

'Sarah, there's no point.'

'You mean you want to believe it?'

'No. God knows I don't.'

'Well, then. Try to remember everything. You may have got it wrong.'

81

There was a pause while he thought. 'I went in – she was on the floor crying. Really heartbroken. It was terrible.'

Sarah looked at her watch. 'What did she *say*?'

'I asked her about Eve and she said, "She's not here." I was alarmed and asked why not and she said, "He's taken her back to your bloody wife" and, "Can't you stop them?"'

'Just now you told me she said, "Make them stop it".'

'Oh, Sarah, you're being like a policeman.'

'But it might make a difference. You must tell me *exactly* what she said.'

'What's the point? I know it's true. It all fits. That's why she's always on his side – that's why she didn't really care about Prue – that's why she didn't want me back.'

His agitation made Sarah calmer than ever. 'What did she say next?'

'I helped her back into the flat – she was really in a dreadful state – and she said, "He told me to go – he was so angry ... but I didn't mean it." Something like that.'

'Well, that only proves they had a row. Nothing about your wife.'

'No, she went on. I tried to get her to explain but she was crying so much I couldn't get any sense out of her.'

'Exactly, you may have got yourself upset over nothing.' And if she got caught in the rush-hour traffic, Geoff would ask questions.

'She said, "Don't you care about what they do?" and, "I've tried so hard, I can't bear it, you've got to stop them."'

'Is that all?'

'Isn't that enough?'

'It doesn't prove Gavin and your wife are having an affair.'

'What else could it possibly mean?'

'Well, obviously Gavin and the girl had a row – probably about the baby. She's done something wrong and she's jealous of your wife for being good with babies – and she wants you to stop him running back to your wife with the baby so she can have a proper chance to play mother.'

'Do you really think it could be just that?'

She could see he was longing to believe her. 'I think it's a lot more likely than them having an affair.'

'Oh – she said, "It's not fair, she's got everything and I've got nothing." I forgot that.'

'That just sounds like a child not getting her own way.'

He didn't answer. Had she convinced him? She glanced at her watch again: she should have already left.

'Look – why don't you simply ring her up and ask her? You've got to know.'

'She's leaving. He told her to go.'

'Is she a student?'

'Yes, that's how they met.'

'Well – can't you track her down at college?'

'You're very calm.'

It sounded like criticism. She got up. 'Chase her up at college and get her to spell it out. It may be all nothing.' She kissed him. 'I hope so. Darling, I must rush, Geoff will murder me.' All she could think of now was getting home. 'I'll ring you tomorrow – I'll be desperate to know what happened.'

'But Cassie's expecting me – and I can't face her till I know.' Now *he* sounded like a child: puzzled, scared.

'Ring her and say you can't come.' She picked up her bag and made for the door.

'What excuse can I give her?'

'Work – illness – anything. D'you need an excuse?'

'No. Not really. She doesn't deserve one.' From one extreme to the other.

'Don't judge her yet. I'll ring you tomorrow.' She blew kisses at him, desperate to escape.

'Thank you. You've been wonderful.'

She was touched to see he meant it.

After she had gone Manson simply obeyed her instructions. He went into the bedrooom and phoned Cassie. Sarah was right, of course, and the pictures of Prue gave him strength.

Cassie answered at once. 'Peter! What's happened to you? I've been worried.'

'I'm not coming back tonight.' When he heard her voice he felt so sickened, it was all he could do to speak to her.

'He's awfully sorry you had a wasted journey – he brought

Eve down and he quite forgot you were coming to fetch her ... '

'I won't be down until Saturday.'

'But why? What's the mattter?' She sounded so normal.

'Something cropped up.'

He hung up. He actually hung up on her without saying good-bye. Cassie was astonished, then angry, then alarmed. She replaced the receiver and went back into the sitting-room. Eve on the sofa gave her a sudden beaming smile, as if nothing in the world could be wrong. Cassie said, 'I'm glad you think it's funny.'

The traffic defeated her and the worst happened: his car was already there when she turned into the drive. She parked carelessly and ran into the house, her mind polishing excuses. The simpler the better, probably. Too blatant to be a lie. Nothing she had used recently.

He was in the bedroom, changing.

'Geoff. I'm so sorrry. Is that really the time? My watch stopped.' She adjusted it quickly. 'I thought I had heaps of time. Never mind, I'll get changed. Oh, I've had the most frightful afternooon – I'm exhausted. Have you been home long?' She could feel his rage in the silence. He kept his back turned. 'Shall I get us a drink? I'm sure we both need one. What would you like?'

He swung round. 'I'd like to know where you've been.'

'Shopping. I've been all over the place – got masses of samples to show you for carpets and curtains, it's really exciting –'

'No. After that. When you'd got over the excitement of shopping.'

'What do you mean?'

'You've been out again since then. Your precious samples were all over the hall floor when I came in. Where were you?'

There was something exhilarating about a quarrel. No matter how much she dreaded it beforehand, once it began she was never afraid.

'I went for a drive.'

'Why?'

'Because I felt like it.'

84

'Where did you go?'

'Around.' Already she felt innocent, as if it were true.

'Don't I have the right to know where?'

'The *right*?'

'Of course I am only your husband. I don't suppose that entitles me to anything.'

She said, 'I drove to the end of the road and then I turned left. I stopped at the traffic lights because they were red. When they turned green, I drove on and then I turned right.'

'Oh – shut up. You've made your point.'

'No, I don't think I have. When you start talking about husbandly rights and being entitled, I feel I'm in the middle ages. I didn't know marriage meant being interrogated like a criminal every time I go for a drive round the block. And if it does mean that, then I think I was better off without it.'

She went into the bathroom and slammed the door to round off her exit.

After Vicky had gone, Gavin made supper. He hadn't realized how used to her he had become. Suddenly the flat seemed very empty and he was more alone than ever.

Manson sat by himself in his living-room. The prospect of so much activity, so many confrontations, exhausted him. He poured another drink.

Cassie was reading in bed, trying to believe there was nothing to worry about. She looked round the empty room, glanced at the clock. There couldn't be any reason for his not coming – just a mood. But it weighed on her: she felt heavy. Exhausted, yet unready for sleep. She turned out the light.

*

When the bell rang, Gavin's only thought was that Vicky must have come back. When he opened the door he wasn't sure if he felt relivd or disappointd.

'Oh. Cassandra.'

'Who were you expecting?'

'Nobody. Come in.'

He followed her into the kitchen, said automatically, 'Where's Eve?'

'My daily's looking after her.'

'Is that okay?'

'She's had five of her own.'

He saw her looking at the débris of toast, the milk bottle on the table. Squalor, by her standards. He felt conscious of being unshaven, scruffy.

'Would you like some coffee?'

'Yes. Thank you. Is that lunch or breakfast?'

'I'm not sure.' He poured the coffee. 'It's good to see you.'

'You mean, why am I here? I want to talk to you.'

He was immediately alarmed. 'Did he give you a bad time last night?'

'I didn't see him.'

'Didn't he show up at all?'

'He rang and said he wasn't coming till Saturday. I tried to explain about Eve but he wasn't interested. He sounded very odd.'

'What sort of odd?'

'Distant ... and as if he was angry about something but trying to hide it ... and in a hurry to get off the phone.'

'Did he say why he wasn't coming?'

'No. Just that something had cropped up.'

She looked worried. He tried to be soothing. 'Well, I guess you'll find out on Saturday.'

'I'd rather not wait till then. There was something about his voice that worried me.'

'You mean he was in one of his moods?'

'No, it was more than that.'

'Are you having premonitions again?' A feeble joke. It didn't work.

'The last time I had them,' she said, 'I was right.'

'Maybe something went wrong at the office.' He didn't know what else to suggest.

'I rang the office this morning. He's not there. And I rang the flat. No reply.'

'He's gone to ground.'

'Yes.'

There was a silence while they both thought what that could mean. Casssie said reluctantly, 'Was ... Vicky still here yesterday when you got back?'

'Yeah, but not for long.'

'She didn't ... say anything?'

'What about?' Careful now.

'I thought ... she might have mentioned if she'd seen Peter – if he was upset or anything ... '

'No. I didn't think to ask her.'

Now they both had the same fear and neither dared to put it into words.

Cassie said casually, 'There's nothing ... she could have said to upset him, is there?'

And he answered too quickly, 'No, of course not.'

When Vicky saw Gavin on the college steps, all her despair vanished. It was going to be all right – just like the movies. She had cried all those tears for nothing. They would forgive each other and start again. He came up to her, confirming her fantasy.

'Gavin,' she called.

'I've been looking for you.'

'I knew you'd change your mind,' she said rapturously.

'Don't be stupid. I want to know what happened yesterday after I left.'

As if it wasn't enough to have her hopes raised and tumbled so fast, she had a new sensation: terror.

'Happened?'

'Did he show up?'

'Yes.'

'And?'

'I told him you'd taken the baby ... and he left.'

'Just like that?'

'Well, he hung about a bit trying to cheer me up.' If only he would stop questioning her; she had never been good at lying. And there was so much at stake.

'You didn't say anything to him, did you?'

'What about?'

'You know what about. He didn't go home last night and Cassandra said he sounded very odd on the phone.'

'I was crying and he tried to be nice. We didn't talk at all.'

He said grimly, 'I hope for your sake that's true.'

She watched him go. Even after he disappeared through the gates, she couldn't move. The implications of their conversation paralysed her.

'Feeling better today?' Manson's voice startled her.

'Oh. Hullo.' He must have been hiding somewhere: she had not seen him approach.

'I came to find you – I wanted to know how you were.'

'I'm all right, thank you.' She looked round for escape.

'Did you find somewhere to stay?'

'Yes. Sort of. I'm on somebody's couch.'

'I saw you talking to Gavin. Have you made it up with him?'

'No, he's – no, we haven't.'

She almost stammered from nerves; she saw him look at her appraisingly.

'Are you busy just now?'

'No, I've finished for today, but – ' Foolishly truthful.

'Then you could come and have coffee with me.'

'Oh. Well ... '

He said firmly, 'You'd be doing me a great favour. There's something I want to ask you – about Gavin.'

She longed to refuse. 'All right. But I haven't got long ...'

'Five minutes.'

In the street he took her arm as if he feared she might run away: a sensible fear, she thought.

'Is there a café nearby?'

'There's one at the end of the road – but Gavin might be there.'

'Quite. Let's go somewhere nice – and get out of this rain.' He hailed a taxi. 'The Savoy, please.'

Inside the taxi she shrank into her corner and said brightly, nervously, 'I've never been to the Savoy.'

He was not to be diverted by trivia. 'Yesterday – ' he began.

'I'm sorry about yesterday. I hope you didn't misunderstand anything I said.'

'On the contrary, I understood you perfectly. But I'd rather Gavin didn't know about our little talk.' He paused; he had planned it all, but it was still hard to say. 'When my wife told me what happened between them, I promised her I'd never tell him I know. We all have to meet so often because of the baby, it's much easier if he thinks I don't know.'

Silence. She looked at him, amazed. 'Your wife told you?'

'Yes, of course. We don't have secrets. But she said it was over. That's why I got such a shock yesterday when you seemed to think it was still going on.'

He held his breath: would it work?

'Oh, he said it was over too. But I didn't believe him.'

Well, he had asked for it. Why was the shock so great? He tried to keep going in his role. 'I never expected him to tell you.'

'He didn't really. I guessed. Then he admitted it.'

She had been almost enjoying this newly sophisticated talk: it made her feel grown-up at last. Then she saw in his face that he had only just found out. The full horror of what she had done closed in on her.

'You didn't know. Oh God, you didn't know.'

He sat with his eyes shut. He looked terrible. Vicky was very alarmed. Suppose he was ill: what if he had a heart attack or something?

The taxi drew up outside the hotel.

'We're here,' she said urgently. 'We're at the Savoy. Are you all right?'

He was silent for so long she wondered if he had fainted.

'I'm sorry,' he said at last. 'I feel rather ill – do you mind if I go home?'

'Where's home?'

'Sloane Square.'

'Sloane Square, please,' she said to the driver, feeling busy and important. As they moved off she tried to think what to say, to put right the damage she had done. 'Look, you've got it all wrong. I only said it to get back at Gavin. I was so upset I wanted something dreadful to happen to him. That's why I said it. I wanted you to punish him for me. But it wasn't true. I was lying. Oh, please – you must believe me.'

His eyes half-opened; he squeezed her hand. 'You're very kind.'

Outside his flat he took out money, tried to give it to her.

'Please – take the cab home. I'm sorry about the coffee.'

'Don't be silly. I'm not leaving you. You're not well. You shouldn't be alone.'

Together they paid the cab and she accompanied him into the flat. She had the feeling that she was assisting an invalid.

In the living-room she made him sit down and hovered round him.

'Are you all right?'

'Yes, I think so.' He could hardly tell; he was not conscious of himself. One thought swamped his brain: Gavin and Cassie. It was true.

'Shall I get you some water or something?' It was yesterday in reverse.

'No, I don't want anything. I'll be all right in a moment. It's always better to know exactly where you are.'

He felt her look at him with pity.

'I could kick myself.'

'No, I'm grateful. Really.'

She said sadly, 'You shouldn't have pretended you knew. I'd never have told you if you hadn't done that.'

Her compassion was unbearable. He got up and poured himself a large drink. Facts. He had to know the facts.

'Did he tell you when it started?'

'Wouldn't it be better if you tried not to think about it? That's what I've been trying to do.'

'Please tell me.'

'When Prue was in hospital.' He couldn't help reacting. She was alarmed. 'There, you see, you're only upsetting yourself more. She never knew. He was sure of that.'

'And how long did it last?' He had to make himself ask these questions.

'I don't know. Till a bit after she died, I think. He said it wasn't very long. But he sounded awfully fond of her – of both of them, I mean.' She floundered, trying to make it sound better. 'That's why I was so jealous. He's never been fond of me like that.'

Manson finished his drink and poured another. Cassie and Gavin. While Prue was in hospital and after she died. The enormity of it was almost too much to comprehend. He felt ill when he thought about it.

'Mr Manson,' Vicky said, 'you've had an awful shock. I don't think whisky's very good for you right now.'

But somehow all this energy had to be diverted, this urge to kill. He swallowed the second drink. What was this child doing here?

'Doesn't all this revolting mess teach you anything about him?'

'Yes, he's terrified of you finding out. Please don't tell him you know. He'll kill me.'

'No, I meant ... can't you see what a lucky escape you've had? Someone who can behave like this and not even feel ashamed ... how could you ever be happy with someone like that?'

'We weren't happy at all, most of the time. But it was better than not being with him.' She looked surprised, as if he didn't understand.

'You're so young.' Younger than Prue?

She said indignantly, 'I'm twenty.'

'How can you still want him back? When you know how he treated my wife – and my daughter? Can't you see how totally evil he is?' She didn't answer. 'Your parents must be very worried about you living like this.'

'Oh, they don't care what I do. Mum's busy with her new husband and Dad says I've got to learn from experience and make my own mistakes.'

He was shocked. 'He can't mean that.'

'Yes, he does, he's not like other people's fathers.' He could tell she was trying to sound brave and cheerful. 'He believes in everyone being free and independent and doing their own thing. He says whatever I do, it's my decision and he won't interfere.'

'And you wish he would.'

Clearly she was torn between loyalty and truth. 'No, but ...

sometimes I wish he'd be . . . more of a father and less of a person. D'you know what I mean?'

The telephone rang. He was furious at the interruption. 'Yes?'

Sarah said doubtfully, 'Peter?' He sounded like someone else.

'Oh, it's you.' He modified his voice.

'You sound very grim. Was it bad news? I've been worried all day.'

'Yes, it was bad news.'

'That's incredible. I can't believe it.' She didn't know what to say.

He said brusquely, 'Look, I can't talk now, can you have dinner with me?'

'No, I can't rock the boat any more this week. We had an awful row yesterday. But I could meet you for a drink. Is that any good?'

'Can you come here?'

She hesitated. 'All right.'

She had not meant to make love but of course they did, though neither of them really felt like it. There was still something about it that made it easier to talk afterwards. She said gently, 'I expect they were both lonely and sort of . . . thrown together. You and I were here, after all, and your daughter was in hospital – they must have felt very isolated.'

'There's no excuse for what they did. My God – how can they both pretend to love her – and behave like that?'

She could not find a way to explain to him – at least not a way he could accept.

He went on bitterly, 'It's the end of my marriage, of course. I suppose I should have realized what she's like when she boasted about that other affair – but I never dreamt she could sink as low as this.'

She didn't like the derogatory tone. 'It was probably just on impulse. She may be very sorry she did it.'

'She will be – when I've finished with her.'

The vindictiveness frightened her. 'Oh, don't – I can't bear it. Everyone's trying to punish everyone else – it's awful.'

'I'm sorry – did he give you a bad time last night?'

'It was our worst row yet.' Bits of it echoed in her head. 'I don't think I should have got married, that's all.'

'Well ... if you ever want to run away, you can always come here.'

'That's sweet of you, but it didn't work last time.'

'It's a bit different now.'

'Is it?' She couldn't see how. If anything, it was more complicated than ever.

'I'm ... totally free.'

'I wish I could say the same. I didn't know that marriage could be such a prison.' She hardly noticed that she was guiding the conversation from his troubles to her own.

'He seemed ... a nice boy when I met him.'

'Yes, he is. And he loves me very much. That makes it worse.'

'You don't love him.' He made it sound simple.

'I'm very fond of him. He's good and kind and generous. But he can't give me any space. When we got married we agreed nothing would change. He'd always let me be free before – that was what I liked so much about him. I'd never have married him otherwise. But he's changed completely.'

'I must try to learn from all this.'

He was making her feel guilty and she resented it.

'It's not just the freedom to have affairs – it's freedom in general. I might just be out for a walk – or seeing my sister – or shopping – or meeting you, okay – but it's having to give an account of myself each time that kills me. I know lots of people think that's normal, and good luck to them, but we didn't set it up like that and I feel I've been cheated.'

'You're not in love with him, and he is with you. That's all there is to it.'

He hadn't understood.

'I can't accept that. You're just using labels. I don't see why being in love should mean total ownership. I don't expect Geoff to be faithful to me.'

'But he is, isn't he?'

'Probably. But that's to please himself, not me.'

'Oh, Sarah. You're right. You shouldn't have married him.'

She laughed. 'I've shocked you. Lying here in your bed – deceiving my husband – I've actually shocked you.'

'No. But you've made it hard for me to ask you a favour.'

'What?'

'This week-end is going to be very difficult ... the first time I see them ... now that I know.'

'Oh, you're not going to have a showdown.' The prospect of other people's fights, beyond her control, terrified her.

'I shall do what's necessary.'

'God, you're frightening me.'

'Only right now I don't feel strong enough.'

She said automatically, 'How can I help?'

'In all this time – ever since ... the funeral ... I haven't been able to visit her. I've never been to the grave. I don't even know what they've put on the headstone. Cassie tried to discuss it with me but I wouldn't let her. I couldn't. Now – I've got to go there. I must be with her again before I see them. It's the only way I'll ever be strong enough for all I've got to do. And I can't go alone.'

'You want me to go with you.' Was that all?

'Would you? I know it's a terrible thing to ask.'

'No. I don't mind. It's just ... tricky to organize.'

'Could you manage tomorrow?'

When she got home Geoff was arranging flowers all over the hall.

'Good God,' she said. 'What on earth are you doing?'

'Surprise.'

'It certainly is. They're beautiful. And you're home early this time – I'm not late, am I?' She wanted to make a joke of their last row.

'Of course you're not late. I came home early specially – I wanted to arrange all this before you got back.'

'It's lovely.' She kissed him.

'Come upstairs. I want to show you something.'

'I've heard that one before.' She followed him upstairs, feeling light and cheerful. A welcome change.

In the bedroom there were more flowers all over the room and champagne in an ice-bucket. She didn't know how to react.

'Good heavens. What is all this?'

'Peace-offering. Am I forgiven?' He began opening the bottle.

94

'What for?'

'Behaving like a male chauvinist pig. It won't happen again.'

His generosity amazed her. 'I'm sorry I was so rude,' she said.

'You were justified. I had no right to question you like that.' He passed her an envelope. 'Could you open this for me? I've got both hands full.'

'What is it?'

'Have a look.'

He opened the champagne and poured two glasses while she took two airline tickets out of the envelope.

'Paris,' she said faintly.

'Well, we didn't have a proper honeymoon. You do like Paris, don't you?'

'Yes, I do.' She studied the tickets more closely. 'Tomorrow. But what about the office?'

'I've taken a couple of days off.' She could feel him studying her. 'Aren't you pleased?'

'Yes – I'm thrilled.'

'Convince me.'

She thought quickly. 'Darling – the awful thing is, I've promised to have lunch with my father tomorrow. It's his birthday. I can't disappoint him. I nearly forgot it, only Barbara rang to remind me.' The extra detail seemed to add conviction.

'That's all right. Of course you must go. We can get a later flight.'

She said, 'If we ... went in the evening, I could get my hair done and everything.'

'You pick the flight you want and I'll change the tickets. All right?'

She felt a warm rush of affection for him. Affection and pity.

'You're very good to me,' she said.

'I happen to love you, that's all. Come on – drink up.'

*

Sarah drove him to the cemetery. As they got nearer and nearer to their destination his feeling of panic grew, and from being totally silent he suddenly found he couldn't stop talking.

'For months I didn't believe it. I couldn't talk about her in the past, the way the others did. I was so sure she'd walk in. She was so beautiful.'

Sarah said uncomfortably, 'Yes. I remember.'

'Losing her was so . . . ' He thought about it for a long moment and remembered too much. 'I don't know how I survived. I thought nothing so bad could ever happen again. But to know how they treated her – those two people who were supposed to be close to her, to love her –'

'Don't get upset again, please.'

She didn't want to hear. He tried to keep quiet and the memories racked him like toothache. Prue. They were nearly there and he was going to tell her –

'It's strange,' Sarah said, 'last year I spent a lot of time wondering what your home was like, and the village. Trying to picture you at week-ends. I never imagined we'd be here together . . . making this kind of visit.'

By the time they reached the cemetery and parked he was trembling all over, but she didn't seem to notice. Perhaps it didn't show: perhaps it was only on the inside.

'I'll get the flowers,' she said, reaching into the back seat. 'They're beautiful.'

Silence. She looked at him anxiously. He felt he was choking.

'I can't go in.' When he closed his eyes he could see Prue: alive, laughing, close to him.

'It'll be all right.' Sarah squeezed his hand. 'You're not alone.'

'I can't do it. I wanted to tell her . . . to ask her . . . but I can't. If I go in there – it's going to make it true.'

She said gently, 'Darling, it is true. You'll feel better afterwards, I'm sure you will.'

'No.' He could feel himself sweating with fear. 'Can you do it for me? Take the flowers and give them to her . . . and tell me what they've written about her.' He was close to tears. Sarah kissed him on the cheek and got out of the car with the flowers. After she had gone, he sat and shivered, alone with Prue.

Sarah walked slowly between the graves, carrying the flowers. She was dazed by the grief she had just witnessed. It made her hope she would never love anyone enough.

She looked about her for Prue's grave. The cemetery was crowded. So many dead people. In the distance she saw a dark young man planting something. When she got nearer she saw he was crying and she stopped. The inscription read: 'Prue, cherished daughter of Peter and Cassie Manson, beloved wife of Gavin Sorenson and mother of Eve, 1956 – 1976'.

She had never liked Prue, but the words moved her. The young man's tears moved her too. She felt thoroughly uncomfortable standing there, clutching her flowers.

'I'm sorry, I'm intruding.'

'No.'

'You must be Gavin.'

'Yes.'

She liked the way he wasn't ashamed of his tears.

'I'm Sarah.'

'Of course. I should have known.'

She gave him her handkerchief and he took it. Neither of them was embarrassed at all, which pleased her.

'Thanks.'

He wiped his eyes. She thought about Prue being loved so much. He was not at all what she had imagined. Manson had painted a monster.

'This is very good of you,' he said politely.

She indicated the flowers. 'They're from her father. He asked me to bring them.'

'Oh, I see. That explains a lot.' They stared at each other, fascinated. At last. The unknown enemy, revealed. And it was just a person. Rather nice and hesitant. That was all. 'I always wanted to meet you. I couldn't imagine what you were like.'

'I was curious about you too.'

There was a strangely tense pause. He saw a thin blonde girl, Manson's mistress, Prue's rival, but she looked real. He had not expected that. He said, 'You must have seen it all from the other side.'

'I'm not sure what I saw.' She seemed genuinely confused. They looked at each other with longing: there was so much they could have said, given time. 'I must go now,' she said reluctantly.

He was suddenly desperate. 'If you ever want to talk about it – you know where I live.'

'Yes.'

She walked away as he watched.

When she got back to the car Manson was still sitting there, as as if she had never left him. Like a statue. She was unnerved by his stillness.

'There's a beautiful inscription,' she said.

'Tell me another time.'

He looked away and after a moment she realized he was not with her. She got in the car and drove off, trying to adjust her mind to the man she had met, as well as the man in the car. She felt exhausted and wished to be alone to recover, but that was not possible.

Paris was a strain, but she thought she coped with it well. It was a shock when they got back, as they were unpacking, to hear him suddenly say, 'Come on Pussycat, you're back now – so you can stop pretending.'

'What?'

'Why didn't you want to go to Paris?'

'I did ! And I enjoyed it –' It was true, within limits.

He repeated gently, 'Why didn't you want to go Paris?'

She thought about it. How to be honest without being hurtful? 'I'm not sure. It was a lovely idea – but you made such a honeymoon thing of it – I suppose I was afraid I couldn't rise to the occasion.'

He tried to make a joke of it. 'That ought to be my line.'

'I'm sorry. I never seem to feel in the mood these days.' She resented having to apologize.

'I was beginning to wonder if there was something my best friend hadn't told me.'

'No.'

'If I changed my deodorant ... my toothpaste?'

'You're lovely.' She meant it but she was angry as well.

'You don't make me feel very lovely,' he said, as if he knew.

There was a nasty silence. They said simultaneously:

'Geoff, can we talk ... '

'We must talk ... '

They stopped and laughed, embarrassed.

'Well, we're agreed on that, anyway,' Geoff said.

'Yes.'

'You go first.'

'No, you.' She would not express how much she hated discussing her feelings and she did not know why.

Geoff said eagerly, 'I was going to say we must talk about what's wrong. Analyse it. Sort it out. There are dozens of ways we can make things better once we know what the problem is. Now – you haven't been really happy since we left Frankfurt. Right – we can go back there if that's what you want. You don't like this house – we can move. You're bored – tired – right – we can get a housekeeper and you can go back to work. You see? It's easy. And those are only three possibilities – right off the top of my head. There must be others. But do any of these appeal to you? Or all of them?'

She knew he was good and kind and loved her, but he sounded as if he were addressing a board meeting.

She said, 'I was going to say – I'm not very good at being married.'

He didn't seem at all perturbed. 'We can't expect to get it right at once. My parents were married nearly thirty years and they said they were still learning. It's like business. It must be. You don't get anything for nothing. The harder you work, the greater the profit. And you plough it back into the business.'

He looked so pleased with himself. She didn't know whether to love him, hate him, or pity him. She was touched, but angry that he had muddled her.

'And that's how you see marriage?'

'Why not?'

'My parents split up,' she said aggressively.

'So what?'

'If a business isn't sound – if it's making a loss – you don't go on pouring good money after bad.'

99

He looked at her with love. 'You do if you have faith in the business. If you know it's just a bad patch.'

Cassie heard the car and went into the hall to greet Manson as he arrived.

'Peter. You're early. Why didn't you ring?'

'Weren't you expecting me?'

'Yes, of course.'

She went up to him to kiss him but he turned away suddenly to pick up some letters on the hall table. The coldness puzzled her. Then she noticed he was without luggage.

'Where's your suitcase?'

'In the car.'

'Aren't you going to bring it in?'

'Later. I could use a drink.'

'Yes, of course.'

In the sitting-room she poured drinks automatically, while he stood at the window and stared into the garden.

She said, to make sure he was prepared, 'Gavin's coming later to see Eve. You don't mind, do you?'

'I assumed he'd be here.'

'He's awfully sorry about the other day – giving you a wasted journey. He had a row with his girlfriend ... and rushed off with Eve without thinking.'

'Yes, I know.'

'Oh, she told you, did she?' She gave him his drink. 'Do sit down, Peter, you look so uncomfortable standing there.'

'I'd rather stand.' Still the same cold voice. Like a horrible stranger.

'Are you all right? You sounded very odd on the phone the other day. I was quite worried.'

'Not so worried you felt obliged to ring up again.'

She flinched. 'I rather got the impression you wanted to be left alone.'

'Yes, I did. Just like you. In fact, it suddenly occurred to me how very unfair I've been to you, forcing my way back, assuming I was ... welcome. It must have been quite an effort for you, pretending you still cared for me. What a wonderful sense of duty you must have, to put on such an act.'

She was still puzzled but now angry as well. 'Peter, what's the matter with you?'

'Of course, from your point of view, you've overdone it. If you hadn't been so convincing I'd never have come back. So you've only yourself to blame. You actually made me believe there was some feeling left and we could start again. What a joke.'

'I don't understand you. What's happened?' A touch of fear. Had Gavin lied? What could Vicky have said? She pushed the fear away.

'Where's Eve?' Manson asked suddenly.

'Upstairs.'

'I'd like to see her.'

'And I'd like an explanation.'

He looked at her with contempt. 'Don't worry. You'll get one.'

The door-bell rang. She felt a great surge of relief mixed with apprehension. 'That'll be Gavin.'

'Of course.'

'Well, I hope you're not going to behave like this in front of him.' She went to answer the door as Manson went to see Eve. 'And try not to wake her,' she added sharply.

Gavin said, 'Hi,' before he saw the fear in her face. 'What's happened?'

'I'm not sure. Come in.'

He followed her into the sitting-room, reassured to find it empty. 'Where is he? Not here yet or not coming – please God?'

'Upstairs with Eve. I've never seen him like this. He's been bloody rude to me but it's more than that. He's sort of . . . turned vicious. I'm scared.'

'It's okay. I'm here.' But it wasn't okay at all. It confirmed his worst fears, and hers. She lit a cigarette and he watched her hands shake.

'Gavin, something must have happened. Did you talk to her?'

'Yes.' He made a quick decision. 'She swore there was nothing but when I went to the grave this week . . .'

They heard Manson's footsteps on the stairs.

'He's coming back,' Cassie said in a whisper; then louder: 'Would you like a drink?'

'Yeah, thanks.' He tried to relax : perhaps it would still be possible to evade the issue. And if not – suddenly he was pleased and surprised to find that part of him even welcomed a showdown.

Manson came in. 'Well, here we are again, all of us.' He had an air of sinister energy about him, a kind of bustling malice that Gavin had not seen since before the wedding.

'Hullo, sir.' For once they looked directly into each other's eyes and saw pure hatred.

'All three of us. Or should I say four? I've just been to see your daughter. She gets more beautiful all the time.'

'Yeah, that's right.'

'She must take after her mother.'

They were both startled to hear him refer to Prue for the first time since her death. It sounded like a declaration of war.

Cassie served the meal that no one wanted and they all sat at the table facing each other. The silence oppressed Gavin and he could see its effect on Cassie, so he made one last attempt at social hypocrisy.

'I sure am grateful you're not going to Scotland yet awhile, sir.'

Manson said, 'Yes. I imagine you are.'

'Well, it would have been very awkward for me.'

'In many ways.'

'I do count on seeing Eve, as you know.'

'And when you see her, does she remind you of her mother?' His tone was savage.

'Yes. Naturally.'

'Because she's so beautiful?'

'Yeah.'

Cassie trembled. There was a power emanating from Manson she had not seen before and it terrified her. 'The food's getting cold,' she said.

Manson went on as if there had been no interruption. 'However – beauty is one thing, character another. Don't you agree?'

'I guess so.'

'You guess so. And does my lovely wife also *guess so*?'

'Of course.' He reminded her of a river; that was it. Calm for so long, he had suddenly overflowed and was in full flood. He was unstoppable. He would destroy all in his path.

'Then we're all agreed. That being the case, let's hope that sleeping child upstairs doesn't inherit too much of her mother's character.'

'What d'you mean, sir?'

'What do I mean sir? I'll tell you exactly what I mean. I hope she'll be a better judge of people than her mother. I hope she won't be so trusting. I hope she'll be able to tell the people who'll make her happy from the people who'll do her harm.'

Dazed with terror, she heard herself say calmly, 'Oh, Peter. For God's sake stop raking up old scores.'

'Old scores? You really don't understand, do you? But you will. I promise you that.'

'If there's something you want to say to me, sir – '

'We *all* have Eve's welfare at heart.'

'Yes, of course.'

'Even you.'

'I resent that.'

'Oh, you resent it, do you? Not so much as I resent you beating up my daughter. Has it ever occurred to you how nearly that child of yours upstairs didn't get born? How you might have killed her inside her mother?'

It was inevitable now. She knew that. They were all going to face it. Yet she still had to try.

'Peter, please stop it.'

'Stop it? What is there to stop? It's all over, isn't it? So you keep telling me. I mean there *is* a grave, isn't there? That I ought to visit, if only I had the courage. How do *you* manage to visit that grave, that's what I'd like to know? Does anything like guilt or shame ever touch you both – or are you too far gone for that? Do you ever take that precious child to see the mother you murdered?'

His anger filled the room, swamped the table like a wave. Gavin stood up.

'I can't take any more of this.'

'Oh, you can't take it. Why not? You've taken everything else. You took Prue and you managed to kill her and I couldn't stop you. But your child is never going to lie in hospital the way my child did – trusting, forgiving, pregnant – while her mother fornicates with her husband.'

Dead silence. Then they both spoke at once.

'You don't understand –'

'It wasn't like that –'

He went on : 'When I look at you two, I want to vomit. You –' He looked at Gavin – 'well, you don't know any better, I suppose, it's natural to you to behave like that, but you –' Cassie shut her eyes ' – how can you call yourself a mother?'

He made a sudden move towards her. 'I'd like to kill you both.'

Instantly Gavin was between them.

'Keep away from her.'

'Get out of my way.'

Gavin stood his ground. Manson hit him.

4

REPRISALS

MANSON was astonished how quickly everything degenerated from drama into farce. The exaltation he had felt, the almost orgasmic sense of self-righteousness as he denounced them both, the blessed release when he finally struck Gavin – it all fell away and he was exhausted, cold with anti-climax, and shocked that he of all people could have succumbed to the violence he had always deplored in others. No matter that they deserved it. He had given way to something that was against his principles. It made him feel as unclean as they were, no longer uplifted like an avenging angel. He sat down heavily at the table: he felt ashamed and foolish.

Cassie said to Gavin, 'Are you all right?' She helped him up.

'Yeah. It's nothing.' He was anxious to make light of it.

'It doesn't look like nothing. Lean your head back.' His nose was bleeding; she put ice from the wine-cooler in a table napkin. 'Hold this against it.' Her solicitude sickened Manson. He poured himself a drink. 'I suppose you're proud of yourself,' she said to him.

'Prue would have been,' said Gavin abruptly, surprising them both. 'She always wanted us to have a fight and she wanted me to let you win. She'd have been delighted – except for one thing. The way she saw it, we should have fought over her – not her mother. That wouldn't have pleased her at all.'

Cassie suddenly lost control. 'But you did fight over her – didn't you?' She turned on Manson. 'I didn't hear you say one word about my being unfaithful to you. If you were angry – jealous – hurt. Not one word. All you cared about was what I'd done to Prue. But she never knew. We were very careful not to hurt her. Even after she told me about you and your mistress.'

'So you did it for revenge,' Manson said heavily. 'Not very flattering.'

Cassie still wanted him to understand. 'No. We were lonely and worried and frightened. It was ... comforting to be together. There was no one else around. We're not proud of what happened –'

'We're not ashamed of it either,' Gavin said.

' – but it wasn't the way you imagine.'

Manson picked up the only detail that interested him. 'Prue never wanted a fight. That's a disgusting thing to say.'

'You don't know the first thing about her.' Gavin flung the bloodstained cloth on the table.

'I know my own daughter. And she's not here to defend herself – thanks to you. You killed my daughter and you ruined my marriage.'

Cassie heard herself shouting. 'If anyone ruined our marriage, it was Prue. From the day she was born she came between us. You always loved her more than me. When I had the twins and nearly died – it didn't matter. When I had an affair with Sven – you didn't notice. All you could see was Prue.'

In the silence that followed she realized she had been wanting to say that for twenty years.

'What an evil woman you are,' Manson said, 'to be jealous of your own child.'

'Yes, I was jealous of her – and I still am. I've got good reason to be. For all her twenty years she had everything she wanted. She had your love and his love and the child she wanted. She had it all. I've never had everything I wanted for more than a few months.' She barely recognized this screaming voice.

Manson said coldly, 'I don't think there's any point in going on with this conversation. You're obviously hysterical.'

'Can't you face the truth for once in your life? Your beloved daughter was spoilt, cruel and selfish, we both made her that way. That's the truth. But it didn't mean I didn't love her.' She stopped for a moment, remembering that painful love. 'I loved her very much.'

Manson stood up. 'In case it's of any interest to you, I intend to divorce you, citing him as co-respondent. I shall of course obtain custody of Eve. You're not fit to have the care of a child.'

He left. Each thought the other might stop him but neither moved. Once they were alone, it was all suddenly real and they felt much too exposed.

'He's just trying to frighten you,' Gavin said.

'He's succeeded.' She poured herself a drink.

'I didn't know you felt that way about Prue. Not for so long. You never said.'

'I'd rather not talk about it.'

He came over and hugged her. 'Cassandra, I'm sorry. I've done nothing but make trouble for you.'

All the times she had longed to be hugged and now she could only pull away. 'I want to be by myself. I've got a lot of thinking to do.'

'He doesn't mean it. He can't.'

'Oh, he means it all right. I know him. The only question is, can he do it?'

'Surely not.'

'I don't know.'

'He can't take Eve away. She's mine. I'm her father.'

The irony of it almost made her laugh. 'If you only knew – you're so alike.'

'What?'

Suddenly she couldn't bear his presence a minute longer. As far as she could see, her life was in ruins and it was largely his fault. 'Gavin, please. I've got to be on my own.'

'I did love her too,' he said. 'I loved you both. I still do.'

'I know.'

He gave in. 'Take care of yourself, Cassandra. I'll call you tomorrow.'

After he had gone she lit a cigarette and poured another drink. She felt very tired. All the shouting had drained her. She couldn't believe they had all said those things. And they would all have to go on living and face each other again. Upstairs, Eve cried. Cassie went to her with a sense of relief.

It was one of their better times. They were sleepy, they had laughed a lot over dinner, they had drunk plenty of wine but not too much. Sarah was beginning to enjoy all the old sensations she thought she had lost with him. She wanted to please him, too, as well as herself : there was a lot to make up for.

The phone rang. At first they tried to ignore it but it went on and on. Eventually Geoff picked it up and said furiously, 'Yes?'

Sarah felt sudden panic. But he hung up almost at once.

'They didn't speak.'

'Mm.'

'I hate that. Who the hell was it?'

Somehow she knew, although there was no reason. 'Wrong number. Or a drunk.'

'It couldn't be Freddy, could it?'

'At this hour?'

He wouldn't leave it alone. 'Maybe I should ring him.'

'But he'd have spoken.'

'Yes.'

'It's just a mistake.' She cuddled up, wanting to distract him, and they tried to pick up where they had left off, but the mood was gone. They rolled apart. She began to feel sleepy. Maybe she'd been wrong. He wouldn't ring up in the middle of the night. *Surely*.

'Have you thought any more about what I said?' Geoff's business voice.

'What about?'

'Us. Whether you want to go back to Frankfurt or move house or go back to work.

'Oh. Not really.' Why did they have to go into all that *now*?

'Well, it's up to you. I don't mind. Whatever's going to make you happy.'

'Mm.'

His voice droned on. He had given the matter a lot of thought. 'As I see it, Freddy really ought to be in Frankfurt, unless you specially want us to be there. He's more useful to me there and there's less responsibility – while he's learning the ropes. It's exactly what the old man did with me to give me a chance. Well, you remember. So that means we really ought to stay here. But we could still move house, if you really hate this place. Or, better still, get someone in to run it, so you could be free. How d'you feel about part-time work? Then you wouldn't be tied but you'd still have your independence. Mm? What d'you think?'

When he looked at her she was asleep.

Sunday morning. Cassie had thought she wouldn't sleep but she did in the end, and woke to wish she hadn't. The transition from thinking that life was normal to remembering what had happened was so awful, she would have preferred to stay awake.

She didn't know what to do with the day. She glanced at the Sunday papers and put them down. She took food out of the fridge and put it back. All bought with such love and care, and now there was no one to eat it.

Yesterday's disaster nagged at her. The more real it became, the more she felt she should do something about it. But she didn't know what to do.

Gavin was trying to work but he only read the same paragraph over and over again. None of it made sense. He got up, wandered round the room, looked out of the window. Finally he went into the hall and rang Cassie. He was worried about her. He had screwed up her life and she was upset : she would need reassuring.

The phone rang and rang. There was no reply.

He hung up, worried. Where was she? More important, where had she taken Eve? Were they both on their way to see him, perhaps?

He took his book into the bedroom and lay on the bed. Prue's photograph mocked him from the bedside table. What was Cassie doing? Would there really be a divorce? He couldn't believe it, but the punch yesterday had been real enough. He felt his jaw gingerly. His lip was cut too. But he didn't grudge Manson the satisfaction : he had earned it.

Just as he was settling down to read again he heard a key in the front door. Then footsteps in the hall. They passed the bedroom door and went into the living-room. He got up stealthily and followed them.

Vicky was packing her books. Taking them off the shelves and putting them in a cardboard box. She hummed tunelessly as she worked : it was something that had always irritated him about her. He waited, anger mounting (what a nerve she had to walk in like that), until she sensed his presence and spun round, startled.

He said, 'I hope you're satisfied.'

'Oh, you gave me such a fright. I thought you were out.'

'That's pretty obvious.'

'But you said I could come and get my things when you were out.' She looked puzzled.

'That's right.'

'I thought you'd be visiting the baby today.'

'I would have been.'

She finally noticed his swollen lip. 'What's the matter with your face?'

He said savagely, 'Ah, now you're getting somewhere. You may be slow but you get there in the end.'

'Has something happened?'

'Oh, come *on*, you knew he was gunning for me and you let me walk right into it. Didn't have the guts to warn me, did you?'

She was shocked. 'He hit you?'

'You could say that, yeah.'

'Oh, I'm sorry. Have you put anything on it?' She came towards him.

'Get away from me, haven't you done enough harm? For Christ's sake, why did you have to tell him?'

'But I didn't, really. I may have said a few silly things when I was upset but I didn't actually *tell* him, honestly. I wouldn't do a thing like that. He tricked me. He pretended he knew all the time – he said his wife had told him.'

Either she was lying or she was even more stupid than he had thought.

'And you believed him. You must be thick.'

'But there *are* people like that. He said they didn't have any secrets. How was I to know he was lying?'

He tried to spell it out for her. 'You didn't have to *know* anything. All you had to do was to keep your mouth shut – and you couldn't even do that.'

'Neither could you. If you hadn't told me, I couldn't have told him even by mistake.'

'You did it on purpose.'

'No, I didn't, but you shouldn't have told me.'

'You guessed.'

'You could have denied it. It's hardly something to boast about – going to bed with your mother-in-law.'

He hadn't expected her to stand up for herself. 'It was a lot better than going to bed with you.'

'That's not fair.'

'You don't seem to realize what you've done. Because you're so bloody stupid or spiteful or both, he's only going to divorce her and name me and try to take Eve away from us both.'

He could see he had finally succeeded in distressing her, but she was too hurt and angry to retreat. 'Then it serves you right.' He lost control and slapped her. She promptly burst into tears and ran out. 'She'll be better off with him.'

He was suddenly shocked by his own behaviour – it brought back too much of the past – and he ran after her. 'Vicky. I'm sorry. Come back. Vicky, please.'

But it was too late. She'd gone.

After tea Cassie drove the boys back to school. They bounced around in the car so naturally, they almost made her feel that nothing had happened. She admired their energy, too.

'That was smashing!'

'You ate like a pig.'

'So did you.'

They made grunting noises.

She said, 'You won't want any supper then, will you?'

'We might.'

'It's always grotty on Sundays. They give us rabbits' food.'

'They must have seen your ears.'

They wrestled good-humouredly. She looked at them with love and astonishment. They were so uncomplicated, in spite of everything. She was grateful. It took an effort to let go of them.

'Well ... off you go. I'll be down again soon.'

'Will Dad come next time?'

'I expect so.'

'I wish he'd come today.'

If only they wouldn't spoil it. She couldn't cope with their anxiety as well as her own.

'I told you, he's busy today.'

'He wasn't ill again, was he?' Andrew, worried.

'No, of course not.'

'Only he has been ill an awful lot.'

'He can't help it. He doesn't do it on purpose.' David, defensive.

'He will come to the match, won't he?'

She said, 'I'm sure he will. Go on, you're going to be late.'

'Bye, Mum.'

'Bye.'

They all hugged each other and she watched them run into school. She almost envied them. Previously, her worst nightmares had been about being a child again in a classroom. Now she recognized that there were, incredibly, worse fates.

Manson couldn't think who was ringing his door-bell. The day had passed in a dream. He kept re-living the previous day as an endless, repetitive, action replay. It was quite a surprise to find that anything else could happen.

Vicky said, 'I hope you don't mind . . .'

'No, of course not.' He had to be polite. 'Well – come in.'

'Am I disturbing you?'

'Not a bit. Are you all right?'

She came in without a qualm. 'I didn't know where to go.'

'I'm glad to see you.'

'Are you really?'

'Yes, of course. Can I get you anything?' In his present state, he only dimly remembered who she was.

'No. Thank you.' She looked at him strangely. 'I'm sorry, I shouldn't have come.'

'Don't be silly. Has something happened?'

She said in a sudden rush, 'Oh, I do wish you hadn't told him you know. He'll never forgive me now, he's so angry, I'll never get him back. I wish you hadn't done it.'

'How d'you know what I've done?' She was going much too fast for him.

'I've just seen him. I begged you not to tell him.'

'I'm sorry. I had to.'

'You didn't have to hit him.' To his horror, she began to cry. 'Oh please don't get divorced, it's horrible. You're going to make me feel it's all my fault. Please stay with your wife and let him keep the baby, that's all he cares about really.'

'Why are you so upset?'

'Could I have some aspirin please? I've got a headache.'

A sudden terrible suspicion occurred to him. 'He – didn't hurt you, did he?'

When Cassie got home she found Gavin waiting on her doorstep.

'Hi. I called you but you weren't answering so I ... came down. I was worried about you.'

'I had to do something so I went to see the boys. I thought that might help.'

'Did it?'

'Not really. I kept thinking about what I might have to tell them.'

He picked up Eve and cuddled her – the object of his visit, no doubt.

'It's going to be all right,' he said, without much conviction.

'Is it?'

'It's got to be.' He looked at Eve. 'He can't take you away. You belong to me.'

Cassie said, 'Well, I'd better start getting her ready for bed.'

'I'll give you a hand.'

'No.' She was surprised how much resentment she still felt. 'D'you mind if I don't ask you in? I'm sorry. I expect I'm being silly but I keep thinking Peter might turn up and if you're here he'll only ... imagine things.'

'Okay. If that's how you want it.'

She could see he was shaken. 'I know I'm locking the stable door after the horse has bolted and all that ... but I can't help it.'

'You really do feel guilty.'

'Yes, I do. And I don't find the idea of divorce very pleasant either.'

He was hurt and tried to make light of it. 'How long am I banned for?'

'You're not ... Oh, just a few days. Till I've spoken to Peter. Till we get something sorted out.' Then she suddenly had to say it. 'Oh, why *did* you have to tell that girl?'

'Showing off, I guess. I'm sorry, Cassandra.'

'Well, it's done now.'

'I wanted to talk to you.'

'Not now. Gavin, please.'

'She came to see me today. And I hit her.'

'Oh no.' She turned away, exhausted, and picked up Eve.

'I'm so ashamed. I don't know what to do.'

Even now he seemed to expect her to help him with his problems. 'We'll talk another time. I'm sorry. I just can't take any more now.'

Vicky was amazed by the transformation. Once Manson understood Gavin had actually hit her, he became suddenly active and lucid, scurrying about to get a cold-water compress for her eye and applying it with surprising concern.

'How does it feel now?'

'It's just sort of throbbing. It's nothing really. The cold water's lovely.'

'I'll get some ice. That might be better still.' He hurried into the kitchen, shouted to her with satisfaction, 'Now d'you see what sort of person he is? You ought to report him.'

'Who to?'

'The police, of course. Somebody's got to stop him.' He returned with the ice. 'Now this is going to be really cold. Hang on.'

'Ooh. Yes, it is.'

'Better?'

'Yes. Thank you.'

'You could take him to court, you know.'

'Oh, I couldn't.' She loved his attentions to her eye but she wished he'd stop coming up with such silly ideas.

'Why not? There's no reason on earth why you should tolerate this kind of treatment, you're not even –'

'No.' She could have done without that reminder, too.

'I mean – you don't have to live with him. How's it feel now?'

'Not so bad. I think you've frozen it, like a tooth.'

'Let me look.'

'It doesn't show, does it? I don't want everyone knowing.'

He stared at it closely. 'No, there's only a slight graze at the moment. But it may swell up tomorrow. You really ought to see a doctor, you know. Just to be on the safe side.' She felt herself starting to smile; she couldn't help it. 'Well, you can't be sure it's all right. He may have done some damage we can't see. What's the joke?'

'My father's a doctor,' she said. 'I suppose I ought to see him.'

By the time Manson drew up outside her father's flat, Vicky knew they were both mad. She should never have let him bring her here.

'I'm not sure this is a good idea,' she said, understating wildly.

'Nonsense, of course it is.'

'He'll only say I'm making a fuss about nothing.'

'Surely not.'

It was not possible to explain properly about her father. She tried and tried but she could never make people understand.

'He will. He's very stoical, especially about other people.'

'D'you want me to come in with you?'

Horror. 'Oh no, that would make it worse. I mean, thanks all the same, but he'd think I was being childish. Well ... ' She got out of the car reluctantly.

'Let me know how you are.'

'Yes. Thank you.' She went up the steps to the door and turned. He was still there, parked, and watching her encouragingly, with a look of concern she now found irritating. How to escape? She waved. He waved back. She put her hand over the bell-push and to her relief heard the car drive off. Without ringing the bell she turned and walked briskly away.

A voice called out in Welsh: 'I'd know that bum anywhere.' Her father's voice. The front door slammed. He must have come out the minute she left. What rotten luck. She turned and found it was even worse: he had Anna with him.

'I was coming to see you,' Vicky said, feeling stupid.

'Of course. Walking backwards as usual.' He switched to English in deference to Anna.

'I changed my mind.'

'Why not?' He looked amused. 'You remember Anna, don't you?'

'Yes. Hullo, Anna.' She was elegant as ever, making Vicky feel scruffy and childish.

'Hullo, Vicky. How are you?'

'All right.'

They all eyed each other uncomfortably.

Anna said, 'I'll wait in the car.'

He gave her the keys. 'Thanks. Won't be long.'

Anna said, 'Bye, Vicky. Nice to see you.'

'Bye.' She bitterly resented her father saying he wouldn't be long.

Anna got in the car and Vicky stared at her father, willing him to give her all his attention.

'How all right are you?' he said.

'Gavin hit me.'

'Oh dear, how nasty. What did you do to annoy him?'

'Why d'you always assume I'm in the wrong?'

'That's not what I said. But you wouldn't be living with someone who hits you for no reason at all – or would you?'

'He's thrown me out.'

'I'm sorry. That's always a bad one.'

Was that *all* he was going to say?

'Would you look at my eye, please. Now I'm here.'

'Which one?'

'The left.'

He inspected it briefly. She was sure he made more fuss of his patients, and they were strangers.

'Seems all right. Bit less make-up than the right one but no damage.'

'Someone put cold water on it.' Someone who *cared*, she wanted to say.

'No harm in that.' He kissed her forehead briskly, 'You may have a bit of a shiner tomorrow. See your GP if you're worried.'

'I wanted to see you.'

'But I'm not your doctor.' He actually started to walk away.

'No, you're only my father.'

'It would help if you rang up first, you know.'

'Oh – to make an appointment, you mean.'

He said, 'Come and tell me all about it when I'm not so busy.'

'You're always busy.'

He smiled. 'All right, have a nice wallow. It might do you good. We'll talk another time.'

Sarah made a grand entrance at the top of the stairs and did her street urchin whistle to attract Geoff's attention. She was proud of being able to make such a loud, shrill, vulgar noise, so much at odds with her new evening dress and fox fur stole. Geoff looked up. He had been pacing the hall, complaining they were going to be late, but now she could see from his face that she had been worth waiting for. She had almost forgotten the events of the night. She felt peaceful and good-tempered. She liked Geoff's friends and she was looking forward to dinner.

'Why do they have to live in the wilds of Essex?' she asked, as he started the car.

'I suppose they like it.'

'They must be mad.'

'You're wonderfully intolerant. What's wrong with Essex?'

'Well, if you can't – Oh !' She let out a squeak of surprise. As they turned out of their gates, she saw Manson's car parked under a tree only a few yards away.

'What's up?'

She said the first thing that came into her head. 'Oh – I – I meant to get some flowers for Marian.'

'Whatever for? She's got a garden full of them.'

She was surprised how steady her voice sounded. 'Yes – of course.' She watched Manson's car in the mirror till Geoff turned the wheel. So the nightmare was real. 'Still, it would have been a nice thought,' she said.

*

When the phone rang in the morning Manson picked it up and listened without speaking. You couldn't be too careful. It might be Cassie, trying to worm her way back, to make him forgive her, to cover up her shame.

Sarah said, 'Peter?'

'It's you.' He was so relieved.

'What on earth were you doing yesterday?'

'When?' He could hardly remember yesterday. It seemed to have blurred in the night. But Saturday was still painfully real.

'When? Outside our house in the evening. You gave me the fright of my life.'

It came back to him vaguely. 'I wanted to be near you. I didn't know what to do.'

'But Geoff might have seen you.'

'I'm sorry. I didn't think he'd recognize me.' In fact he had not thought at all. He had been past thought.

'Oh, *Peter*.' She sighed. 'What happened at the week-end?'

'I can't tell you now. Are you coming over?' He was desperate to see her.

A long silence.

'I suppose so. As soon as I can. I've got things to do.'

Gavin met Vicky by arrangement on the college steps. He gave her the cardboard box containing her books; she gave him the front door key to the flat. Then they just looked at each other.

He said, 'I'm sorry. I really am.'

'Are you?'

'Don't you believe me?' He had never seen such a cold look on her face before.

'I thought you liked hitting women. Why should you be sorry?'

When the door-bell rang, Manson was surprised and pleased. He had not thought Sarah would arrive so soon and he was tidying up; somehow he had let the place become rather a mess without realizing it.

He opened the door and saw Cassie. 'Can I come in?'

'There's nothing to say.' He was shocked.

'I think there is.'

The sheer habit of courtesy made him let her in, though he longed to slam the door in her face.

She looked around. 'I didn't want to come here, you know. It reminds me. I didn't even want to see it.'

'Then you should have stayed away.' He turned his back to show her how he felt.

'You must have been very comfortable here ... with her.'

'Is that all you've come to say?'

'Don't you find it even slightly flattering that I can still be jealous – after all these years? Would you rather I didn't care what you did? Peter, I just want to remind you we've both got a lot to forgive. I think that ought to help. Are you listening?'

'I hear you. I don't have to look at you as well.'

'We all said a lot on Saturday. At first I was afraid we'd said too much – things we couldn't ever forget. But then I decided it was better that way. We don't have to forget, we meant all those things – at the time. It was probably quite healthy to say them. But that doesn't mean we can't try again. Does it?'

He turned round in a sudden panic. Sarah might arrive at any minute.

'Don't you understand? What you did – with him, of all people – you're untouchable.'

'For the moment. Yes. I see that. Perhaps for a long time. But is that really enough to break up a marriage? Gavin and I had so little time together. You and I have come through so much over the years. Do you really want to throw all that away?'

He said, 'I only know I could never live with you again.'

Sitting in the taxi, Sarah felt tired and old. She wished now she had not been to the doctor before seeing Manson. It was too much for one day.

Cassie said stubbornly, 'I don't want a divorce.'

'You should have thought of that before.'

'And I don't believe you do either. We're not good at living alone, either of us. We've tried it. I was miserable and I think you were too. If you cite Gavin, everyone will know what happened. Gavin won't mind that – but you and I will. Very much. And if you try to take Eve away – '

'Ah, now we're getting to it. That's all you really care about, isn't it?'

'No – or I wouldn't be here. But it's all Gavin cares about and he'll fight you. I think he'll win.'

'Because you're going to help him, no doubt.'

'If I have to ... He's got a right to his own child. Nothing he's done justifies you trying to separate them. Anyway, you can't look after a baby.'

'I shall hire someone who can.'

His air of omnipotence infuriated her. 'It costs the earth. You can't even afford this place, let alone a nanny. What are we all going to live on?'

'So it's money you're worried about.'

'Among other things, yes. Someone's got to be practical.'

He suddenly remembered Sarah. 'I'd like you to leave now.'

She went on as if she had not heard him. 'I went to see the boys yesterday. Have you thought about them at all? How do we begin to explain something like this to them?'

'I've got nothing more to say to you.'

'I'm not leaving till you promise to reconsider.'

Desperate to get rid of her in time, he said the cruellest thing he could think of. 'You disgust me.'

The taxi drew up outside Manson's block of flats. Sarah was about to get out and pay, but she paused to check her make-up. At that moment Cassie came out of the building and Sarah, putting away the hand-mirror, saw her. The narrowness of her escape terrified her. She sat in the taxi, shaking, and watched Cassie, who seemed very distressed, run across to her car and drive off.

She said furiously, 'You might have warned me.'

'I'm sorry, she just turned up. I'd no idea she was coming.'

She was still shaking. 'One minute earlier and I'd have run slap into her.'

'She didn't see you, did she?'

'No. Anyway, she doesn't know me. But I saw her. She looked awfully upset.'

'Yes. We had ... an argument.' He didn't seem very concerned.

'What's going on?'

'D'you want a drink?'

'It's awfully early.' She paused. 'Yes, please. It wasn't you who rang up on Saturday night, was it?'

'I'm sorry.'

She was outraged by his casual tone. 'How could you? What's Geoff supposed to think? And yesterday, hovering round the gate like that when we went out to dinner – he has *met* you, don't forget. If he'd seen you, he would have recognized you.'

'Yes, I know. I shouldn't have done it.'

'What got into you?'

'I had a dreadful week-end.'

'And I wasn't available. I'm sorry.' She tried to push her own troubles to the back of her mind. 'Tell me what happened.'

He paced about the room while she sat and watched him. 'Oh, we all three made a disgusting exhibition of ourselves ... said a lot of things we'd been trying not to say ... I hit him ... I didn't know I could do such a thing ... I'm going to divorce her and take Eve away.'

'But can you do that?'

'I don't know. I'll find a way.'

'Then why was she here?'

'She wanted to try again.'

'And?'

'I said no, of course.'

It had all gone much too far. She was alarmed. 'Oh, Peter, are you sure?'

'How can you ask me that? Her own daughter's husband. It's revolting. She's contaminated.'

'You've been married a long time.'

'What's that got to do with it?'

Sarah got up and poured herself another drink. He sounded so positive. He astonished her. 'I envy you sometimes,' she said.

'Me?'

'You're so sure what to do. Any situation you're in – even if you behave badly, at least you're positive about it. You don't seem to have doubts. Whereas me – I just get in one mess after another and I muddle along and I'm never sure what to do for the best. I hate being like that.'

He looked at her in amazement. 'What's the matter?'

She couldn't keep it to herself any longer. 'I think I'm pregnant.'

Barbara said, 'Are you sure?'

'I just rang my doctor for the results of the test. I'd been hoping all morning but no luck. It's positive.'

'It always is.' She cast around for something cheerful to say. 'Hey – why are we depressed? You've got a rich husband.'

'Yes.'

'Well, then. That's the main thing.'

'Is it?'

'Of course it is. Oh, I know you didn't want to do it straight off but still, what's the difference, get it over with, that's what I say. You might as well. It's not so bad. And at least you won't be lurching about like me, throwing up with one eye on your watch, afraid they'll dock your pay if you miss the bus to work.'

'No.'

'He's always wanted kids, hasn't he?'

'Yes.'

'Well, that's all right then. John was always furious – as if I'd done it on purpose to spite him.' She peered at Sarah's gloomy face. 'Cheer up.'

'Sorry.' She poured some more cider. It was all Barbara had to offer. She had no appetite for lunch and the council flat always depressed her. She wished now that she had not come, but there was no else she could talk to.

'Look,' Barbara said, 'it doesn't hurt all *that* much and they can give you stuff to help.'

'I know all that.'

'When I had Sharon it was easy as shelling peas. Only it doesn't do to tell *them* that.'

'Who?'

'Men, of course. Better if they think you've suffered. Then they make more fuss and you can hold it over them for ever more. That's worth a few presents. Well, in your case, I mean, not mine. For obvious reasons. Ah, you're really feeling down, aren't you?'

Sarah said sharply, 'I'm not sure whose it is.'

The pub was crowded but Geoff and Freddy managed to get a table to themselves for lunch. There was a lot to discuss.

'D'you think he'll do it for less?'

'I'm not sure. He says that's his last offer.'

'But you think he's bluffing.'

'Probably.'

'Well, if anyone can get him to come down a bit, it's you.'

Freddy grinned. 'It's a dubious talent.'

'Nonsense. It's invaluable.'

'What if he can't afford it?'

'Then he'll say no.'

'And do we say yes?'

'Come back to me on that when it happens. If it happens. They don't often slip through your fingers. Now – about Beihoffer.'

Freddy looked pleased with himself. 'I think that's going to be all right. But I'd like you to see it first.'

'Can you call in tonight?'

'It's cutting it fine but I'll try.'

Barbara said, 'You're having me on.' But she saw from Sarah's face it was true. 'You idiot – you've been up to your old tricks.'

'Don't be cross, I can't bear it.'

'Cross? I just think you're bloody stupid, that's all. You get it all handed to you on a plate and what do you do? Go out and look for trouble. Who is it this time?'

'The same one.'

'Not that old bloke – your ex-boss? You want your head examined, you do. Why him? Whatever for?'

Sarah said wearily, 'What's the point of going on about reasons? You wouldn't understand.'

'I suppose you've been using me to cover up again. Geoff doesn't suspect anything, does he?'

'I don't think so.'

'Think so ! You better be sure.'

'No, he doesn't.'

'Thank the lord for that. Then you're okay. Drop the other one sharpish and tell Geoff you're pregnant.'

Sarah was shocked. 'Let him think it's his?'

'Maybe it is.'

'And maybe it isn't.'

'Well, you can't tell him that, can you?' She paused, horrified. 'Is that what you were going to do?'

Sarah said, 'It's . . . such a big thing to lie about.'

'You've had plenty of practice.'

'Not about something as important as this.'

'It's no good getting squeamish now,' said Barbara, brisk as ever. 'Just make up your mind you've got to tell one more whopper. Make it a good one and make it your last. Who knows, it may even be true.'

'It seems . . . so wrong.'

'What about the rest of it?'

'That's different.' She meant it. That was how she felt.

'Oh yeah? Try telling him that. Look, love, if you tell him the truth and he throws you out, you won't get a penny. He'll be ever so hurt – can you imagine? He'll never forgive you. And it may be his child all the time.'

'I know. I know all that. You're right. But I don't think I can do it.' What was the use of logic when all her feelings were against it?

'You've got to. Either that or get rid of it.'

'Oh, I couldn't do that,' she said instantly, automatically.

'Then you've got no choice.'

Cassie sat in her car and smoked and waited for him to come home. It seemed a long time. When he finally appeared, she felt weak with relief.

He came up to the car at once, surprised to see her. 'Cassandra – what's wrong?'

'I wanted to see you.'

'I thought I was out of bounds.'

She ignored that. 'Can I come in?'

'Yes, of course. Where's Eve?'

'With my daily. She's quite safe.'

Inside the flat he began automatically to tell her his troubles first.

'I went to see Vicky. I told her I was sorry but she wouldn't believe me.'

'I expect she does – but she'd rather make you feel guilty.'

'She's succeeded.' Then he looked at her more closely. 'Are you okay? You look a bit washed out.'

'I went to see Peter.'

'And?'

'Could I have a drink?'

'Sure – I think there's some Scotch left.' But he looked and there wasn't.

'Never mind.'

'What did he say?'

'He said I was untouchable. He said I disgusted him.' Even now, just repeating the words made her shiver.

'He's crazy.'

'That's how he feels.'

'He'll get over it.'

'I don't think so. He was very cold, very bitter. He couldn't wait to get rid of me. I shouldn't have gone.'

'Why did you go?' Gavin, practical as ever. 'You might have known he'd be like that.'

'I had to ask him to reconsider.'

'You really want to go on living with him?'

'I don't want to be alone again. And I don't want a messy divorce. Think what it would do to the boys. And as for custody fight about Eve – '

'That's out of the question. I'll kill him first.'

She felt herself starting to smile. It was all so familiar and comforting.

'That wouldn't be very helpful. They'd lock you up and you'd only see her on visiting days.'

He grinned at her. 'Feeling better?'

'A bit.'

'Talking of visiting days, can I come at the week-end?'

She had nothing left to lose now. 'Why not? You might as well.'

'Great. I'll come on Friday.'

'If this goes on, we'll have to see lawyers and make statements and God knows what. You do realize that?'

'That's okay.'

'You really don't mind?'

'Why should I?'

She was proud of him. 'I told him you wouldn't mind.'

'You were right.'

'And I told him we'd fight for custody.'

'We?'

'I'm on your side about that.'

'You're terrific.'

She smiled. 'Not terrific enough, unfortunately, or I wouldn't be in this mess.'

All afternoon she had been rehearsing in her head and trying to behave normally at the same time till her throat ached with tension. She waited for a suitable moment, opened her mouth and closed it again. Barbara's advice rang in her head. She wanted to do the right thing, not the wise thing, but she was no longer sure which was which.

She took a deep breath. 'Let's go in.'

'Why? It's a lovely evening. You're not cold, are you?'

'No. I wanted to talk to you.'

They were on the patio. Geoff in his bathrobe was still towelling his hair dry.

'We can talk out here, can't we? Have you decided?'

The word made her jump, as if he had read her thoughts. 'What do you mean?'

'About making changes. What you want to do.'

'No. Not really.' She relaxed and that put her off saying any more.

'Flash in the pan, was it?'

'What?'

'All that talk about being restless.'

'I don't know.' Dear God, how could she find the strength? 'Geoff – d'you ever imagine – hating me?'

'Often.' He looked at her cheerfully.

'No – be sensible.'

'I am being –'

'If I did something awful. If I really deserved to be hated, would you throw me out?'

'Come on, Pussycat, don't be silly. What are you on about?'

She felt her eyes sting with tears. Guilt or self-pity? 'I've been a rotten wife to you, haven't I?'

'It's early days. Maybe I've been a rotten husband. I told you. We can't expect everything to be perfect all at once. Anyway, I don't happen to think it's so bad – do you?'

'No.'

'So what's all the fuss about?'

In a sudden rush to be brave she said it. 'I'm pregnant.' She'd meant to go on and say the rest of it, quickly but she couldn't : the word made her freeze.

'Are you sure?'

'Yes.'

'That's fantastic.'

'No –' Now she had to finish it, but he was too fast for her.

'Oh, darling. Oh, Pussycat. Oh! I'm so pleased. Oh, you're beautiful, I can't believe it.' He kissed her, hugged her, looked at her with such adoration she was terrified.

'Please – don't – wait –'

'It's wonderful.'

'No – listen –'

'Oh, I know you wanted to wait, but darling, you won't regret it, I promise you. I'll give you everything you want. I'll make it as easy as I possibly can, you won't be sorry, believe me –'

'Geoff, please listen –' This was worse than anything she had imagined.

'Don't be against it, please. I'm so happy. I've never been so happy. And you'll be happy too, once you get used to the idea, I know you will.'

'No – please –' Still she couldn't get the words out. He kept interrupting her and she was so frightened, she let him. Perhaps she even wanted him to; she wasn't sure any more.

'Darling, I know you think it's too soon but it isn't really, it's going to be the making of us, it's going to make all the difference –'

Just when she thought nothing more could happen, a taxi drew up at the gate. Geoff sprang up. 'Oh – marvellous. Just in time. I'd forgotten I'd asked Freddy to drop in.'

Sarah said urgently, 'Don't tell him.'

'Why ever not?'

'Please. Promise.'

Freddy waved, advanced towards them up the drive. Sarah was desperate.

'Geoff, please. As a favour to me. Just for tonight. It's important. Please don't tell him.'

'Hullo,' Freddy said. 'You look cosy.'

Geoff grinned at him. 'So you made it.'

'I'm on my way to the airport actually, so I haven't much time, but I'd like you to take a look at the Beihoffer contract I told you about – just to make sure I'm on the right lines. I've checked and double checked but you know how it is. Don't want the new boy making a fool of himself, do we?'

Geoff took the contract and tried to study it. Freddy turned to Sarah. 'How's my beautiful sister-in-law?'

'All right.' Even seeing Freddy was painful now. He looked so young and innocent.

'She's a lot more than all right.'

'Geoff – don't.'

Freddy made it worse. 'You know, it does me good to see you two. If I get married young, and I always swore I wouldn't, it'll be all your fault.'

Sarah said, 'Don't rush into anything.'

'Why not? It looks good from where I'm standing.'

'D'you want a drink?' Anything to distract him.

'No, not really.'

'Champagne, I think,' Geoff said.

'No –' She wanted to scream.

'Sorry, Freddy, I can't keep my mind on this but I think it's all right.'

'Really? That's good.' Freddy looked pleased, surprised.

Geoff said, 'Sarah's going to have a baby.'

Everything inside her turned to ice. She watched Freddy's excitement, his delight. 'Fantastic. That's really fantastic.'

'I'll get the champagne,' Geoff said. 'You can wait for champagne, can't you?'

'Yes. I'll miss the plane.' He turned to her. 'Oh, Sarah, how marvellous.'

'She thinks it's too soon but it isn't. I'll get the bottle. You tell her.'

Left alone with Freddy, Sarah stared at the ground. Weeds were growing in the cracks of the patio. She felt ill, as if she were being punished for every wrong thing she had ever done, even those she had not felt were wrong.

Freddy said, 'Sarah, it's wonderful news. Isn't it? Oh, please be happy. Geoff's so happy. All this waiting, it's modern. We're not modern in this family, we're traditional. Mum had Geoff nine months to the day.'

'I just didn't want him to tell anyone yet.'

'But I'm not anyone, I'm family.'

'Yes.'

'It's the best thing that could have happened.'

They heard the bang of the champagne cork inside the house. Geoff came out with the open bottle and three glasses. He made a great ceremony of pouring and Freddy helped him. Sarah watched, dumb with misery.

'There we are,' Geoff said, handing the glasses round.

Freddy said anxiously, 'Champagne isn't bad for babies, is it?'

'Course not. Anyway, the sooner it gets used to it, the better. Start as you mean to go on.'

They toasted her.

'To Sarah.'

'Sarah and the baby.'

Geoff put his arm round her. Sarah started to cry.

*

One thing led, as usual, to another. Freddy stayed and ate with them, caught a later flight. All evening Sarah wondered what to do. The dilemma exhausted her.

When they were finally alone, getting ready for bed, she said to him, 'I wish you hadn't done that.'

'What?' He was still undressing; she was already in bed.

'Told Freddy.'

'It's all right. He won't tell anyone. You can keep it a secret as long as you like. What a bit of luck he dropped in – he was nearly as thrilled as I am. Hey, d'you realize you haven't even told me when it's due?' He paused but she didn't notice; she was too busy trying to make a decision. 'Pussycat? Have you worked it out yet? And names. We'll have to think about names.'

She said abruptly, 'I can't do it.'

'I'll help you. Don't sound so worried. It'll be fun.'

She sat up. 'Geoff, I've got to tell you the truth.'

'What d'you mean?'

'You're going to hate me.'

'I could never hate you. What's all this about? Aren't you sure about the baby?'

'This is so difficult. I don't want to hurt you but I can't go on lying. Please try to forgive me – if you can – you've no idea how sorry I am.'

His face changed. 'Sarah?'

'I've been having ... an affair. I ran into Peter Manson again and ... I'm not in love with him ... but I am very fond of him ... and it was sort of unfinished ... and it made me feel free again, like before we were married ... but it doesn't mean I don't love you because I do. Only you won't believe that now. Oh, please say something, I can't bear it.'

She thought the silence would kill her. Eventually he said, 'I don't know what to say.'

'You hadn't guessed?'

'I thought ... all that stopped when we got married. I tried not to think about it – what you'd done before – I wanted to believe you wouldn't do it again.' His tone grew harsher. 'I wish you hadn't told me, Sarah.'

'But I had to, don't you see?'

'No.'

'Oh please don't make it harder. That's why I didn't want you saying anything to Freddy about the baby ...'

'No.' He was blocking her words, practically shouting at her.

'Because –'

'Sarah, please shut up.'

'I'm so sorry, I'm not sure whose it is.' She waited, but Geoff did not speak. After a moment he began getting dressed again. She watched him in horror and desolation. 'What are you doing? Oh, please forgive me, I can't bear it. Say something. I can't feel worse than I do already. Tell me what to do.'

He said grimly, 'You'd better get rid of it, hadn't you? Unless *he* wants to take pot luck.'

After she heard the front door slam, she lay in bed and cried till there were no tears left.

Gavin arrived with a bunch of flowers. He went over to Eve who was lying in her pram in the shade. He bent over her.

'Hi, beautiful. How are you today?' He tickled her and she

clutched his fingers and laughed. 'That's my girl. See you later, okay?'

He went on into the house. The front door was open, welcoming him. He left it that way.

He presented the flowers from behind his back, and enjoyed her astonishment. 'Surprise. To cheer you up.'

'Oh, Gavin. How lovely. Thank you. That is nice of you.'

She was quite overcome: he'd never done anything like that before. She stopped preparing the vegetables for lunch and filling a vase with water, began arranging the flowers.

Gavin said, 'I peeked at my daughter. She's getting quite brown.'

'Yes, isn't she? Must be nice to have nothing to do but lie in the garden all day in a loin cloth.'

He prowled round the kitchen. 'Something smells good.'

'Lunch.'

'Or maybe the cook.' He felt it was safe to make jokes like this again. They were friends, united by a common enemy. The danger had passed.

'If you can't distinguish between roast beef and Cabochard, I despair of your future.'

'Don't they cost about the same?'

'These days, yes. Just about.'

'It'll never replace Yorkshire pudding, though. Cabochard, I mean.'

She smiled. 'You're very cheerful.'

'I talked to a guy reading law. He said he didn't think they'd ever let a grandfather have custody, with a father and grandmother around, divorce or no divorce.'

'And I rang the Citizens' Advice Bureau. They said the same.'

'That's great.' It was all working out. Of course he'd known it would, but still, it was good to be reassured.

Cassie said, 'Of course what I *should* have done is ring my solicitor. But I hadn't the guts, in case Peter had got there first. Then I thought it might be better if he had – at least I wouldn't have to explain the whole thing from the beginning. Oh well, I'll just have to find another solicitor.'

'It won't come to that.'

'It might. I'm beginning to feel resigned.' She sounded quite brisk and cheerful.

'When he's had time to cool off, he'll change his mind.'

'He *has* cooled off. He's gone all icy and implacable.'

'You're so unalike, I can't think why you ever married him.'

She said at once. 'Were you and Prue alike?'

'No, I guess not.'

'There you are. Anyway, you've never seen him at his best. Losing Prue changed him a lot.'

Even now her loyalty amazed and impressed him. 'I've *never* known him be civil.'

'I meant losing her to you.'

He said stubbornly, 'I still think you'd be better off without him.'

'You're not afraid of being alone.'

'I am too.'

She smiled. 'It's easier when you're young.'

Sarah went to Manson because she could not think where else to go. Geoff had not come home.

'Where is he now?'

'I've no idea. I haven't seen him since. In a hotel, I suppose.'

'I meant what I said on Monday.'

She shook her head. 'I couldn't hold you to that. We weren't sure then.'

'No, I meant it. I don't care which of us is the father. It's your child. That's enough for me.'

'You are extraordinary. I never thought you'd react like this, I thought you'd be shocked.'

He sounded almost proud. 'But I've got you into this mess. If we hadn't met again you'd still be happy with your husband. How can I be shocked?'

The scene with Geoff repeated itself endlessly in Sarah's mind. 'I've hurt him so badly. He just ... closed up. It was awful.'

'If things get impossible – if you want to get away – you can always come here. You know that.'

'But what about your wife?'

'I'll go and see her. We must have a proper talk about divorce. Perhaps I've been too harsh.'

She scarcely heard him. 'If only he'd forgive me. Whether he throws me out or not – I just want him to forgive me.'

'If you come here to have your baby you could help me look after Eve. Or we can hire someone to come in. One baby or two, what's the difference?'

A few words reached her. 'Oh, wait, please wait, you're going much too fast. I can't think that far ahead.'

'Cassie's bound to be reasonable, I know she will if I talk to her calmly. Perhaps we could even share custody.'

One echo was stronger than all the others. 'He said I should get rid of it.'

'No. You mustn't even think of such a thing. It's wrong and dangerous.'

'They say it's very safe if it's done properly.'

Manson was shocked. 'I'm sure he didn't mean it. He couldn't.'

'I think he did. I wonder, would it be like a fresh start if I did?'

He held her hands tight. 'Don't talk like that, please. You must let me help you. This baby gives us a whole new future – don't you see that? I was in despair – and you've given me hope.'

Suddenly the gravity of his intentions came home to her and she was afraid. 'Please – you're very kind but you're rushing me.'

'I'll go and see Cassie. I'll tell her the truth and we'll work something out.'

'No. Don't do anything yet. Please. I *am* grateful but I need time to think.'

'You do want the baby, don't you?'

She pulled her hands away. 'Yes. I thought I wouldn't but now it's actually happened, yes. I want it very much.'

'Then that's all that matters.'

He was being dynamic again. She had not seen him like this since the very beginning. 'It's not as simple as that.'

'It is if you let me help you.'

'No. I've got to work it out for myself.' She felt she was on a terrifying roller-coaster that would not stop.

'Trust me.'

But when she got home, Geoff was there. Incredibly, wonderfully, his car was parked in the drive. She could hardly get her key in the door, her hand trembled so much; she ran up the stairs calling, 'Oh Geoff, you're back.'

'Only to fetch a few things.' He was in the bedroom. Her face fell; she saw he was packing.

'Where are you staying?'

'I don't think you need to know that. I'll pay your allowance into the bank as usual. That's all that really matters, isn't it?' He was totally cold, a stranger. 'You can stay here as long as you like, of course, but since you dislike it so much you may prefer to move out. If you do, perhaps you could write to me at the office, so I can move back.'

She could hardly speak. 'Are we separating?'

'Well, I don't really see how we can live together, do you, till you produce whoever it is. I'm sure that would make for tension, and tension isn't good for pregnant ladies – or so I've heard.'

'But you told me to get rid of it.'

'I didn't tell you to do anything. D'you think you could move slightly to the left so I can get at that wardrobe.' She moved. 'Thanks.'

There was still a wild hope. 'If I did get rid of it – could you forgive me? Could we live together again? Would it make everything all right?'

'Don't be silly.'

'I'll do anything to make it up to you. I mean that.'

He snapped his suitcase shut. 'I think when it's born we should have blood tests. Him and me, I mean. Then we might get a clue about maintenance. Of course we could always pay half each. Or would he rather toss a coin? How about that? Is he a gambling man? Double or quits.'

As soon as Sarah left, Manson got in his car. He had scarcely heard her objections to his plan. It was so obviously the right thing to do – for both of them. It was salvation.

Over lunch Gavin said, 'I guess if he goes ahead with it I'll have to move out of the flat.'

134

They were both in a mood for facing facts. They gave each other courage.

'I don't see why,' Cassie said. 'It was a wedding present.'

'To Prue, not me. And he's never let me forget it. Anyway we can't have the co-respondent being subsidized by the plaintiff or whatever.'

'Petitioner.'

'It really bugs me – all this time he's been thinking I've stayed on there out of greed or laziness and I couldn't explain – not to him – I can't face moving her stuff.'

'If it comes to the point, I'll help you.'

'I told myself I needed the place for Eve and that made it all right but really it's all Prue's stuff. I'm scared to move it. And I'm scared to leave in case I lose her. She's so much in that flat. What if she doesn't come with me?'

Cassie felt the depth of his love for Prue, but she was past envy now. 'She will if you want her to.'

'And yet I'd give anything to forget her sometimes. So what am I hanging on for?'

She knew just what he meant. 'Oh … it takes ages to let go of someone you love.'

'You know, she was all those things you said … selfish and cruel and spoilt. But that only made her more of a challenge. I guess I thought I could change her. If I loved her enough and bossed her around, maybe she'd be different. I think she wanted me to do that.'

'Yes. I'm sure she did.'

'But when she didn't change I was kinda glad.'

She went on listening. She felt he needed to talk.

'You know what it was. I really envied her. She had so much I'd never had. Parents and love and money. All kinds of security. She was so … privileged. I guess I thought some of it might rub off on me. Like people eating the god to get his strength.'

She said gently, 'Hey – that's going a bit far.'

'That's how I feel. She had a kind of magic for me. I wanted to break it or share it. And I couldn't do either. There wasn't time.'

The phone rang. Cassie thought perhaps it was just as well.

They had said enough. Prue's power was as strong as ever, there was no doubt about that.

She got up and went into the hall. At first the voice on the other end of the phone didn't make sense. It went on telling her things she did not believe, asking her questions she could not answer.

'I don't understand. – No – but it isn't. – There must be some mistake. Can I ring you back?'

When she hung up she felt stunned. She could not move. 'Gavin,' she called.

'What is it?' He came into the hall.

'The house,' she said. 'He's put the house up for sale. Without saying a word. That was the agent. Oh Gavin, he really means it.'

Gavin put his arms round her; she clung to him, desperate for comfort. And that was how Manson saw them, framed in the open doorway, as he approached the house. All his good intentions vanished and a wave of nausea swept over him. He turned away, full of rage and disgust, and suddenly noticed Eve in her pram on the lawn. Without thinking, he snatched her up and hurried away down the drive.

5

RESOLUTIONS

MANSON made her comfortable on the bed in a nest of pillows. He leaned over her and she smiled up at him. The resemblance was astonishing. Miraculous, confirmed by the pictures on the wall.

He said, 'You're going to stay with me, aren't you? It's going to be just us, just the two of us. You'll like that, won't you?' At first she was amused and distracted by his attention, but presently she remembered she was wet and hungry, and in a strange place. Her face puckered up. 'No, don't cry, my lovely. It's going to be all right.' He lifted her tenderly. 'Never mind. You mustn't cry. I'll make it all right. I promise. You'll be safe with me. Don't cry. We're together, that's all that matters.'

He walked up and down, rocking the child in his arms, while she went on screaming.

Gavin said sharply, 'Are you still brooding about it?'

They had talked the subject to death; now for the last hour she had scarcely moved or spoken. 'It's difficult not to.'

'Ring him up. It's no good us going over it fifty times. Ring him up and get it straight. Do it now.'

'I don't want to speak to him.' More silence. 'It's incredible. I never imagined he could be so vindictive. He must really hate me. And the boys. Think what he's doing to them. How can he want us all to be homeless?'

'Oh, come on, it's not as bad as that.'

'That's what he's trying to do – turn us all out on the street.'

'You're being very dramatic.'

'It's all right for you, you're not being thrown out of your home.' She sounded bitter.

'He won't do it. He can't. He's only bluffing. It's just the kind of spiteful thing he'd do now he's mad at you.'

'The house is in his name.'

He was amazed. 'Really? That's pretty old-fashioned.'

'Don't lecture me, please. I know I'm not liberated but it's a bit late to tell me now.'

'You better ring him. Get it all sorted out.'

'You mean grovel.'

'Hell, no – but – '

She got up, glancing at her watch. 'Let's not talk about it any more. I've got a headache. Would you like some tea?'

'Is it that late already? We'd better fetch Eve in.'

'She's been awfully good. Can't we leave her a bit longer?'

She looked so tired he felt a rush of pity for her. 'It's okay, I'll get her.'

'I'll put the kettle on.'

He wandered into the garden and crossed the lawn to the pram. His arms reached automatically for Eve before he even saw that the pram was empty. He stared at it for a moment. Impossible. He ran back into the house, yelling, 'Cassandra!'

She called from the kitchen, 'Yes?'

He rushed in, shouting, 'Quickly! Eve's been stolen!'

'What?'

'She's not in her pram.'

Stupidly, they both raced into the garden to look at the empty pram. They could not believe it. They stared at the space as if by willpower they could make Eve reappear.

Gavin was the first to break. He ran back into the house. When Cassie caught up with him he was dialling a number, but she cut off the call before he had finished.

'What are you doing?' He was furious.

'Who are you phoning?'

He said, 'The police, of course.'

'Not yet – we've got to think.'

'What d'you mean, think? She's not there.'

'I know. Just give me a second.' There was a half-formed suspicion in her mind.

'She's missing, my child is missing. We've got to *do* something.'

'I know. I know. Just let me think for a moment.'

'What for? She's disappeared.'

'I know – but she can't – '

'We've got to ring the police. Now.'

'In a minute – it might be wrong – I don't know – it feels wrong – there's something odd – ' She lifted the phone. Some memory stirred : this had happened before.

'Come on, come on.' But when he saw she was not dialling 999 he grew frantic. 'What are you doing?'

'I'm ringing Peter.'

'You're crazy. What for?'

'I've got to tell him. He'll know what to do.' She didn't want to voice her suspicion yet in case she was wrong.

'Anyone knows what to do. I've just told you – ring the police.'

'I must tell Peter first. Damn. It's engaged.' She hung up. Gavin seized the phone. 'Right.'

'No. Please. Let me try again. It seems all wrong to ring them without telling him.'

'We're wasting time.'

'Let me try just once more.' The more he opposed her, the more certain she felt that she was right.

'If anything happens to her, I'll never forgive you for this.'

She dialled again. 'It's ringing.'

Manson watched the ringing phone. He did not want to answer it till it occurred to him it might be Sarah calling back. Besides, the sound might disturb Eve. He had only just got her settled. There was no milk to give her but he had removed her soiled nappy and wrapped her in a towel. She was quiet now, but awake and restless.

He picked up the phone. Cassie's voice. 'Peter? Something terrible's happened. Eve's disappeared. Should we ring the police?' He did not speak. 'Peter. Please answer me. What should we do? Do you know anything about it?'

Eve started to make a familiar snuffling noise, the beginning of a cry. Manson hung up.

'He didn't speak.' Cassie put the phone down and Gavin seized it.

'Typical.' He started to dial. 'Right. Now I don't want any arguments this time.'

Cassie said, 'I think she's there.'

Gavin stoppped dialling, out of sheer surprise. 'What?'

'I think I heard her.'

'Are you sure?'

'No. But I think so. You know that noise she makes just before she starts to cry ... '

'Let's go.' Gavin dropped the phone and they both dashed out to the car.

'I may be wrong,' Cassie said.

'If he's taken her, I'll kill him.'

Manson let Sarah in without noticing how nervous and agitated she was. His vision had narrowed completely to the immediate problem of Eve.

'I can't stay long,' Sarah said, but he scarcely heard her.

'I'm so glad to see you.'

'You sounded very odd on the phone – what's going on?' He led her to the bedroom and opened the door so she could see Eve on the bed. 'You've got the baby?' she said in amazement.

'Yes.'

'But why?'

He was surprised she had to ask. 'I couldn't leave her with them. They're not fit.' He shut the door carefully again.

'But what happened? You were going to talk to your wife. You said you were going to be reasonable ... '

'They were together.' Even as he spoke he saw them again. 'I don't want to discuss it.'

'Peter. Please tell me. How did you get her? Did they agree? Did you have a scene?'

Manson smiled. 'They didn't see me.'

'What? You don't mean you just took her?'

'Why not? She's lovely, isn't she?'

'Yes.' But she seemed disturbed rather than pleased; he couldn't understand her. 'Oh, I do wish you hadn't done it.'

'She was in the garden,' he said, by way of explanation.

'And you took her ... ? Just like that?'

'You'll help me, won't you? We can look after her together.' It all seemed so easy.

'No. I can't stay. I told you. How long have you had her?'

'They didn't even notice.' Surely that was justification enough.

'When did you do it?'

'Oh, I don't know. I don't remember. Earlier on.'

'But they must be frantic.'

He said with pride, 'She's so beautiful.'

'Peter, this is serious.' She sounded angry.

'You must help me. I can't manage alone.'

'But you can't *keep* her.'

'Why not? She belongs with me. She's mine.'

Sarah said, 'Look – you must tell them she's here. They'll be out of their minds with worry.'

'Will you stay with her while I go shopping? I've got to look after her properly and she needs all kinds of things.'

'No. I think we should telephone your wife.'

He stared at her in horror. 'I don't want to speak to her.'

'Then let me ring her. I don't mind.'

'No.' What was the matter with her?

'But you must tell her you've got the baby.'

'Why?'

'Because she'll go to the police, that's why. Maybe you don't care about her feelings any more but d'you really want that to happen?' The door-bell rang. They both jumped. 'Maybe that's them. What are we going to do?'

'We must hide her.' It was obvious.

'No. Please be sensible. You can't get away with it.'

Manson went into the bedroom. So long as he was with Eve, he could protect her. Now – where would be a good hiding-place?

Sarah called, 'I'm going to let them in, Peter? Did you hear?'

He crouched on the bed beside Eve. Now he knew how a trapped animal must feel. He heard voices.

'Is Mr Manson in?'

'Yes.'

'Can I see him, please?'

'You'd better come in, I suppose.' Sarah put her head round the door. 'There's someone to see you.'

He came out reluctantly. It was Vicky. She said brightly, 'Hullo. Sorry if I'm barging in.'

He tried to collect himself. 'Not at all. Sarah, this is Vicky Lewis, Gavin's friend. Vicky, this is Sarah Roberts.'

He saw them eyeing each other with suspicion.

'Hullo,' Vicky said.

'Well, you really started something, didn't you?' It wasn't like Sarah to be so rude; he wondered what had happened to upset her.

'I'm sorry,' Vicky said, offended, looking at Manson. 'I wanted to talk to you – but I won't stay now you've got a friend here. Can I come back another time?'

'Don't run away on my account, I'm just leaving.' Sarah picked up her bag.

'Please don't go, Sarah. Not yet.' He suddenly felt abandoned and panic-stricken.

'I told you I couldn't stay long. I've got an appointment. I would have liked to discuss it with you but there isn't time now.'

In the bedroom Eve began to cry. Vicky was startled.

'That's Eve!'

'Yes!' He was pleased with her instant reaction.

'How did you get her?'

Sarah said drily, 'He kidnapped her, of course.'

'Really? Don't they know?' Vicky seemed gratifyingly impressed.

He said, 'Oh, they rang up when they finally noticed.'

Sarah turned on him. 'What? You didn't tell me that.'

'What did they say?' Vicky asked.

'They said she'd disappeared.'

'And what did you say?'

'I didn't say anything.' He began to be pleased with himself again. He felt clever: he was going to get away with it.

'Lovely,' Sarah said. 'So someone's bound to come round – if it's not the police, it'll be your wife.'

In the bedroom Eve went on crying. He wanted to go to her but he dared not leave Vicky and Sarah alone. Vicky said, 'Oh dear, she does cry a lot, doesn't she?'

He felt helpless again. 'She needs changing and feeding ... I haven't got anything for her yet ... I didn't know ... Sarah can't you take her home with you?'

'No, of course I can't.' She looked shocked at the very idea.

He pleaded, 'Just for a little while.'

'Don't you think I'm in enough trouble already?'

Vicky said hesitantly, 'I could ... take her to my mother if you like.'

'Would you? Would you really?'

'Oh, you're both mad.' Sarah made for the door. 'I'm going.' She slammed the door behind her, but they still watched it, as if she might come back.

'She's very upset,' Vicky said. 'D'you think she'll ring your wife?'

'Possibly.' He felt a sense of urgency now. He hurried into the bedroom to fetch Eve. 'There, my lovely. Hush. It's all going to be all right. Not long now. We'll soon have you comfortable.' When he came back, with her in his arms, he found Vicky at the window, watching Sarah's departure. It disturbed him. He wished they had not met. He gave Eve, still crying, to Vicky. 'She'll be all right with you, she's used to you,' he said hopefully.

'Well, I'm not very good with her but I'll do my best.'

'Your mother will know what to do.'

'Yes.' She looked doubtful.

'Where does she live?'

'Oh – Edgware.'

'You'll need money for a taxi.'

'No – really.'

'But you must.' He forced money into her hand, suddenly feeling it was not such a good idea after all, but what else could he do? Cassie might be here any minute. And Gavin, no doubt. Both full of righteous anger. What hypocrites they were, and how nearly they had fooled him. He had almost decided to be merciful. He felt sick all over again when he thought about it.

'And you've been using this method ever since you came off the Pill, have you?'

The examination was over. The doctor was back at her desk, making notes, and Sarah, when she finished dressing, sat opposite her.

'Yes. The doctor in Frankfurt said it was the next safest method.'

143

'So it is – usually. You've been very unlucky.'

She could still see his face in her mind, hear his voice insisting on safeguarding her health. 'I could kill him, I really could. If only he'd let me stay on the Pill. I'd risk anything – I don't care what side-effects I might get, anything would be better than this.'

'Well, I'm afraid there's no doubt you're pregnant. About seven weeks. How d'you feel about it now you've had time to get used to the idea?'

Why should getting the results of the test make her used to the idea? 'Awful. I'm not used to it at all. I can't go through with it.'

The doctor said gently, 'Why not?'

'Because I don't know who the father is – my husband or my lover. I can't have a baby like that, it's impossible.'

Silence. The doctor was unshockable, of course, despite her cosy appearance. Sarah guessed she was about forty, with the look of a nice, understanding aunt. But like all doctors, Sarah thought, she asked stupid questions.

'Why is it impossible?'

'It's so unfair – it's cruel – I can't do it to him.'

'Who?'

'My husband, of course. He's been so good to me – I can't hurt him like this. He was shattered when I told him, he said I should get rid of it. Then he walked out. I don't think he's coming back. And he made awful jokes about blood tests.'

'A blood test might not prove anything – except who *wasn't* the father. Your husband and your lover might even be the same group.'

'Yes, I know all that.'

Another silence. Why couldn't she just say yes or no to the abortion? Why all these pointless questions?

'You've told me how your husband reacted. What about your lover?'

'Oh – he just sees me and the baby as a way out because his life's such a mess.' She hardly recognized the Manson she had seen that afternoon. He seemed demented to her.

'He wants you to have it?'

'Yes – but I can't.' She was surprised now that she had ever thought she could. Total panic had set in.

'Not even if you were sure it was his?'

'No. I couldn't rely on him, the state he's in. Anyway, it's not that serious an affair.'

'You're telling me how you feel about him – not having his child.'

'It's the same thing, for me. There's not enough love – he's more like – well, he's a lot older than me – it wasn't that kind of relationship – not to have a child.'

'You – definitely don't want his child?'

'No. It's too late. Maybe last year – it was different then – but this has happened just as I was feeling the affair was nearly over – you see, last year it was all unfinished. And then I got married.'

She had not known for sure how she felt about the whole thing until she heard herself stating her feelings so clearly. Perhaps the questions were more helpful than she had thought.

'What if you were sure it's your husband's child . . .?'

'Oh – I'd have it.'

'Willingly?' The doctor looked at her thoughtfully.

'No. I'd just have to. He wants children so much.'

'And you don't?'

'I'm not sure. I'm really muddled up about it. I always thought . . . one day . . . eventually I'd have them . . . only much later. That's why I was always so careful. I wanted . . . time to think.'

'Was it a shock when you missed your period?'

Sarah began to feel she was taking an oral examination and the doctor, smiling encouragingly, was hoping she would come up with the right answers.

'It was the worst nightmare of my life. After being on the Pill for seven years – I was so used to being safe – I just couldn't believe it. At first I tried to pretend it was just my system getting back to normal. I tried very hard to believe that.' She remembered clearly how she had conned herself as the weeks went by. If only she hadn't wasted so much time.

'What else did you feel?'

'Oh – along with the panic and horror, a crazy feeling of "Aren't I clever", and "What would it be like if?"' Was she being too honest? It was the terrifying ambivalence that was worst of all.

'What would it be like?'

'Ghastly. Not me at all. I'd be alone with a baby – that's the *fact*. No job, no husband, no money. Having fantasies about radiant motherhood just isn't realistic – it's straight out of an advert.'

'Would it make a difference if you had plenty of help and support?'

'What kind of help and support?' She was suddenly suspicious : the conversation had taken the wrong turn.

'Well, talking about your feelings.'

'You mean to you?'

'Yes, you could come here whenever you felt – '

'Yes, very nice, thank you, but it wouldn't pay for rent and food and clothes, would it?'

'No.' The doctor looked slightly embarrassed.

'Anyway, suppose I didn't like it when it was born – because of not being sure about its father?'

'That might not matter once it was actually here.'

'No – maybe not – but what a risk.'

'Yes. It is a risk. But it might be worth taking.'

Another silence. Sarah felt desperate. Just *tell* me, she wanted to scream. I thought you were on my side. You're a woman too : you ought to know how I feel.

'Look,' she said, 'do you want me to say I'm going to kill myself? I won't say that, I'll just find another doctor. I'll lie if I have to. I'm sorry I've told you the truth. It doesn't work.'

The doctor said soothingly, 'I'm not trying to be hard on you. But we don't have abortion on demand. To recommend a termination I've got to be satisfied your mental health would be more damaged by having the baby than by not having it. It's my job to help you make the right decision – that's why I've been trying to make you look at alternatives.'

Had she let her ambivalence show? She had heard it was important not to let them know you had any doubts. But how could you help having some?

146

'I don't see any,' she said. 'It's all fantasy. I just want to save my marriage. I didn't realize how much till this happened. If I have an abortion my husband may come back – we may have a second chance. Why ruin all that?'

'Does it feel like a baby already?' The doctor was watching her closely.

'No. But it would by the time it was adopted.'

'How does it feel now?'

The more she was pushed to consider having it, the more impossible it seemed. She felt herself beginning to suffocate. 'If you want the truth ... like a monster with two heads. It seems to belong to them both. It's just like the muddle I'm in – it really sums it up. No, it's worse than that, it's going to make the muddle go on for ever. It's pointless. It's going to ruin everything. It's like being taken over by both of them and they're so possessive already. I can't bear it.'

When they reached the corridor. outside Manson's flat, Cassie suddenly lost her nerve. 'Oh, Gavin, what if she's not here?'

Gavin rang the bell. ' She's got to be here.'

'It's like that dream – where I had to tell Prue ...'

Manson opened the door as if he had been expecting them, but his face was blank, as if he did not know them.

'What do you want?'

Gavin shoved past him into the flat, flinging the door wide. 'Where is she?'

'I don't know what you mean.'

Cassie said, 'Peter, please – no matter what we've done – don't punish us like this.'

Manson turned away and Cassie followed him back into the flat. Gavin was searching everywhere, like somebody mad.

Manson said coldly, 'I suppose you can't stop him behaving like this.'

'He's desperate, can't you see?'

Gavin shouted, 'Give me back my child.'

'I might say that to you.'

Cassie trembled. 'Oh don't, don't – please don't start all that again. Peter. You have got her, haven't you?'

'No.'

'He's lying.' Gavin went to search the other rooms.

'But I heard her,' Cassie said. 'When I rang you I heard her crying.'

'Then you're very imaginative. Have you rung the police?'

'No, I rang you first. Then I heard her so I knew you'd taken her. It was just like that day in the garden.'

'Then you've made a mistake, haven't you?'

Gavin came back. 'She's not here.'

Manson looked smug. 'You see? You'd better ring the police, hadn't you? Or d'you want me to ring them for you?'

'He's bluffing. He's hidden her somewhere.' Gavin turned on Manson. 'When I find her, I'll make sure you never set eyes on her again.'

'You've both been very careless, haven't you? Anything may have happened to her by now.'

'Don't.' Cassie couldn't stand any more.

'I thought you'd look after her better than that. But I suppose you had other things to do.'

'Come on, let's get out of here.' Gavin made for the door and she followed him. Then he suddenly turned and shouted at Manson, 'But we'll be back.'

Manson shut the door in his face.

Outside on the pavement they stood around irresolutely.

'What now – police?'

She said humbly, 'Whatever you say. I'm sorry I've wasted so much time.'

'No – you were right. He *has* got her – or he knows where she is.'

'D'you really think so?'

'Yeah – don't you?'

'Yes – but I was afraid it was just wishful thinking.'

'No – now I've seen him I'm sure. I wasn't before. I just went along with you having a premonition. But it's true – he's not worried enough.'

She longed to believe him. 'That's right. When you think how he used to fuss over her – he ought to be frantic.'

'And instead he's almost pleased. He's getting his own back.'

'He'd never hurt her . . . So she must be safe.'

'Right. But where?'

'None of our friends would help – they'd all ring me.'

'You've been out.'

'No, he wouldn't risk it.' She tried to think. 'It must be some-one at the office. Rupert wouldn't touch a baby. *Monica*. It must be Monica. But I don't know where she lives and I don't know her married name.'

'Someone at the office will know.'

'Yes.' She glanced at her watch. 'We'd better hurry.'

Just as they reached the phone box Gavin said, 'Would he trust Monica not to ring you?'

'I don't know. Probably. She's very loyal.'

'There's someone else he could trust.'

'Who?'

'Someone he could be sure wouldn't dare ring you.' He paused; he looked embarrassed. 'I'm sorry, Cassandra, I didn't want to tell you, but one day at Prue's grave – I met a girl with flowers from him – she said her name was Sarah.'

*

Gavin came out of the phone box and got back into the car. He handed Cassie a piece of paper with a name and address on it.

'I pretended I was a long lost cousin from the States. The girl on the switchboard was real keen to help.' He looked pleased with himself.

'I should have remembered. Peter told me she was married.'

'I guess you weren't listening too hard. There's loads of Roberts in the book but only one Sir Arthur. They flew home for the funeral and there were pictures in the papers, apparently. They're filthy rich, it seems. The switchboard girl was most impressed, not to say envious.'

Cassie was studying the A to Z. 'You're feeling better, aren't you? I mean you're really sure she's there.'

'No – but I'm sure they'll know where she is. It's so obvious once you think of it. I'm sorry I had to tell you about her.'

Cassie was surprised how calm she felt. 'It doesn't matter. She's a ghost.'

149

'It makes him bawling us out look pretty sick, though, don't you think?'

She gave him the A to Z. 'Hold this open there.'

Geoff's house was a surprise to them. They found it easily enough, but it was more imposing than they had expected and oddly daunting, closed in on itself, like a prison or a museum. She parked but she didn't want to get out of the car. 'I keep thinking of Prue,' she said. 'How angry she'd be.'

'Don't think of Prue. He's doing enough of that for all three of us. That bedroom of his is like a shrine – pictures plastered all over the walls – it gave me the shock of my life.'

'Don't tell me any more.' He got out and she followed him reluctantly. 'I hate barging in like this.'

'It's the only way. And she must feel guilty as hell.' He rang.

'Suppose she isn't here?'

'They'll know where she is. Oh, come on, come on.' He rang again, several times.

'Don't – you'll only make them cross.'

There was a grille in the door, with bars, and inner doors like a dining-hatch. This suddenly opened, framing the face of a middle-aged woman.

'Hullo?' She spoke with a strong foreign accent.

'Can we see Mrs Roberts?'

'Madam not home.'

'Please. It's very important.'

'No. Madam not here.'

'Have you seen a baby?'

'Baby?'

Cassie tried to explain. 'We're looking for a baby. My grand-daughter. This is my son-in-law. We're very worried. We think she may be here.'

'Madam no baby. Too soon.' She smiled at them indulgently, as if they were foolish.

'Have you seen her today?'

'Madam out.'

'It's hopeless. She doesn't understand a word.'

'Good-bye.' She made to close the hatch.

'No, wait please.' Cassie turned to Gavin. 'I'll have to ring

Monica.' She begged the cleaning lady, 'Please can I come in? Just for a moment. It's very important. Just to make a phone call.'

'Madam not here.' She clung stubbornly to her main point.

'I know, but can I use the telephone? Can I leave a message?'

'No, Madam – is not possible.'

'Please, it's very urgent.'

Gavin lost his temper. 'Look – my daughter's been kidnapped and your bloody Madam knows where she is.'

'No understand.' He had antagonized her. She closed the hatch firmly in their faces.

Gavin beat on the door with his fist.

'Don't – it won't help.'

'So what do we do now?'

'I don't know.' She was suddenly exhausted.

'She's out somewhere – hiding her – I'm sure of it.'

'I wish I were sure.'

'What d'you mean?'

'Oh, Gavin, suppose we're wrong. Suppose Peter didn't take her.'

'No. It has to be him. He wasn't worried, remember. Hang on to that.'

'But if he didn't, I feel it's all my fault.'

'You're crazy. Look – okay – we've drawn a blank here – right – let's go home and ring everyone – police – Monica – Rupert – your husband – this wretched girl – everyone. All night if need be. Okay?'

She was close to tears. 'Mm.'

'Come on. He knew where she was, I'm sure of it.'

Now that it was all settled Sarah felt worn out with relief. All she wanted to do was go home and sleep.

The doctor was saying, 'You can have a local or general anaesthetic, as you wish – if it's local you can go home the same day – it doesn't hurt – you may feel a bit uncomfortable, that's all.'

She forced herself to ask, 'And what actually happens?'

'A canula is inserted and the contents of the uterus are sucked out. It takes about ten minutes.'

'Yes, I see.' She hoped she did not sound as appalled and terrified as she felt.

The doctor looked at her sympathetically. 'Nobody does this without a lot of thought. If you want to change your mind, that's fine. Would you like me to ring your husband?'

'I don't know where he is.' Better not to think of that now. 'How soon can I have it done?'

'Well, you're lucky, we're in quite a good area. You shouldn't have to wait more than two weeks. In some places the consultants are a bit tricky. You do want an N.H.S. termination?'

Two weeks? 'I can't wait that long. If I pay, can I have it done quicker?'

'Yes, probably. Maybe next week.'

'I'd rather pay.' Waiting would be worse than anything.

'I don't want to recommend you unless we're both sure this is the right thing for you.'

'I'm sure.' It hardly mattered now whether she was or not: the main thing was to get it over.

The doctor said, 'I have to ring up another doctor and make an appointment for you to see him. D'you want to do that now?'

'You mean I have to go through all this again?' She couldn't believe it.

'You need two signatures – yes – I'm afraid so.'

Sarah closed her eyes. 'It seems never-ending.'

'It's a lot quicker and easier than it used to be.'

'Yes, I'm sure it is. Only it never happened to me before.'

Vicky sat on the steps of Gavin's flat with Eve on her lap. Passers-by looked at them curiously. Vicky was singing 'Ten Green Bottles', the only song she could think of to go on indefinitely, because every time she stopped, Eve began to whimper. She was surprised to be so successful: no one had ever liked her voice before. She didn't enjoy it much herself. But success palled after a while: she had to wait too long. By the time Gavin and Cassie drove up, she was bored, cross, and extremely tired.

Gavin jumped out of the car. 'I ought to kill you for this. What have you done to her?'

He grabbed Eve from Vicky.

'I thought you'd want her back. Aren't you pleased?'

Cassie followed more slowly. 'Don't be silly, Gavin, she must have taken her from Peter.'

Eve started to cry. Vicky was gratified. 'I said I'd take her to my mother for him. He's going to be awfully cross. But I couldn't let you go on worrying.'

'We're very grateful,' Cassie said. She looked exhausted. 'Really, I can't tell you how grateful we are. Gavin?'

'Yeah. Thanks.' He went up the steps with Eve in his arms.

Vicky said, 'I'm afraid she's awfully wet and hungry and all that, but there was nothing I could do for her.'

'It's all right,' Cassie said. 'We'll see to her now. You've been marvellous.'

Vicky looked longingly at Gavin, but he was fussing over Eve. 'Well. I'll be off then,' she said.

Cassie smiled at her. 'Don't you want to come in for a drink or something?'

Vicky watched Gavin opening the front door. 'No, I'd rather get home.' She was embarrassed at the way Cassie was trying to make up to her for Gavin's coldness. It was humiliating.

'We really can't thank you enough,' Cassie said.

Vicky shrugged. 'Oh – that's all right. There wasn't much else I could do. And I thought it might . . . oh well.'

Cassie said gently, 'I'm sure it does.'

Frankfurt was bright and sunny. Geoff and Freddy walked along the towpath.

'Aren't you going to say anything?' Geoff had expected an instant response: indignation, support, advice.

'D'you really want me to?'

'Don't be daft, I'm past caring. You can say what you like about her.' There was still no reply. 'Well?'

Freddy surprised him. 'I'm wondering why you're here.'

'Where else could I go? I had to talk to someone and there's nobody else I can trust.'

'You could have stayed at home and talked to Sarah. D'you love her?'

'Yes – damn it. No. I don't know. What's the point of asking me that? It's all over.'

'Funny, I didn't think you'd give up so easily. After all you said about working at marriage. I believed all that stuff, you know. You were very convincing. Pity you didn't mean it.'

'You know I meant it.'

'Oh yes? So you throw in the towel at the very first setback.'

Why didn't Freddy realize how much it hurt? 'My wife is having another man's child. I'd hardly call that a setback.'

'No, it's jolly bad luck.'

'Is that all you can say?'

'I could say a lot more but you won't like it. First of all, it's probably your child anyway. Secondly, you've both got a choice what to do about it. The one thing you don't have is the right to leave her alone when she needs you.'

'I don't owe her a thing.'

'Maybe not, but what's that got to do with it if you love her?'

'Oh – you don't understand. You're too young.'

'Because I don't agree? So you come all this way for a yes man.'

'No, of course not.' Geoff felt uncomfortable : Freddy had never talked to him like this before. But he had asked for it.

'All right, your pride's hurt, that's jolly painful but it's not really important, is it? Doesn't Sarah matter more than your pride? Doesn't your marriage matter? Look, this time last year you were desperate to marry Sarah. You knew she had other guys but you didn't care, you told me it didn't matter. She's not behaving any differently now, is she? Just been unlucky, that's all. And you walk out on her.'

'I thought . . . if we were married . . . she'd change.'

Freddy was using his most severe professional voice, as if he, not Geoff, were the elder brother. 'I hope you told her that before the wedding. Otherwise it makes a pretty dishonest contract.'

'So you think I should go back to her.' Geoff suddenly realized that he had come all this way not merely for comfort but to be told to follow his heart and reassured that Freddy would not despise him for doing so.

'I think you'd be a fool to stay away if you love her. What's the good of being all justified and self-righteous if you're bloody miserable and lonely? And she must be in a hell of a state. Suppose she did something silly?' Geoff looked at him in horror. 'Well, aren't women meant to be a bit odd when they're pregnant? And she's all alone.'

Barbara helped Sarah into the waiting taxi and it moved off. Sarah huddled into her corner away from Barbara, who watched her anxiously.

'Are you all right?'

'Mm.'

'Are you sure?'

'Yes.'

'You look a bit pale.'

'I'm fine.'

A long silence. Barbara studied her. 'Was it awful?'

'No, not really. They were all very kind.'

'I never thought you'd go through with it.' She couldn't restrain her curiousity. 'How d'you feel now it's over?'

'Relieved.' It was true and yet there was so much else she felt, so many contradictory feelings that she couldn't explain to Barbara.

'Oh well, that's all right then. So long as you're sure you've done the right thing.' Then she saw Sarah was crying; she squeezed her hand. 'I'm sorry, love. Why don't I just keep my big mouth shut, right?'

Sarah looked out of the window: there seemed to be children everywhere, and women with prams.

Barbara said, 'Never mind. It's all for the best. He'll come back and you can have another one and do it all properly next time. Cheer up. We'll soon be home and you can put your feet up. I'll make you a nice cup of tea – or a stiff drink.'

Sarah shook her head. 'No. You drop me off and take the taxi home.'

'What? I'm not leaving you alone in that house.'

'I'd rather. Honestly.' The prospect of being alone with Barbara ministering to her was appalling.

'I won't say another word. I promise. I'll just be there.'

'I'd rather be by myself. I just want to take a pill and go to bed.'

'You're not going to do anything silly . . .'

'No, of course not. Don't worry about me, I'm fine. You've been marvellous.' And in a way she meant it. Certainly there was no one else she could have asked.

Barbara said, 'I've been bloody useless.' And for a moment true sisterly affection blazed between them.

Then a great weariness came over Sarah. 'Oh, it's all the same. I just couldn't face going home alone. But you've got me over that. Now all I want to do is sleep.'

When Manson opened the door to Vicky she was shocked at his appearance. She had never seen him looking less than conventionally neat and tidy, well-dressed and conformist. Now he was in a dressing-gown and unshaven, as if for several days. He peered at Vicky uncertainly and seemed disappointed, as if he had been hoping she might be someone else.

She said, 'I wanted to apologize.'

'Mm?'

'I didn't dare come before.'

He shook his head vaguely and went back into the flat, leaving the door open.

'May I come in?' She waited but there was no reply, so she came in anyway. 'I feel awfully guilty about last week, but I simply couldn't take her to my mother – Gavin was so worried – he'd never have forgiven me. You must see that. Are you very angry with me?'

Manson picked up a tumbler of whisky. 'She's not here, you know. They've taken her away.'

'Don't you remember? I took her with me. You gave me money for a taxi. I felt awful about that. You must have it back.' She held out a five-pound note, but he ignored it. 'Please. I took it under false pretences. You must take it.'

He didn't look at her. He drained the glass of whisky and said carefully, 'She won't come back now. I waited and waited, but she's not coming.' Then, swaying slightly, he went into the bedroom.

Vicky didn't know what to do. She put the money down, looked around, waited. 'Mr Manson,' she called eventually. 'Are you all right?'

Silence. She began to get worried and followed him into the bedroom. He was sitting on the bed, pouring whisky into his glass. The wall behind the bed was filled with pictures of Prue at all stages: Vicky got quite a shock. She felt like an intruder.

'They were jealous of her, you see. That's why they killed her.' Manson put his head in his hands.

'Who are we talking about?'

No reply. Presently he surfaced, drank the whisky and poured some more. Vicky was alarmed.

'She was so beautiful,' he said.

'Yes.' She looked around the room. 'Mr Manson, I don't think you're very well.'

'That's why they hated her. It was envy. She was so beautiful they wanted to destroy her. I tried to save her but I couldn't.' He drained his glass.

'Please don't drink any more. Wouldn't you like to lie down? You look awfully tired?'

'I couldn't save her. She wouldn't listen to me.' He lay down heavily on the bed.

'That's right, you have a good rest.'

'I miss her so much.' He sounded as if he might be going to cry, but he didn't.

'I know.' She took the empty glass from his hand and put it down. With a lot of effort she managed to lift his arms and legs and get the quilt over him. His eyes were closed and he looked peaceful; he even started to snore. Vicky picked up the telephone and dialled. When her father answered, she said, 'Hullo, Dad are you busy?'

Sarah didn't hear the front door close; she didn't hear the footsteps on the stairs. But she was dimly aware of somebody saying her name.

Geoff stood beside the bed. 'Sarah. Are you all right?'

'Mm?' She tried to wake up, but it was like hauling herself out of some subterranean place.

'I've just ... called in. I should have rung you first, I know, but I didn't have ... well, I wasn't sure you'd want to see me.'

She said faintly, 'Geoff?'

'You're not ill, are you?'

'No. Just very tired.'

He walked around the room, trying to explain to her. 'I shouldn't have stayed away so long. I didn't know what to do. In the end I went to Frankfurt. I had to talk to someone, so I talked to Freddy. I hope you don't mind.'

'No.' She could barely take in what he said.

157

'I thought he was just a kid but . . . he's got the right instincts. Look, I want to say I'm sorry. Can you forgive me? I should never have gone off like that.'

'I'm so glad to see you.' He was here: that was all that mattered.

'Are you really? That's wonderful.' He sat on the edge of the bed.

'How did you know? Did Barbara tell you?'

'Know what? I haven't seen her.'

'She said you'd come back but I didn't believe her.' It was all coming true, like a dream.

'Look – I must talk to you. Are you properly awake?'

She made a big effort. 'Yes. I'm listening.'

'I think . . . we can still work something out. Let's not do anything in a hurry, let's just go on as if . . . well, let's decide what we're going to do after you've had the baby. We may both feel different then. We may be . . . quite sure it's mine or – well, we may not even mind any more. Let's wait till then and see how we feel.'

'That's . . . very generous.'

'It's not. I don't want to lose you.'

'But there's no need. I've done what you said. It's all right now.' She was so glad to have something to give him in return.

'What d'you mean?'

'I've had an abortion.' His silence worried her. 'Aren't you pleased?'

'You don't mean it. You can't.'

'But you said I should.'

'No.' He jumped up.

'You did. You told me to get rid of it.'

'Did I say that?'

'Yes. You did.'

'But I didn't mean it.'

'How was I to know?' She was frightened now.

'You should have known.'

'How could I?'

He paced up and down the room distractedly. 'Because – no matter what – I couldn't – it's awful – how could you think I meant it?'

158

'I did it for you.' At that moment it seemed to be true.

'How could you do such a terrible thing?'

'I wanted to give us another chance.'

'But it might have been—' He stopped. 'Why didn't you tell me?'

'You weren't here,' she said bitterly.

'It's too horrible.'

He went out. Sarah sat up and yelled with all her strength, 'Geoff. Please come back. Don't leave me again. Geoff!'

She heard the car start and drive away.

*

Evan Lewis's kitchen was a true work of art, designed and elaborately equipped for a dedicated cook. Vicky always had the feeling that she was interrupting a priest or a surgeon at work. She assumed he was listening while she talked, but he appeared to be much more interested in preparing vegetables.

'Is that all?' he said, when she had finished.

'What d'you mean?'

'His daughter's dead, his wife had it off with his son-in-law, and you nicked his granddaughter – no wonder he's depressed and knocking back the Scotch. But I don't see what I can do about it.'

'How can you be so callous?'

'I can hardly go barging into a complete stranger's flat and say, "My daughter thinks you're cracking up – let me have a look at you" – now can I? Doctors aren't supposed to tout for patients – remember? Besides, don't you think one member of this family interfering in his affairs is enough?'

The word hurt. 'We're not a family any more.'

'Are you in one of your moods?'

'It's true.'

'We're blood relatives, that's enough. We don't have to shed our blood under the same roof to qualify.'

Useless to argue with him. He always won. 'I want to know what to do.'

'As you're here, perhaps you'd like to make the mayonnaise?'

'No, I wouldn't. You're so fussy about it.'

'I taught you, remember. You ought to get it right.'

'Who's it for?'

'Christine.'

'What happened to Anna?' She liked to keep track of his women.

'Nothing happened to Anna. Her husband's at home this week.'

Vicky started on the mayonnaise. 'Why do you always cook for them?'

'I enjoy it, they appreciate the novelty, and it's cheaper than taking them out. Besides, a meal at home can be interrupted in all kinds of delightful ways that are hardly possible in a restaurant. You must have noticed that yourself.' He saw her flinching. 'Sorry. Still hurts, does it? You haven't made it up with him?'

'Tell me what to do about Mr Manson.' She didn't want to change the subject.

'You could try leaving him alone for a change. The poor devil's probably exhausted with his wife and his mistress popping in and out all the time – he hardly needs you as well.'

'It's not like that. He's old enough to be – '

'Quite.'

'Everybody isn't like you.'

'Ah, you've noticed that already, have you?' He came over and inspected her mayonnaise. 'Careful, don't rush it.'

'If you want me to do it,' she said sharply, 'leave me alone to get on with it.'

'Fair enough.' He was unruffled. He went back to his vegetables and for a while they both worked in silence.

'Please tell me what I can do to help him,' she said eventually.

'If you absolutely must do something, I should ring up rather than call round. It gives him more of a choice. He's probably very tired. He may need to be alone.'

'I hadn't thought of that.'

'That's because you hate being alone. He may like to know you're there if he gets lonely, but you could be overdoing it.'

'He was so depressed.'

'Yes, he's obviously ill. But we can't force help on him if he doesn't want it.'

'If I can get him to agree – will you see him?' She always believed he could work miracles.

'If he asks me to, that's different, of course.'

'I'll try.'

'Don't try too hard. You could make him worse and he won't see anyone. Besides, he may get over it, left to himself. In his own good time. Lots of people do. Doctors aren't magic, you know.'

'But I want to help him.' It seemed to be the only thing left she could do.

'Not everyone can be helped. That's something you've got to learn. It took me a while, believe it or not.'

'He's so unhappy. He got that baby all muddled up with Prue.'

'That's understandable, especially if he was drunk.'

Her father's calmness exasperated Vicky. She burst out: 'I hate Prue. She's caused so much trouble and she's still causing it, even now she's dead.'

'You mean you're jealous of her.'

'Yes, I am. Why should she have everything her own way, everyone loving her and giving her what she wants? Ruining people's lives and making them miserable and getting away with it. Why shouldn't I hate her?' She heard herself shouting.

Her father said quietly, 'She's dead and you're alive.'

Manson was still in bed. He looked terrrible. Sarah sat beside him, not sure whether to be comforting or brisk.

'If you're not ill,' she said, 'you really will feel better if you get up. I've stayed in bed for days but it didn't do me any good. I was only hiding.' She remembered it well. All those days of thinking that the worst had finally happened. 'Can I get you anything?'

He shook his head. 'Stay with me.'

She held his hand. 'Peter, I'm worried. My daily says a middle-aged woman and a young man came to see me that Friday when you took the baby. Was it your wife and Gavin? She said they were asking about a baby. Did you tell them about me?' He didn't answer. She went on, 'They were looking for the baby at my house. Why did they think she was there? How did they know where I live? What did you say to them?'

He said, 'Don't leave me.'

161

She gave up. 'Look – I'm sorry – I can't come here any more. It's all too much. I can't cope. I don't want to let you down but it doesn't feel right any more – we should never have started again, it was all a mistake. I think you feel the same really, don't you? We're not doing each other any good.'

He looked at her in bewilderment. 'The baby. You promised. You and me and the baby.'

'No. I didn't promise anything. And there isn't a baby.' He stared at her, horrified. 'I'm sorry. I couldn't go on with it. I wanted Geoff to come back. But it didn't work.'

'What have you done to my baby?'

'It wasn't yours. Oh, I don't know. Maybe it was. Anyway, I couldn't have it.' She heard herself speaking angrily to conceal her emotions.

'You killed my baby.'

'Don't say that. I had an abortion. It's all perfectly legal.'

'How could you?'

She was shaky and furious. 'Oh, for goodness sake, you're as bad as Geoff. I don't want a baby with two fathers. Can't you understand that?'

'You said you wanted it.'

'I changed my mind.' She started to cry.

'There's nothing left now.' He turned his face away from her.

'Everyone blames me. No one understands. Peter – please. There's nobody else I can … ' He didn't respond. Presently she stopped crying, repaired her face and got up. 'All right. If that's how you feel. I'm going now.' She went to the door. 'Aren't you going to say good-bye to me?' He didn't answer. 'Take care of yourself.'

She left. He didn't speak. He stared at the pictures of Prue and closed his eyes.

Gavin and Cassie were having tea. She was amused to note he was in his most proprietary, fatherly mood.

'I don't think you should put her out the front any more.'

'She's perfectly safe.'

'Oh yeah? Like last time.'

'He won't do it again.'

'How d'you know? He's a maniac. He might do anything.' He got up to look out of the window and check on Eve.

'You'll get indigestion,' Cassie said, curbing her irritation, 'if you keep jumping up and down like that.'

'I don't like her being out there.'

'She's got to get some fresh air.'

Gavin returned and sat on the edge of his chair.

'What exactly did he say when you told him we'd got her back?'

'I told you.'

'Tell me again. Exactly.'

'He said, "You've beaten me." '

'Is that all?'

'That's all?'

'Are you sure?'

'Gavin, we've been over it ten times.'

'Nothing about selling the houses or getting divorced or any of that stuff?'

'No.' She felt weary of the subject.

'It's very odd.'

'Not really. He's given up.'

'He's planning something.'

'No, he isn't. He sounded very tired and depressed.'

'I don't trust him an inch.' He jumped up. 'There's a car.'

'Rubbish !'

'I'm sure it stopped.' He rushed out of the room.

He picked up Eve from her pram, just to be on the safe side. Then he looked round and saw Sarah standing by the gate. He was startled.

'Oh. It's you.' He went over to her.

She half turned away. 'Don't say you saw me. I think I'd rather go home.'

'Why? You must have had a reason for coming.'

'I've lost my nerve.' She looked at Eve. 'Hullo. You look more cheerful than the last time I saw you.'

Eve clutched her finger and chuckled.

'You did know where she was.'

'I tried to make him give her back but he wouldn't. She's beautiful.'

'Yeah.'

'You're lucky.'

There was a curious tenseness about her that he couldn't understand.

Gavin came in with Eve in his arms.

Cassie said, 'I told you she was all right.'

'There's someone to see you.'

'Not Peter.'

'No.' He looked uncomfortable. 'She's scared to come in. It's Sarah.' Cassie was surprised and alarmed. 'I think she means well. Will you see her?'

She thought about it. Curiosity won. 'All right.'

He went back in the hall. 'It's okay. You can go in.'

Sarah came in alone. 'Mrs Manson. It's very good of you to see me.'

It was an odd moment. Historic. Cassie didn't know what to say. For no reason at all, she had often thought this might happen one day, then chided herself for cherishing fantasies.

'It's quite a surprise,' she said.

'Yes, I'm sorry, I should have phoned. But I was too scared. And when I got here I wanted to turn round and drive home again. Only I got caught.'

Cassie smiled. 'I didn't know I was so alarming.'

'It's my guilty conscience.'

'Why have you come?' She stared at her, fascinated. So this was Peter's mistress.

'I wanted to say I'm sorry. I saw the baby at your husband's flat but I couldn't make him give her back. I should have rung you then.'

'We were probably out looking for her. At your house.'

'Yes. But I should have done something. I didn't have the guts.'

She looked round. Cassie thought how pale she was. How young and fragile.

'That's not your only reason for coming, is it?' she said.

'No. The others are harder to explain.'

There was a long, awkward silence.

Cassie said, 'Would you like some tea?'

'You don't have to be polite to me. I'm sure you hate me, you must do.'

'Why should I hate you?'

'After all I've done.'

'Do I know *all* you've done?' Sarah didn't answer. 'You're right, I did hate you. Last year. But I don't any more. I think I'm too tired. No – I remember, I stopped hating you when Prue died, I don't know why. I started feeling sorry for you instead. That's not meant to sound insulting.'

Sarah said, 'I always wanted to meet you but I couldn't think how to manage it.'

They looked at each other with a strange mixture of sympathy and hostility. They had so much in common. All that jealousy – had it been for nothing?

'Well – you've managed it now,' Cassie said. 'What did you want to say to me.'

Sarah didn't answer for a long time.

'Just sorry, I suppose. I should never have got involved. The whole thing was so much more complicated than I ever realized till it was too late.'

'Yes.'

'I'm afraid I've done a lot of harm without meaning to.'

'So have I. That is how it's done.'

'I shouldn't have come back this year. That was even worse. But I have been punished, believe me.'

'I'm sure you have.' She suddenly wanted to take pity on her. 'You know, we could sit down if you like.'

'No, thank you. I mustn't stay long.' She looked tired and nervous, as if she had been through some ordeal.

'You can still run away if you want to. I won't stop you.' They sat down opposite each other. 'You're even younger than I expected.'

'I feel very old at the moment.' She looked embarrassed. 'It is all over between me and your husband. You must believe that.'

'Peter and I are separated. He has a right to his own life.'

'Well – I won't be in it. I've messed that up for good this time. And my marriage. I've made a horrible mess of everything and I don't know what to do.'

165

Cassie was amazed to see she was close to tears. 'Can I help?'

'I don't see why you should.'

'Isn't that why you came?'

There was no answer. She kept thinking that this girl was hardly older than Prue. Her head ached with the thought.

Sarah said, 'I thought – I wanted to tell you everything but I can't. I just want you to forgive me. Can you do that, without knowing it all? Can you forgive me, no matter what I've done? Nobody else can and you're the person I feel most guilty about.'

Cassie looked at her in the silence. She felt Sarah's burden as if it were her own. It didn't seem to have anything to do with Peter.

'Yes,' she said, 'I can forgive you.'

Sarah was impressed. 'And him? Can you forgive him?'

'I think that's between him and me, don't you?'

'I've just said good-bye to him.'

'Are you trying to give him back to me – like something you borrowed and don't need any more?' Cassie heard herself being suddenly bitchy.

'No. I didn't mean it like that.'

'Sorry. I must still be feeling a bit raw. I didn't realize.'

Sarah said, 'I meant – I think he's very lonely. He feels I've let him down. He won't talk and he stays in bed as if he's ill. I'm worried about him, that's all. Would you go and see him? Just to make sure he's all right. I think he needs you.'

Manson was drinking heavily. There didn't seem anything else to do. When he sobered up, reality was so awful, he had to get drunk again. He went round the room taking down the pictures of Prue in reverse order, starting with her wedding pictures and ending with her as a baby. The pictures seemed to sum up his life as well as hers. That puzzled him a bit, but he went on being calm and methodical. There was only one fact to grasp after all: that there was nothing else to live for.

The telephone rang, but he ignored it. He went on drinking and taking pills. There were such a lot to take. He put the photographs in a neat pile under his pillow. He'd thought it would be more emotional than this, actually doing it, but he was so tired, and what with the pills and the drink, he could hardly think straight. He just knew she was out there somewhere and he wanted to get to her because nothing here was any good.

The phone rang again, but he hardly heard it, and eventually it stopped. He thought how peaceful it was all going to be without telephones. He got into bed and tried to finish the pills and the whisky, but he was nearly sick. That alarmed him. He lay down heavily, and when he tried to turn off the light, his hand couldn't find the switch.

Cassie watched Sarah playing with Eve. They got on so well. She was envious and impressed.

'Okay, Cassandra, I'll see you next week-end.' Gavin at the door.

'All right.'

He looked at Eve with Sarah.

'Take care of her for me,' he said to Cassie.

'I won't let her out of my sight. Don't worry.'

'I still think I should have her with me in the vac.'

'You won't get much work done.'

Gavin went over to Eve and kissed her good-bye. Cassie felt slightly dizzy to see Gavin and Eve and Sarah and herself all in one room. It seemed to make nonsense of all their feelings.

'Now you be a good girl,' Gavin said to Eve, 'and don't run off with any strange men, d'you hear me.'

Sarah looked at her watch. 'Mrs Manson, you've been awfully kind, but I must be going.'

'I'm glad you came.' And she meant it.

Gavin suddenly said, 'Could you give me a lift to the station?'

'Back to town if you like.' She turned to Cassie. 'Is that all right?'

'He's a free agent.' The final irony.

'I'm sorry. Am I dropping bricks again?' She looked like a guilty child. Cassie didn't know whether to hug her or hit her.

The porter blocked Vicky like a slab of concrete. He was so uncomprehending, he drove her mad.

'Can't you let me in?' she said. 'You've come this far and you've got a master key.'

'I don't know. It's only for emergencies.'

'This is an emergency. I've rung and rung but he doesn't answer.'

'Maybe he's out. Or away for the week-end.' He looked around the corridor as though some other tenant might come to his aid.

'No, I'm sure he isn't,' Vicky said. 'I looked up from outside, the lights are all on.'

'Well, I don't know.' The porter scratched his head. 'You'll have to take responsibility. It's not something I'd do off my own bat.'

'Yes, yes, anything, only please hurry.' She had no reason to think so but she was sure that something terrible had happened.

The porter said dubiously, 'It's nothing to do with me if the tenants want to leave their lights on when they're out. They pay the bills, not me.'

'But I think he's ill. In fact I'm sure he is.'

'This ain't nothing to do with the police, is it?'

'No, of course not.' She was furious: it seemed such a petty question.

'You're not one of them inquiry agents, are you? I don't want no trouble.'

'No, I'm a friend and I'm worried. Please open the door.'

'Oh well, all right then.' He was happy or at least willing to unload the responsibility. 'But I'm not sure as I'm doing the right thing. I don't want no part of it. It's all your doing.'

They found Manson lying on the bed, unconscious. There was no way of knowing if he was alive or dead. Vicky shivered: for a moment she was even glad the porter was with her.

'Oh, my Gawd,' the porter said. 'I knew it was trouble. He's done himself in.'

Vicky picked up the phone and dialled.

'Dr Lewis, please. It's an emergency.'

6

EMERGENCIES

VICKY watched Manson, unconscious on a stretcher, being placed in the ambulance. The porter was with her, and a small group of neighbours, avidly watching.

'He does look bad,' the porter said with satisfaction.

'He's going to be all right.' Vicky was trying to convince herself. 'He's got to be.' She spoke fiercely. 'I wish all those people would go away.'

'Where're they taking him?'

'The Schroeder.'

'Looks to me like he ought to be in hospital.'

'It's the same thing, don't be silly.' The porter looked offended. 'And it's the nearest. No —' she said to the ambulance men who were shutting the doors, 'I'm coming with him.' They looked doubtful. Vicky played her ace. 'It's all right, my father works there.'

She got in with them and they drove off. The porter and the onlookers dispersed, disappointed that the show was over so quickly and there wasn't any blood.

The telephone rang and rang. Cassie was upstairs with Eve. She ran down to answer.

'Hullo?'

There was a voice she didn't recognize.

'Mrs Manson. I'm sorry, I've got some bad news for you.'

'What? Who is this?'

'It's me, Vicky. I'm ringing from hospital.'

'Hospital?' The word struck a chill.

'It's Mr Manson. He's had an accident.'

'What?'

'He's . . . taken an overdose and he's unconscious. I just found him.' Cassie didn't answer. 'Mrs Manson, are you still there?'

'Yes.' She could barely take in what Vicky had said.

'I'm sorry to give you such an awful shock. Can you come?'

'Yes, of course.' She hardly dared ask, 'How bad is he?'

'I'm not sure.'

Vicky sounded scared. Cassie said, 'I'll come right away. Which hospital is it?'

'It's the Schroeder Clinic in Pont Street. Can you find it?'

'Yes. But there's Eve ...'

'Can't you leave her with someone?'

'It's quicker to bring her – and she's been so unsettled since he ...' She stopped.

'Bring her with you. I'll look after her.'

'I'll ring Gavin. He can take her.' She re-dialled in a hurry. But there was no reply. Gavin was not home.

They were awkward and silent in the car. Presently Sarah said, 'Mind if I put on some music.'

'Sure. Go ahead.'

They both felt safer and more relaxed with the music playing. He didn't make conversation from a sense of duty, just to be polite, and she was rather glad.

The scene with Cassie went round in her head. She had longed to tell Cassie everything as if she were an understanding mother. All about the abortion. But that would have been selfish.

'Are you in a hurry?' she said to Gavin.

'Not at all.'

'I was wondering if we could stop for a drink.'

'If you like.'

'It's been such a funny day. I feel a bit shaky.'

Evan Lewis came through the swing doors. Vicky rushed up to him and flung her arms round him.

'All right.' He stroked her hair. 'All right. I'll go along to Casualty and see how he's getting along, shall I?'

She nodded. The feel of him and the sound of his voice had their usual calming effect.

'D'you want to wait in my room?'

She shook her head. She wanted to stay as close to Manson as possible, sending out waves of energy.

'I won't be long.'

She watched him go and then sat down again, willing Manson to stay alive.

Cassie rang Gavin's door-bell again and again. No reply. She couldn't believe it. First no answer on the phone and now this. Just when she needed him. She picked up Eve in her carry-cot and went back to the car. She would have to take her to the hospital. It did not seem fair to have to bear all this anxiety alone.

When Evan came back Vicky hardly dared to look at him. 'He's going to be all right.'

'Honestly?' She slumped, with relief.

'They're just washing him out now. He'll be fine. You did well – you were very quick.'

The unaccustomed praise made her squirm with pleasure. At last she had impressed her father. Behaved like a real responsible adult, made him proud of her.

'Can I see him?'

'Tomorrow perhaps.'

'You're really sure he's – '

'I'm sure. You can go home and rest easy – you've done your bit.'

'I'm waiting for his wife,' she said importantly.

'Are you taking charge of the whole family?'

'She's bringing the baby. I'm going to take it to Gavin.'

'Ah. That explains everything.' He smiled gently, making fun of her.

'No. It's not just that. She's very worried. I've got to be here to meet her. After all, it's partly my fault he did it.'

'Your fault? How can it possibly be your fault?' He sat down beside her as though she were a patient.

'Telling him about her and Gavin, of course.'

'You're being very greedy, taking so much responsibility. How d'you know that was why he did it? If he did it. Maybe it was an accident.'

'I don't think so.'

'Then how d'you know he wasn't meant to find out? They could have been just using you.'

'Using me?'

'Or did you tell him on purpose?'

The pub was crowded. The noise and warmth and people made Sarah feel better already, as if life could be normal again. It had been going on all the time like that, only she had slipped out of it.

'What would you like?' Gavin said when they got to the bar.

'I'm getting them, it was my idea.'

He insisted. 'What would you like?'

'Scotch-on-the-rocks, please.' She gave in happily.

'Two Scotch-on-the-rocks.'

When Cassie arrived at the Schroeder Clinic with Eve, the first person she saw was Vicky sitting on a bench in the foyer. Cassie was too frightened to ask how Manson was. All the way in the car she had been thinking 'What if he dies – now – and we've not had chance to – '

Vicky rushed up to her. 'He's going to be all right.'

'Are you sure?' She felt faint with relief.

'Come and meet my father. He'll tell you.'

The whisky was good, cold and strong. It made them both feel better, made the spectre of Cassie recede.

'Here's to your lovely daughter,' Sarah said.

'She is pretty good, isn't she?'

'You're lucky. I never really liked babies before.'

'Neither did I. She was Prue's idea. I guess you might say ... the best thing Prue ever did.'

'I met Prue once. She was very beautiful. But we hated each other on sight.' She stopped. 'Oh, what am I saying? She must have told you all that.'

'Yeah, she did.'

They stared at each other, fascinated, trying to check their impressions and decide what they thought. Both felt they had been misinformed.

'It's really very odd – meeting someone you've heard so much about.'

'Do I look the part?'

'I'm not sure.'

'Aren't I the monster he described? Haven't you spotted my cloven hoof yet? Look – I'll show you.' He made to take off his shoes. 'Oh, sorry, I can't – odd socks.'

Sarah laughed. She felt as if she hadn't done that for a long time. 'I feel much better now I've seen Mrs Manson,' she said. (And she could understand Gavin having an affair with her, too.)

'Why did you want to?'

'To apologize. And tell her it's over.'

'Really?'

'Oh yes. I mean it this time.'

'What happened?' he said cynically. 'Did your husband find out?'

'Yes. But that's not the reason. It just didn't work any more.'

'I can't imagine what you ever saw in him.'

'Of course you can't. You're biased.' Even now she had to stick up for Manson.

'The thing that gets me is he's got one set of rules for himself and another for me and the rest of the world.'

'He can't help it. Anyway, so have lots of people.' She felt a twinge of guilt.

'Not me.'

'Are you sure?'

Vicky took Cassie and the baby into Evan's office. Cassie got an immediate shock: he reminded her of Sven. She pushed the thought away.

'Dad, Mrs Manson's here. Can you tell her about her husband?' Cassie put down the carry-cot.

'Mrs Manson, this is my father, Dr Lewis.' She was proud of him and his status.

Cassie and Evan shook hands.

'Your husband's going to be fine.'

'Really?' He was staring at her as though he recognized her too. 'Can I see him?'

'Not yet. They're still tidying him up. I'll check with Casualty for you in a minute. Is this your granddaughter?'

'Yes.'

He said to Vicky, 'I thought you were going to take her back to her father.'

'He's not in,' Cassie said.

'Would you like to phone him?'

'I've just called round and he's still not back. I can't think where he's got to. He ought to be home by now.'

Evan said smoothly, 'Would it help if Vicky took the baby to your husband's flat? Then you could pick her up when you're ready.'

'Yes – but ...'

'Only a suggestion.'

'I haven't got a key,' Cassie said.

'I have.'

They both looked at Vicky in surprise.

'Very far sighted,' Evan said.

Vicky looked embarrassed. 'It was on his dressing table. I thought it might be useful. For him going home, I mean. I brought his pyjamas and a toothbrush as well.'

'For him staying in.' He was teasing her.

'Yes.'

'You think of everything.'

'I was only trying to help,' she said defensively.

'And you'd probably had enough of sleeping on your friends' sofa.'

'I didn't think of that.'

'No, of course not. Off you go, then.' He turned to Cassie. 'If that's all right with you.'

'Yes. It's a good idea. You don't mind?'

'Not a bit.'

'I'm very grateful,' Cassie said.

Vicky picked up the carry-cot. She suddenly had the feeling that she had been got rid of rather neatly but she was not sure why.

She said to Cassie, 'I'll see you later then. Shall I keep ringing Gavin for you?'

'Please. He must be back soon.' When they were alone Cassie said to Evan, 'It's very kind of her.'

'Not at all. She likes being useful.'

Silence. The tension was extraordinary. Was she imagining it?'

'When may I see my husband?'

'I'll find out for you.' He picked up the phone. 'He won't be awake, of course.'

Cassie made herself ask, 'Did he do it on purpose?'

Evan hung up and stared at her. She wasn't imagining it. She stared back, unable to move or look away.

'Hard to say, at this stage. It was a lethal dose but only just. Depends on whether or not he expected to be found in time.'

'I don't see how he could have done.'

They took refuge in talking about Manson.

'All the alcohol made it worse. Is he normally a heavy drinker?'

'No.'

'Then it *could* have been an accident.'

'But you don't think so.'

'My daughter seemed to think he'd been very depressed lately.'

'Yes. That's true.'

Evan picked up the phone again. 'Well, let's see how he's getting on.'

The pub was warm and relaxing. Gavin and Sarah were eating sausages: they had found they were suddenly ravenous.

'Why did you come over here in the first place?' She had always wanted to know more about him.

'I was dodging the draft. The whole Vietnam bit – I just couldn't see any sense in it.'

'But why here? Why not ... Canada? Or Sweden?'

'I was keen on an English girl at the time.'

So it all came back to that. 'Prue.'

'No, somebody else. She ditched me and then I met Prue.'

'Don't you want to go home? There's an amnesty now, isn't there?'

'I don't have much to go back to.' He didn't sound self pitying, merely matter-of-fact.

'No family?'

'The aunt who brought me up. If we never meet again it'll be too soon for both of us.'

She smiled. 'That bad.'

'She was very religious. The worst kind of Puritan bigot. And – I guess I wasn't the easiest kid in the world. She thought I had "bad blood" – whatever that means.'

'What happened to your parents?'

'I don't know about my Dad. My Mom ran off with a truck driver when I was nine. I guess she got sick of my aunt telling her how she'd disgraced the family. I don't really blame her. I tried to run off too but they kept on bringing me back.'

'Who?'

'The cops. Neighbours. Do-gooders. A kid on his own is kinda conspicuous. You feel such a fool – setting out on the great adventure – the real Mark Twain bit – and then they catch you.'

So they'd both had rotten childhoods, Sarah thought. It made a bond. 'How did you get to university?'

'I worked my way through – that's pretty normal in the States – I did all kinds of jobs – I washed up and drove cabs and I dug ditches. It's pretty easy really if you don't care what you do. I just wanted to get on and get out.' It sounded impressive, the casual way he told it. 'Would you like another drink?'

'It's my turn.' She got up.

'I'm old-fashioned.' He got up too.

'I don't believe you. Anyway, I insist.'

He was sorting his money. 'Old-fashioned but broke. I'll have to give in gracefully.'

Alone in Evan's room, Cassie lit a cigarette and tried to calm herself, sort out her impressions. He was not really like Sven. For one thing he was not going bald. But they were the same height, and build; the same age. So were millions of people. No, it was more than that – a look, a manner. The same dark, stocky air of being in control. Reassuring and menacing at the same time.

Evan came back. 'You can see him now ... Aren't you going to put that thing out first?' He stared disapprovingly at her cigarette.

'Oh. I'm sorry. I wasn't thinking.' Not like Sven, an inveterate smoker.

Evan pointedly opened a window. 'You're not an addict, are you?'

'I don't think so.' She was annoyed. 'I realize it must be annoying for non-smokers.'

He smiled at her. 'Oh, I'm more than that. I'm an ex-forty-a-day man. So I have all the reforming zeal of the convert.'

Sarah came back with drinks. They decided they were still hungry so they had more sausages as well. She suddenly realized she was actually enjoying herself for the first time in weeks.

'And then what?' she said.

'And then a job – I guess.'

'What kind of job?'

'That's a good question. To satisfy *him* it would have to be something high-powered at Unesco or the U.N. I can't imagine anything less would do.'

'And to satisfy you?'

'I'd like ... well, I've been a student so long and it's all theory. I'd like to get out there and see how people really live and what it's like. How the theories apply to real life.'

'Get out where?'

'Anywhere. I used to think Africa but it's too late for that. They're not going to welcome a white sociologist at this stage of the game. South America maybe. India. I don't know. But I would like to be some use to someone.'

She thought about it. 'It sounds as if you're running away from something.'

'Sure I am – the whole Manson family. I've had enough. I'd like to pick up my daughter and run.'

'Can't you?' The idea of flight was infinitely attractive.

'That's the whole point. Once you've got a kid, you can't please yourself. I've got to think what's best for her. She's a bit young to be dragged round the world. Who's going to look after her when I'm working? I feel guilty enough already – she's had a hell of a time the past few months being passed round and fought over. The best thing I can do for her – probably – is take some dreary teaching job at some tin-pot university and hire a nanny. Can you imagine ...'

'It doesn't sound like you.' Already she felt she was getting to know him.

'No, it isn't. But it would give her a home and a settled life.

That's what everyone tells me she needs and who am I to argue? I didn't turn out so well without one, did I?'

Sarah said vehemently, 'But what really matters is – you and her, isn't it? What you think is best. Not what other people say.'

'I believe that when I'm feeling tough. But other times I don't really think I have a lot to offer.'

'At least – she's here and you love her.'

'Yeah.'

The urge to confess was suddenly too strong. 'I've just had an abortion.' She watched closely for his reaction.

'That's tough luck.'

'It was my decision.'

'Of course. But it can't have been easy.'

'No. It wasn't. And everyone's so angry with me.'

'Who's everyone?'

'The two of them.' She was so relieved he was being sympathetic. He wasn't judging her like the others.

'What did you say to me? It's what *you* think that matters.'

'But I don't *know* what I think.' She hesitated.

'Whose was it?' he asked, just as she was wondering if she dared mention that.

'That was the worst part – I wasn't sure.'

'Is that why you got rid of it?'

'Yes.'

'The only reason?'

'And my husband told me to . . .'

'Maybe you just didn't want it.' She couldn't answer. 'That's not a crime, is it?'

'Some people think it is.'

'I don't. How about you?'

She said honestly, 'I feel very funny about it. I keep changing my mind.'

'Would you put the clock back if you could?' She thought about it and shook her head. 'Well – that's a start,' Gavin said.

Cassie sat by the bed holding Manson's hand. He looked so pale. Was he really going to be all right or were they all deceiving her? The reality of what he had done appalled her. How could he get as desperate as that? Did he hate her so much that he wouldn't turn to her again, no matter how bad things were?

A nurse put her head round the door. 'I shouldn't stay long if I were you, Mrs Manson. He won't know you're there.'

She went away but Cassie couldn't move, although part of her knew it was pointless. She wanted to be near him, yes, but she was also punishing herself for not being there when he needed her.

She lapsed into a painful reconstruction of the past. All they had been through – to end up like this. Deep in thought, she was startled when Evan came in.

'Satisfied?'

'Yes, he . . . doesn't look too bad.'

'He'll be fine.' He paused. She was very aware of his presence.

'Well, good night.'

'Oh – are you going off duty now?'

'I wasn't *on* duty. I'm much too exalted to work nights. I only came along because of Vicky.'

'And my husband.'

'It was a package deal.'

'I'm very grateful to you and Vicky.'

'But I haven't done anything yet.' There was a long silence. She knew she wasn't imagining the tension between them. He said abruptly, 'Are you going to sit there all night?'

'I don't like to leave him.'

'He's not going to wake up till tomorrow. If you don't get some sleep you'll be useless when he wants to talk.'

'I suppose you're right.'

She felt a strange mixture of relief and reluctance. She got up and kissed Manson on the forehead, feeling self-conscious in front of Evan.

They went out together.

Going down the corridor Evan said briskly, 'Now what are you going to do?'

'Oh – collect the baby and go home.'

'Where's home?'

'Surrey.'

There was a pause.

'That's a long drive. Wouldn't you like to have dinner first? I hate eating alone.'

*

They drove back slowly, mindful of how much they had drunk. When they opened the door of the flat the phone was ringing, but by the time Gavin reached it, it had stopped.

'They always do that,' Sarah said.

'Yeah. Like buses when they see you running.'

'Never mind. If it's important they're bound to ring again.'

The mood between them was good. Easy and relaxed.

'Come in. You don't have to rush home, do you?'

'No. Home's the last place I want to be.'

They went into the sitting-room.

'Would you like a drink? I think I've got some Scotch.'

'Yes. Thanks.'

He searched. 'Oh. There isn't any left.'

'Oh yes there is.'

'Where?'

'Right behind you.'

He turned round. Triumphantly she produced the half-bottle from her handbag.

'When did you get that?'

'While you were in the loo.'

'You're brilliant. I'll get some ice and some glasses. Don't go away.'

Sarah wandered reminiscently round the room. How strange it was to be back here, in this flat, and with him, of all people.

He came back. 'God knows how many drinks I owe you by now. So much for masculine pride.'

'Oh, you're not going to be boring about it.'

'No, I'm grateful. But I just can't tell you how tired I am of always being broke.'

'Maybe you need that high powered job after all.' She hoped not: she was surprised to find it soothing to be with someone poor. Like Simon; except that he wasn't. She felt confused.

'Oh, sure I need it. Only I'm not a very high-powered person. If I only had myself to consider I wouldn't mind bumming around the world for a few years. I'm sure I'd learn more that way than in any job.'

They clinked glasses.

'Sounds like fun.'

'Fun for me, not Eve.'

Cassie was so envious of Evan's kitchen that she forgot to be self-conscious or even aware of him as a man. In his own home he seemed, curiously enough, less threatening.

'What a very impressive kitchen,' she said.

'Is it? I hope so. I tend to agree with the man who said "I don't live in a bedsitter. I sleep in the kitchen".' He gave her a drink.

'Thanks.'

'Have a seat. Or would you rather prowl? I don't mind.'

'No.' She sat.

'I think a cheese soufflé might be nice. While we're waiting for the lamb.'

'Can you really be bothered?'

'Why not? I enjoy food – don't you?'

'Shall I do something to help?'

'No, that's not allowed. I'm sure you do quite enough cooking in your own home. Why on earth should you do more of it in mine?'

'This is very kind of you,' she said politely.

'Really? I don't think I've been accused of that before. We both need to eat – you're tired and I enjoy cooking – particularly for someone else.'

Silence. She could feel the tension creeping back.

'Dr Lewis –'

'Evan –'

'About my husband. I don't know how much Vicky has told you . . .'

'Yes, it is a little tricky.' But he didn't seem to mind. 'Your family and mine are already so interwoven, I feel we're practically related.'

'It's rather embarrassing.'

'Oh, I thought it was quite cosy. I'm a bit short of relatives myself.'

Gavin said, 'Why is home the last place you want to be? Did you have a fight with your husband?'

'How did you guess?'

'A bad one?'

'A very bad one. It could be our last. And all this money I'm spending so freely belongs to him.' But she didn't really care: she felt she was on the run, like a crook in an old film.

'Is that why you married him?'

She liked his blunt questions. 'Not exactly. It helped, of course. But really I think I was looking for somewhere to hide. We had a good friendship and good sex – I thought that was enough. I didn't want to be in love again – it hurts. I wanted to forget about Peter. And there we were, Geoff and I, in a foreign country and it was Christmas and we were homesick and – suddenly we got married.'

'You mean it seemed like a good idea at the time.'

'That's it.'

They laughed.

'What went wrong? Apart from meeting *him* again, I mean.'

She didn't have to think: she knew. And she had a feeling he'd understand. 'Oh – I blame myself really. I have this dreadful urge to rock the boat. As soon as I get everything just right I . . . have to smash it up. It's too peaceful, too settled. My sister thinks I'm mad. I suppose I'm punishing Geoff for falling in love with me. He wasn't meant to do that and I can't stand the responsibility.'

'It can get a bit heavy.'

Cassie was suddenly aware that she was enjoying herself when she ought to be thinking about Manson. She said, 'If my husband . . . did try to kill himself . . . then it's really my fault. We were separated – he'd had a very unpleasant shock recently – and there'd been a lot of trouble over the baby – he must have felt he had nothing left to live for.'

'And if it was a mistake?'

'He must have been in a pretty bad way to make a mistake like that.'

'So either way it's your fault.'

'I may as well admit it.'

He grinned and shrugged. 'If you're trying to claim entire responsibility, I'm afraid you're too late. My daughter was ahead of you. She's convinced it's at least partly *her* fault.'

'How?'

'That's what I asked her. To put it crudely – because she let the cat out of the bag.'

'She made a mistake, that's all. I did the real damage.'

Evan refilled their glasses. 'You're a very determined lady. Everything has to be your fault. Wasn't there anyone else in your husband's life who might have depressed him?'

'Yes. He'd just lost his mistress.' But the word didn't seem to relate to Sarah.

'Couldn't that have had some effect?'

'I suppose so.'

'Anything else?'

Cassie hesitated. She wasn't sure how much she wanted to say.

'Oh, it all goes back to Prue. He's never got over her death.' Another hard, irrelevant word.

'And was that your fault?'

'No ... but ... I didn't love her the way he did.'

'Two people hardly ever do love in the same way. Each other – or somebody else.'

'It was worse than that. I was very jealous of her. My own child.'

He said casually, shocking her. 'Did you wish her dead?'

'No.'

'People do, you know.'

'Well, I didn't.'

'Even if you simply hate someone and they die – that can make you feel you've killed them. Children often feel that when they lose a parent.'

'Yes, I know all that.'

'Sorry. You've read *Teach Yourself Psychology* like everyone else and you don't need my lecture for beginners.'

'I know you're only trying to help.'

He smiled. 'It's probably the worst vice there is. Certainly the most irritating. I keep trying to cure my daughter of it but I can't cure myself.'

She thought how calm he was, but in an oddly dynamic way.

As if he had everything under control and she needn't panic any more. It could all be said and accepted. Nothing was as terrible as she had imagined.

'You're right, of course. I do feel I killed her. So many times I wished she'd never been born – then I might have had a real marriage. Now she's gone and it's all in ruins anyway.'

Relief. She'd unloaded it all onto him.

'Would it help if I told you I killed my mother? She wouldn't let me have a pair of roller skates – too dangerous, she said. We argued and fought – I kicked her – she hit me – but she wouldn't give in. I hate you, I said. You're a rotten spoilsport, I wish you were dead. She was driving to the station to meet my father. There was another car on the wrong side of the road – a drunk – it was on a bend and she couldn't swerve in time. She was never a very good driver. She was careful but her reflexes were slow. The drunk got away with a broken leg.'

Cassie felt stunned. 'I never thought you were talking about yourself.' She was struck by his generosity in telling her.

'It took me a long time to work through it. So I shouldn't really be trying to take your guilt away. You may need it.'

'D'you mean to punish myself?'

'Not exactly. It may be to make up for something you feel deprived of. Guilt means responsibility, after all, doesn't it? And power.'

He served the soufflé.

Gavin dumped two plates of beans on toast on the table. 'I'm sorry, this seems to be all there is.'

'It's a treat, I love them. I so seldom get them these days.'

He mocked her. 'Poor little rich girl.'

'Shut up. Anyway, it takes me back. I had this lovely boy-friend who used to give me beans on toast. He was a student and broke and I used to go round and cry on his shoulder. Simon, his name was. He was ever so nice.'

She was getting quite drunk by now and talking much faster, with great energy and vitality.

'Why didn't you marry *him*?'

'He didn't ask me. In fact he went off with someone else. I was most upset.'

'When was all this?'

'Last year.' It seemed a lifetime ago.

'At the same time as –'

'Geoff and Peter – yes. Are you shocked?'

'No, just impressed by your stamina. Why did you need three?'

'They were all so different. I could be a different person with each of them. And anyway they made me feel safe . . . like having three insurance policies. One of them was bound to come up trumps.' She giggled.

'And one of them did.'

'Yes.' There was a pause while she thought about it. 'There's something wrong with the theory, isn't there?'

'It sounds like a lot of effort for a small reward.'

They both thought that was very funny. Sarah refilled their glasses.

'I've never had more than two affairs going at once,' Gavin said, 'and that seemed quite enough.'

'You mean Prue and her mother.'

'Yeah, but before that. I meant ever in my life. I guess I get too involved. Or I don't have the energy.'

'You know, whisky goes really well with baked beans. I didn't know that before.'

'You're right, it does.'

Sarah leaned her elbows on the table and expounded her theory. 'You see, I think two is a bad number. You want either one or three. One if it's perfect and three if you want to spread the load. Two just sets up a kind of nasty competition.'

'I'll bear that in mind, next time. Right now, I'm off the whole thing. It's more trouble than it's worth. If they were recruiting for a monastery, I'd sign on the dotted line.'

'How funny – I feel exactly the same.' She was delighted to hear it, in her present mood, although she did in fact think he was attractive.

'Oh, you'd be a wow in a monastery.'

'No, you fool. I mean I'm off the whole thing too. Only I thought it was something to do with the abortion.'

'Well, it can't be that in my case.'

They laughed. He had to make an effort to remember that this was Manson's former mistress. She was such fun, so sexy and vulnerable. If only he didn't feel switched off.

Sarah said, 'I think the worst part is people thinking they own you.'

'Yeah. I know what you mean.'

'You go to bed with them or you marry them –'

He laughed. 'There is a difference.'

'Yes, but the principle's the same. Suddenly it's all "Where have you been?" and "What time do you call this?" and all kinds of yukky scenes. They start telling you about their rights and they try to make you feel guilty.'

'Do they succeed?'

'No, I just get furious. It's like that nightmare I have. Someone's trying to suffocate me, and I panic, but it's not just panic, it's rage.'

He said with conviction, 'I'm sure rage is much healthier than panic.'

'How do you feel when they do it to you?' She wanted to know him.

'Oh – I guess I just want to push them away.'

'There you are. You see what I mean.'

'Yeah – but it's supposed to mean they love you and all that.'

'I don't care what it means. I don't like it.'

They sat and looked at each other, feeling comfortably alike. The whisky gave them a welcome illusion of cleverness and lucidity. They felt they were making important discoveries that would enrich the world.

Cassie finished the last of the cheese soufflé. She was most impressed. 'That was really delicious. Better than mine, dammit.'

'My mother taught me. She was much better at cooking than driving. Sorry, sick joke. In actual fact she cooked for a living. That's how my father met her. In the end it was cheaper to marry her than to keep going to the restaurant.' He got up. 'Ready for lamb?'

'Yes, please.'

He cleared away. 'Pour us some wine then, would you?'

Cassie poured. She felt a great wave of guilt for enjoying herself when Manson was so ill.

'I taught Vicky to cook,' Evan went on, 'much against her inclinations, so your son-in-law will have been well fed, if nothing else.'

'That will have made a nice change. My daughter couldn't boil the proverbial egg.'

'Actually, boiling an egg properly is quite difficult.'

'Yes, I know.' She paused. 'It does seem ironic. Here I am enjoying a gorgeous meal when my . . .'

'When your husband lies in my clinic sleeping off his overdose. Quite. But I promise you, he wouldn't appreciate cheese soufflé and roast lamb just now.'

He served the lamb. Crown roast. She could hardly believe it. Would he have gone to all this trouble for himself?

'That looks marvellous,' she said.

'It should be all right.' He dished up the vegetables. 'Courgettes and potatoes. You're not dieting, I hope.'

'No.'

'That's good. I can't stand women who diet. And it's usually very thin women who do it, have you noticed?'

'I haven't thought about it.' The personal tone embarrassed her slightly, making her more aware of his physical presence. He wasn't overweight but he certainly wasn't thin. Neither was she.

'My wife used to diet. Constantly. And she was extremely thin. Just this side of anorexia nervosa. Very frustrating for a dedicated cook like me.'

'Was that why she did it?'

'You're learning fast.'

Mention of his wife made Cassie curious. Where is she now?'

'Not about to burst in upon us, I promise you that. She's living happily in Edgware with her second husband. Probably watching television and eating slimming biscuits.' Cassie laughed. 'Duo Mawr, I've actually made you laugh. That's quite an achievement.'

'You're being unfair. Having a suicidal husband isn't a joke.'

'No – but he's going to live. Or had you forgotten?'

They ate for a while in silence. Cassie found herself desperate to know more about him. 'How long have you been divorced?'

'Oh – it must be about seven years by now. No – probably

nearer five. We had a couple of years wrangling after we had separated.'

'You sound very cheerful about it.'

'Is that an accusation? It was hell at the time, as they say, but we've both got over it, luckily.'

He made it sound so easy.

'Before all this happened ... my husband was talking about divorce. I was very upset.'

'Do you want to go on living with him?'

'I feel such a failure. We've been married twenty-four years.'

'And were none of them happy?'

She tried to be fair. 'Yes. Quite a few. Most of them in fact. Moderately happy.'

'Did you specially want to reach your Silver Wedding?'

'I just assumed we would – naturally.'

There was a pause. She felt he was genuinely trying to help her.

'I have a theory about marriage – probably invented to deal with my own guilt, but I think it's still valid. If we valued all relationships, including marriage, by their quality instead of their length, we'd be a lot better off. For instance, you'd think being moderately happy for twenty-four years was quite an achievement. Instead, you're fretting because your marriage isn't going to last for ever. In our case, we were very happy for five years, tolerably happy for seven and progressively miserable for three. Don't you see, the fact that it's ended doesn't turn it into a total failure. It's only the last bit that was nasty. You've had your allotted span, that's all.'

'It's a lovely theory.' She envied him.

'But you can't accept it.'

'I'd like to. I really would.'

'But guilt is more fun.'

'That was rotten.' Being teased by him was surprisingly warm and friendly. Almost fun. It was a long time since she had had fun.

'Look,' he said, 'it's largely a matter of expectations. If you get ten pounds in the post and you're only expecting five, you're thrilled – right? But if you're expecting fifteen, you're disappointed. The amount you've actually got remains exactly the same.'

'You think we expect too much of marriage?' She had the feeling this was his favourite theme. He was on familiar ground.

'Don't you?'

'You're quite a crusader. I bet you felt just as guilty as I do at the time.' She was beginning to be brave.

'Of course I did. But you don't catch me as easily as that. I've got the ultimate justification: if I hadn't left my wife, she couldn't have divorced me and married the man who is now – she tells me – making her so much happier than I ever did. Talk your way out of that.'

Having said so much about Geoff, it was natural they should drift on to Vicky. The whisky was making Gavin mellow and repentant.

'I really feel bad about her – she's a nice kid. She tried her best and I gave her a rough time.'

'Not intentionally?'

'No – but if someone keeps lying on the floor, you tend to walk on them.' He made to refill Sarah's glass.

'No, I mustn't have any more, I've got to drive.'

'D'you think you should? We've both had quite a lot.' He was trying to cling to the remnants of common sense.

'Maybe I'll take a cab. In which case – yes – I will have another drink.'

He poured it for her. 'Will your husband be worried about you?'

'With any luck he won't be there.' She picked up her glass and looked at it thoughtfully. 'Oh dear. I don't want this.'

'Then don't drink it.'

'I only bought the bottle to spin out the evening. I don't want to go home at all.'

She began to cry slightly: drunk, maudlin. Gavin put his arm round her in a brotherly fashion. He didn't feel too well himself.

'Then don't. You're welcome to stay.'

'I'm not making a pass at you. Honestly.'

'I know. I can sleep on the couch. And I don't want you to make a pass at me, I'm dead beat.'

'That's all right then.' The crying switched abruptly to laughter. 'I'm making an exhibition of myself, aren't I?'

'Come on, let's get you to bed.' He noticed how pale she suddenly was, as if she might be sick, but to his surprise he wasn't disgusted, only concerned.

'Don't you ever get drunk?'

'Sometimes. I'm not exactly sober now, only you haven't noticed. Come on.' He tried to guide her. 'The bedroom's this way.'

'I know where the bedroom is. I was here before – remember?'

'Oh yes – I'd nearly forgotten.'

The whisky helped them both to take that particular memory in their stride.

'I ought to apol – apol – apologize for using your flat like that.'

'It was a long time ago.'

'Could I have a big glass of water, please?'

'Sure you can.'

He went and got her one and watched her drink it all in one go, like a thirsty child.

'Oh. That's better. Thank you.'

'Okay now?'

She wiped her mouth on the back of her hand. 'Look – this is silly. You're going to be ever so uncomfortable on that couch. Why don't we share the bed? I promise I won't jump on you.'

'Be all the same if you did. Not that you aren't very – '

'Oh, don't bother, don't bother with all that, please.' She sagged against the bedroom door.

'Okay.'

'I'm so tired.'

'All right. Come on.'

She lay down. She said suddenly with touching, childish fear, 'And I don't want to be alone.'

Vicky was asleep on the couch, her book open in her lap. She had meant to ring Gavin again, to ring him all evening and all night if need be. Eve slept in the carry-cot beside her. They had both fallen asleep unintentionally, long before they meant to.

Dinner was over. Coffee was over. Brandy was over. Cassie could not remember when she had enjoyed an evening so much.

'I really must be going,' she said reluctantly.

'Back to Surrey.'

'Yes.' Back to problems, she thought. Back to reality.

'So you can get up at crack of dawn, presumably, and drive all the way back to London to visit your husband.'

'Yes.'

'You're mad, woman.'

'I've really had a lovely evening and a gorgeous dinner. You were quite right, it wouldn't have helped to sit by the bedside all night – but now I really must – '

' – be going.'

'Yes.'

The more he stared at her, the more nervous she became. He put his hand on top of hers.

'Are you frightened of me?'

'No. Of course not. Why should I be?'

'You're shaking. Are you cold?'

'No.'

'You're not frightened and you're not cold. Then why are you shaking?'

'I don't know.' It was so long since she had anyone but Peter, and meeting Sarah had made her realize that Peter had been merely kind.

'Don't you? What an interesting medical condition. Do you often shake for no reason?'

'No.' She removed her hand.

'Then there must be a reason. Why don't you stay the night and we'll find out what it is.'

'Do you have a spare room?' She had not wanted anyone so much for a long time. Since Gavin, in fact.

'Yes, it belongs to my daughter. And that's not what I'm offering you. But of course you know that.'

'I think you're taking an unfair advantage.'

'Why? I'm not your doctor. I'm not even your husband's doctor. What's unfair about telling you I want to sleep with you? A lot of people might even think it was a sort of compliment.'

'Yes. I do.' She shivered; Sven had used the same direct approach and all kinds of memories were evoked.

'But you find me repulsive.'

'No. Not exactly.' She smiled.

'Well, d'you want to sleep with me or don't you? If you want to make love, we will, and if you don't, we won't. It's a very simple choice.'

Confronted with choice she panicked and lit a cigarette to steady her nerves, give herself time to think.

He said with calm deliberation, 'Oh, now you really have hit on the one and only way of making sure you get the spare room.'

Cassie hesitated, but only for a moment. Stronger even than desire, a great wave of recklessness swept over her. She stubbed out the cigarette.

*

Morning. Door-bell. They woke, but without realizing what had woken them. They just knew they were suddenly awake. Reality was awful, the thick tongue, the aching head, the knowledge it was all their own fault. But they were both pleased to find the goodwill remained the same.

'Hi,' Gavin said.

She smiled. 'Hullo. Who are you?'

'Did you sleep okay?'

'I must have done. I don't remember getting into bed.'

They both noticed how far apart they were, and still partly dressed.

'How's your hangover?'

'What hangover?' Everything buzzed and spun. She felt dizzy.

'Okay, okay.' His skin crawled: he felt hot and cold all over, and very unreal.

'How's yours?'

'All right if I keep very still.'

They both giggled in spite of their discomfort: the feeling of friendship was paramount. Then the door-bell, startling them. It was the first time they had been aware of it.

'Oh hell,' Gavin said, 'who's that?'

Sarah was alarmed but preferred to be flippant. 'Milkman? Postman? Your creditors?' He got out of bed and she turned her back to give him privacy. 'It's all right. Just remember this is England and you're innocent till proved guilty. More or less.'

He went to answer the door and she turned over, trying to go back to sleep. But she couldn't. Her hungover brain was flooded with images of herself and Manson, in this flat, in this bed. Why was it so vivid when it seemed an age ago? Was she even the same person any more?

Manson was sitting up in bed when a short, broad, dark-haired man came in. He resented him immediately: he wanted to be alone.

'Mr Manson. How are you feeling today?'

'Much better, I think.'

'I'm Dr Lewis, Vicky's father.' He sat down as if he owned the place. Perhaps he did.

'Oh, I see.'

'She found you unconscious yesterday in your flat.'

'So it's Vicky I have to thank for being here.'

'If you feel like thanking her.' He looked at Manson shrewdly: it was uncomfortable.

'Of course I do. If she hadn't found me, I suppose I might be dead by now.'

'That's what I mean.'

'Look here, you surely don't imagine I intended to kill myself.' Presumably that was the right thing to say. 'That's ridiculous. It was an accident. I should have thought that was obvious. I had a lot to drink and I couldn't sleep so I took extra pills. I lost count. I forgot how many I'd taken. That's all. It was quite idiotic and very careless of me. But you can rest assured it's taught me a lesson. I realize what a narrow escape I've had.'

Silence. He felt the other man was peering into his soul, scraping out specimens, analysing them.

'Mr Manson, I'm not your doctor. For one thing, I'm a neurologist, for another I feel I know too much about your background from my daughter. But I would like you to have a talk with my colleague, Dr Schroeder. He's a psychiatrist and I'm sure you'll find him helpful.'

'I expect I would – if I needed a psychiatrist. But I don't. And I'm sure Dr Schroeder has enough to do seeing people who are really ill – without wasting his time on me.' He had never felt such a sense of panic. Horror, not relief, had ensued on waking up: now all he could think of was escape.

It had been bad enough to find Vicky at the door. But she was so full of herself. It wasn't sufficient to bring Eve back: she had to hang about and go on talking.

'And I only just got him there in time. Just think, if I hadn't found him he might have died. And we're not sure but we think he did it on purpose. Isn't that awful? He must have been really desperate and nobody cared enough to be there.'

'That's all I need.' His head ached alarmingly: even his normal heartbeat seemed to make it thud.

'What d'you mean?'

'Now we'll have nothing but guilt – everyone weeping and wailing – blaming themselves. Why the hell did you have to interfere?'

'How can you be so callous? I couldn't just let him die.'

'Why not? It might have saved a lot of trouble.' He thought about this man he had hated so long and all the misery they had inflicted on each other. Why shouldn't it end in death? Prue was dead – why not Manson? And why the hell did Vicky have to turn up now, with Sarah in bed?

'You can't mean that.'

'No. I suppose I can't. But I don't really see why not.'

'Anyway, who's everyone?'

Sarah, fully dressed, came out of the bedroom. Vicky looked startled and then appalled. He gave up, applied his mind to wondering if there was any Alka-Seltzer in the flat.

'Look,' Sarah said to Vicky, 'I'm sorry about this, it's not what you think, but I've got to see Peter.'

'So you're everyone.' Vicky was stony-faced.

'No, I'm just a friend. Please believe me.'

'You don't have to explain to me. I don't count.' She slammed out. He was surprised at the strength of her anger.

'Sorry.' Sarah looked penitent.

'It doesn't matter, it's over. And she'd believe anything, she's in that kind of mood.'

'I suppose I should have stayed in there till she'd gone – '

'Why should you hide?'

'Only I felt so trapped – and I was worried.'

'It doesn't really matter, *really*. In fact it's kinda funny.'

They both sagged against the furniture, wishing there was someone else to make coffee.

'I must go and see him. To think he was doing that – while we were enjoying ourselves. Perhaps they'll make it up now, him and his wife.'

Gavin cuddled Eve. 'Then I really will have to emigrate. He's not getting his hands on Eve again.'

'I'd better go.'

He felt sudden panic. 'Don't just ... disappear, will you?'

She shook her head. 'I'll be back. I'll ring you. I don't have so many friends I can afford to lose a new one. Besides, never mind about you, I want to see *her* again.' She stroked Eve's cheek. 'I won't forget you in a hurry.'

Cassie was sitting by Manson's bed. She thought he looked much better: still very pale but not alarmingly so. And he had recovered enough energy to be indignant.

'Really, Cass, why all the fuss? It was an accident, that's all. Everyone's going on as if I'd committed a crime.'

'I was very worried about you.'

'And now you're angry.'

'No.'

'You sound very angry.'

She said apologetically, 'You know how it is. When the children were late home and you're so relieved to see them you want to knock the living daylights out of them.'

'I'm not a child.' He seemed offended.

'No. But it's the same feeling.'

'If everyone will stop pretending I tried to kill myself, perhaps we can get on to what really matters – how soon I can get out of here. I'm not ill and it must be costing a fortune. It's private, isn't it?'

'Yes.'

'Why aren't I in an ordinary hospital like everyone else?'

'Because Vicky found you and this is her father's clinic.'

So he was right: the wretched man did own the place.

'Why couldn't she send me somewhere normal?'

'I suppose she has confidence in her father.' It was hard to speak casually.

'He's already been in trying to make me see a psychiatrist. Can you put a stop to all that nonsense? I'm perfectly all right.'

She had to ask. 'Peter – did you mean to do it? Honestly?'

'No, of course I didn't, I've told you.'

'Because if you did, I'll never forgive myself.'

'For heaven's sake, why should I try to kill myself?' He looked away.

'Things have been pretty bad for you lately. And you're not a person who gets drunk and takes pills ... just like that.'

'Cass – will you do something for me?'

'Yes. Anything.'

'Help get me out of here. I don't like it and I can't afford it. I don't want any damn psychiatrist. I made a mistake and now I want to go home and sleep it off. I'm tired.'

'D'you want to come back with me? I could look after you. I'd be very unobtrusive.' Guilt and affection made her desperate to help.

'I'm sorry, I didn't mean that. I want to go back to the flat to be on my own.'

She felt rejected. And yet how convenient that would be for her, she thought. But she couldn't allow it.

'You may want to but it can't be good for you. Not after a thing like this. Not so soon.'

'I would be pleased if everyone'd leave me in peace. I know you mean well but I'm never alone – if it's not you, it's doctors, nurses – it never stops – this place is like a railway station – I'd give anything to be by myself. Is that really too much to ask?'

His voice was hoarse, as if he would have liked to shout but couldn't. She tried to keep her mind off what they must have done to save him.

'In your present state – yes – it probably is.'

'But I want to think about everything quietly. How can I do that if people keep popping in and staring at me and asking me silly questions? It's like being in a zoo.'

'We're all trying to help.' She wanted so much to atone for her new happiness.

'Yes, I know. It's driving me mad.'

'The only thing that makes me almost believe it was an accident . . .'

'Oh Cass – not again –'

She was afraid to say the words. 'If you'd meant to do a thing like that you'd have . . . written me a letter – wouldn't you? You couldn't have just . . . gone without telling me.'

'You'd actually want – you'd have wanted to know . . . if it hadn't been an accident.' He looked surprised.

'Of course. I'd have wanted to know the truth. I'd have needed that.'

'I don't think I would. I don't find the truth very helpful any more. Cass, are you going to help me get out of here?'

'If you won't come home with me – will you consider hiring a nurse?'

'But I'm not ill. And we can't afford a nurse.'

'We can if it would help. We can afford anything you need. Would you rather be with Sarah? I don't mind.'

'No. I don't want to be with Sarah.' That was the last thing he wanted.

'But you need someone.' She tried again. 'Peter, tell me what happened.'

'I got very depressed, that's all. I knew we were finished – because of *him* – it was all over with Sarah because of what she did –'

'What did she do?' Was this her chance to find out the real motive behind that visit? But he wouldn't answer.

'I thought Eve was my last hope – and then Vicky took her away. Back to you.'

'I'm sorry, but she had to.'

'Yes, of course, I realize that now. I don't know what I thought I was doing with Eve. I couldn't even look after her properly. But at the time I wasn't quite rational, I suppose. And after you'd all gone, I felt very lonely.'

'That's just what I mean – that's why you shouldn't be alone now.'

He didn't seem to be listening to her. 'So I started drinking. I drank quite a lot. I thought it would help but it didn't. Then I couldn't sleep so I took some pills. They didn't work so I took some more. I was pretty drunk and I forgot how many I'd taken. That's all there is to it, Cass, really.'

'It's all about Prue, isn't it? All these other problems – with me – and Sarah – and Eve – they're just extras. Did you think about David and Andrew at all? They love you very much, you know. They need you.'

'When you're really depressed, you don't think about things like that. It wouldn't even help if you did. Besides, they're better off without me if I'm going to be like this.' He saw her look of alarm. 'I mean – they don't need a depressive father – I'd rather they didn't see me while I'm in this state.'

She relaxed a little. 'You frightened me.'

As she left the clinic, Cassie saw Sarah on her way in.

'Vicky told me. How is he?'

'All right, I think.'

Sarah said hastily, 'I'm only visiting. I haven't gone back on anything I said.'

'You don't have to be defensive. Of course you want to see him.'

'I just feel so guilty. It was such a shock.'

'You and me both.' There was something very unifying about anxiety.

'How is he really?'

'Rather belligerent. All he wants is to get out of here.'

'Did he do it on purpose?' She looked searchingly at Cassie. 'You must tell me the truth.'

'He says not. In fact he insists he didn't. Maybe he protests too much. I don't honestly know. He swears it was an accident.'

Sarah frowned. 'It's not like him to have an accident.'

'No.' She paused. Perhaps Sarah was the person to help. 'Will you try to do something for me? Persuade him to see a psychiatrist. He might listen to you and I'm sure he needs one.'

When Vicky came into Evan's room he was on the phone to a colleague. She sat down and waited till he had finished.

'I went to see Mr Manson just now,' she said disconsolately, 'but he was asleep – or pretending to be.'

'Shame. Never mind, it will do him good.'

'Yes, of course – He *is* going to be all right, isn't he?'

'He certainly is. In fact he's already bleating about going home.'

She didn't like her father's casual tone. 'But I thought you kept them in when they tried to kill themselves. I thought they had to talk to Jim and have tests and all kinds of things to make sure they don't do it again.'

'True. But only if they're willing. I'm afraid medicine is still hampered by this being – nominally at least – a free country.' He saw her dejected look and spoke more gently. 'Darling, can you do me a favour? I've got so many patients to see this morning and there's an auction at Christie's. Are you very busy at college?'

She brightened, 'No. It's nearly the end of term.'

'That's marvellous. Can you go along and bid for me?'

'At *Christie's*?'

'I didn't mean college. And there's some claret I specially want.'

'But I won't know what to do.'

'Rubbish. You've been with me often enough. Here. I've marked all the lots I'm interested in with my limits. Get as much as you can but don't go over a hundred and fifty pounds. There's a blank cheque, and if you spend it on a dress, I'll kill you.'

For a moment she was genuinely diverted from her troubles, as he intended. 'A hundred and fifty pounds – on *claret*?'

Manson still had his eyes shut when Sarah came in but she wasn't deceived.

'I ought to be very angry with you,' she said.

'Don't bother. I've had enough of that from Cassie.'

'You lied to her, didn't you?'

'What if I did? What's it to you?'

'You did do it on purpose. Oh, *Peter*.' She sat down beside the bed.

'What's one life more or less? You can't be concerned about that, surely. If you can kill your baby, why can't I kill myself if I feel like it? What's the difference? Just something unwanted being got rid of. Perfectly normal these days.'

She had not expected to be attacked like this. 'You know

there's a difference – a big one. There's never a good enough reason for suicide.'

'I don't want to discuss it with you.'

'Peter – will you discuss it with someone else?'

He said sharply, 'I hope you're not going to talk any nonsense about psychiatrists.'

'It couldn't do any harm and it might help.'

'Why? I'm not mad, just inefficient.'

'Wouldn't it help to talk to someone impartial? We're all much too involved.'

'Really? I hadn't noticed.'

'That's not fair.' She resented the heavy irony.

'Judging from the way you behave, I doubt if you've ever been involved with anyone except yourself.'

'If you mean I couldn't have a baby just to please you – no. It's too important for that.'

'So important you got rid of it instead. Yes, I see.'

'I had to do what I thought was best.' She was furious. After all, it was not something that could ever happen to him, so how could he judge?

'Best for yourself, you mean.'

'Best for everyone.'

'Why can't you be honest and admit it was inconvenient, so you killed it.'

She was almost shouting. 'It's my body. I've got a right to choose what happens to it.'

'Then so have I.' He spoke quietly.

She knew she was mishandling everything and made a big effort to change direction. Her hangover didn't help. 'I'm sorry. I'm tiring you. We shouldn't be quarrelling again, especially not today. I meant to be helpful but I've only made it worse. Peter? Shall I come back later? Or tomorrow? When you're rested.'

'I don't think I want to see you again.'

'Not ever?' She was shocked.

'I don't think we've anything left to say to each other.' His voice was very cold.

'I'm sorry. I always hoped we could stay friends. I want to help you.'

200

He turned his head away. 'You can help me by not coming back.'

Sarah and Cassie looked anxiously at Evan. 'I can't stop him discharging himself if he wants to – unless we commit him under Section thirty – if I think he's a danger to himself I can apply for a three-day committal.'

'I think you should.' Sarah was very positive.

'It might help – to get him over a bad patch. On the other hand it might make no difference at all – or even make him worse.'

'I'm sure he meant to do it – he more or less admitted it to me.'

Cassie didn't want to believe that. It spoilt all her lovely warm feelings of excitement, memories of the night with Evan. She found it hard to speak to him in front of Sarah.

'But when I saw him he was so positive it was an accident.'

'Don't believe him,' Sarah said. 'Perhaps he wants me to feel guilty instead of you. He's in a very aggressive mood.'

'Then he could be lying to you and telling me the truth.'

Sarah shrugged. 'Or the other way round.'

Manson was outraged at the sight of Jim Schroeder. A tall, slim Australian, fortyish, suntanned, with a carnation in his buttonhole and an air of well-being that could only come, Manson thought, from charging excessively high fees.

'Your wife and Mrs Roberts are very concerned, you know. Why don't we have a talk – just to set their minds at rest?'

'Dr Schroeder, you don't seem to understand me. I thought I'd already made it perfectly clear I don't need a psychiatrist.'

'Mrs Roberts says you told her you meant to kill yourself.'

'Mrs Roberts has a very vivid imagination. I've already explained to my wife it was an accident – why should I tell Mrs Roberts the opposite?'

'You tell me.' He settled himself to listen.

'I can only assume Mrs Roberts likes to imagine I wanted to die because she left me. Perhaps it makes her feel important. Look – since you're here – perhaps you can arrange to have my clothes brought in.'

Schroeder smiled. 'I think it's a bit soon for that. I'd rather wait till you feel ready to talk.'

'You can wait as long as you like, but I'm going home and I'd rather go fully dressed.'

'If you discharge yourself, it's against medical advice.'

'Yes, well, I don't think that's too serious.'

'And you certainly shouldn't go home alone.'

It was all being done so affably. Manson lost his temper. He was not used to these outbursts of anger and they left him exhausted. 'Dammit, that's exactly how I want to go home. There's no one I want to be with – can't you get that into your head?'

The door opened and Vicky's face appeared. She smiled at him. 'Oh, good, you're awake.'

It was the only way out. He had ended up bargaining for his freedom like a prisoner on parole. He signed a statement that he was going home on his own responsibility and he promised to let Vicky keep an eye on him, to set all their minds at rest. When they got back to the flat he felt like a naughty child with a nanny. She even opened the front door for him.

'Here we are. How are you feeling? You go and sit down and I'll make you some tea. Shall I? Or would you rather have coffee?'

'I don't want anything. Thank you.'

'I think you ought to have something. How about some hot milk? I know it tastes awful but it would do you good.'

'No. I really couldn't.' The very thought of it made him feel sick.

'Not even if I put a dash of whisky in it?'

'For God's sake – because I got drunk once – I am *not* an alcoholic.'

'No. Of course not. I didn't mean . . . Sorry.'

They were both embarrassed by his sudden rage.

'*I'm* sorry. I'm very tired.'

'Yes, of course.'

'I think I'll go and lie down.' It was not just to escape: he was amazed at how much the effort of getting up and dressing had exhausted him.

'All right. Could you tell me what you'd like for supper?'

'Supper?'

'Then I can get it before the shops shut.'

'There's no need to go at all that trouble. I'm not hungry.'

'You should eat, all the same. And I'm starving.'

'You're very kind and very sweet and I don't want to hurt your feelings but – I really do want to be alone.' He felt new waves of terrifying anger.

'Yes, I know. But you shouldn't be, not yet, and I promised Jim and Dad I'd look after you. I'm very good at looking after people, even when they don't really want me to.'

'Yes. I'm sure you are.'

'I wish you'd talked to Jim. He's awfully nice once you get used to him. Well, never mind. Perhaps you will later.' She smiled at him coaxingly. 'Now then – how about a nice omelette?'

Sarah watched with amusement while Gavin fed Eve. 'That's quite a messy performance.'

'Yeah. She's at the stage where she thinks it's fun to spit it all out and start over. How was he?'

'Very angry. They're letting him out. I don't think they should.'

'He can't stay in there for ever – more's the pity.'

'It's too soon, but there's nothing I can do.'

Silence. They couldn't agree so they dropped the subject by tacit consent.

'Can I fix you a drink?' Gavin said.

'God forbid. I'm on the wagon – at least till tomorrow.' She stared at Eve. 'Are you going to take her back to Mrs Manson?'

'I don't know. It's kinda tricky now he's sick. She may be all tied up with visiting or he might move back in.'

'How will you manage? You have to get out to libraries, don't you?'

'Oh – I'll find someone to baby-sit.'

Sarah suddenly made up her mind. 'How about me? I could. I'd like to.' She enjoyed Gavin's surprise.

'What would your husband say?'

'That's my problem.'

'It would be a great help. When could you come?'

'Say between ten and four.'

'That'd be great. Which day?'

'Monday to Friday.'

'You mean every day?'

'That was the idea.'

'That's fantastic. You must be crazy.'

'I've got nothing to do. I think I'll enjoy it.'

Cassie had been so afraid it was just a one-night stand and she would be worse off than ever, reawakened, reminded of all she'd been doing without and then made to do without it again. 'All turned on and nowhere to come,' as Gavin had once put it when they talked about frustration. When the florist's van arrived she hardly dared to hope.

'Mrs Manson?'

'Yes.'

The delivery boy gave her a huge cellophane-wrapped bouquet.

'Thank you.' She heard herself sounding calm, as if she were the kind of woman who was used to receiving flowers.

When he had gone she tore open the envelope with shaking hands. The card read: 'Worth giving up smoking perhaps?'

The telephone rang while she was still arranging the flowers. There were so many she ran out of vases and some had to go in a jam jar.

'Hullo?' she said, her heart thumping painfully.

Evan said, 'Hullo, you.'

She almost kissed the phone. 'I've just had the most beautiful surprise. You're very extravagant.'

'I like to do things in style. Or hadn't you noticed?'

'I'd noticed.' His voice brought back all the sensations of the night.

'When are you going to cook for *me*?'

7

DEPARTURES

MANSON was wide awake. He had hoped to sleep heavily after the clinic, but instead his brain seemed endlessly active.

There was a knock at the door. He answered unwillingly; he really wanted to be alone, to think.

'Come in.'

'Hullo.' Vicky appeared with a cup of tea. 'I didn't want to disturb you but I know you've been waking early. It's a lovely morning.'

'Is it?' He couldn't pretend to care.

'Shall I draw the curtains?'

'If you like.'

'Oh – not if you don't want me to.'

'Yes – go ahead.'

She drew them. To please her, he sat up and sipped his tea. She regarded him fondly, almost like a mother with an invalid child, he thought.

'How d'you feel today? Did you sleep better?'

'Yes. Yes, I did.'

'Oh, good.'

He felt quite weak with wishing she would go away.

'How about you?' It was an effort to be civil.

'Oh, I always sleep well. I told you, your sofa's a lot more comfortable than the one I'm used to. Now.' She sat on the edge of the bed, prepared to be horribly efficient. 'What would you like for breakfast?'

He said sharply, 'I think I'll get up today.'

Cassie woke up to find Evan putting a tray on the bedside table. She had slept heavily after making love. Her body ached pleasurably and her mind was cloudy with sleep.

'Greater love hath no man than to make morning tea for his friend.' He began pouring tea.

She heard herself say, 'Oh, Gavin, how nice,' and was instantly horrified.

'Whoops.'

She woke up properly, 'Sorry.'

'Wishful thinking?'

'Never. Amnesia, more like. Can't believe my luck.' She sat up and looked at him with love.

'Your honour, she was a plausible woman.' He got back into bed beside her. 'I raided your garden.' He indicated a single rose in a sherry glass on the tray.

'He'd never have thought of that. I'm surprised you could find one that good in my garden.'

'Don't underestimate yourself. Milk? Sugar? Lemon? I wasn't sure, so I brought all three.'

'See – you don't even know the most basic things about me.'

'Depends what you call basic.'

Manson pushed his plate away. Vicky looked disappointed.

'Can't you eat any more?'

'It was very nice. I'm just not hungry.'

She said encouragingly, 'Never mind, you've done better than yesterday.'

He cleared his throat. 'I've been thinking. I might take a holiday. That might do me more good than anything.'

'Yes – I'm sure it would – what a good idea. Where would you like to go?' She didn't seem upset.

'Oh – I don't much care.'

'Somewhere very quiet and beautiful would be best, don't you think? And warm, of course.' She even began to sound enthusiastic.

'Yes, I expect so.'

'Then you could have a good rest and sunbathe and all that. Could I ask you a favour?'

'Of course.' It all began to make sense.

'If you're going to be away – if the flat's going to be empty – could I possibly stay here? I'd take great care of it, I wouldn't

206

give parties or anything.' She looked at him hard. 'Oh, I'm sorry, I shouldn't have asked.'

He wondered how to explain it to her. 'It's not that. The lease is about to expire and I thought if I go on holiday I wouldn't renew it.'

'But where will you live when you come back?'

'Oh – I'll find somewhere smaller and cheaper. It seems pointless to go on paying rent while I'm away.'

'Yes. Shall I get you some holiday brochures when I go out?'

'What? Oh. Yes. Thank you. That would be very kind.' He was amazed how readily she accepted everything he said. It seemed to confirm his new belief that no one really cared: they were all much too wrapped up in their own affairs.

Cassie lay luxuriating in bed and watched Evan dress.

'I should have made you breakfast.'

'There wasn't time for everything.'

'I like your priorities.'

He kissed her. 'Bye, lovely. Shall we meet tomorrow?'

'If you like.' She felt a chill of disappointment (what was wrong with tonight?) and knew she was being unreasonable, greedy.

As if he guessed, he said, 'Can't make tonight, I've got an appointment. You come to me for dinner tomorrow – about seven o'clock.'

'Fine.' She was instantly cheered by the warmth in his voice. She felt they were friends as well as lovers.

'If I'm late, let yourself in. There's a key in a flower pot.'

'Not underneath?'

'No, I'm highly original. It's under a brick on a brick guarded by earthworms to deter burglars.'

'I used to hide jewellery in a Tampax carton for the same reason.'

'I'm sure we're both quite wrong to imagine burglars are so squeamish, but it's a nice thought.' He kissed her again. 'You're gorgeous. Take care.'

'You too. See you tomorrow.'

When he had gone she tried to sleep again, but she was too happy.

Gavin let Sarah in. He had Eve in his arms.

'Hi. You're early.'

'So I should be on my first day. I'm all keen.'

'I hope she'll behave. I've fed her.'

Sarah asked Eve, 'You sleepy?'

'You're hopeful. She may nod off if you're lucky. I've left everything ready for her lunch in the kitchen. She'll let you know when she's hungry.'

'What about nappies?'

'She'll let you know about that, too. There's a pile of clean ones in the bedroom. Otherwise all she needs is a cuddle and a chance to crawl round the room.'

'Right. I can manage all that.' She looked cheerful.

'I don't think you know what you're taking on.'

'I'll find out, won't I?'

'How did your husband react?'

'Oh – he doesn't mind. I'm having dinner with him tonight, so you won't be late, will you? I want to get my hair done.'

'Back on the dot of four. I'm really very grateful.'

'Don't be silly. I'm going to enjoy it.' She took Eve from him. 'Go on, off you go to your library or museum or wherever you're going.'

Evan, dashing out of the clinic with a shopping basket, nearly collided with Vicky coming in.

'Sorry, can't stop now.' He breezed past her.

'I've got to talk to you.' She ran after him.

'I've only got half an hour to buy dinner.'

'It's important.'

'Walk with me then.'

She fell into step beside him and there was an ominous pause.

'Can I come home?'

'What?'

'He's going abroad – he's going to give up the flat.'

'I thought you had a friend with a sofa.'

'I can't go on staying with Liz. She's sweet but it's not fair on her and Tony – they're never alone.'

'Last time you lived with me, it didn't work, remember?' He had appalling memories of her interference in his sex life:

childish scenes, tears, tantrums. All the textbook jealousy and resentment, only magnified a hundred times. He couldn't tolerate that again.

'I'll be different this time.' An easy promise.

'If you don't get all tight-lipped about my moral welfare.'

Manson was up: washed, shaved and dressed. Sarah was right about that, at least: you did feel better if you made an effort. And he had a lot to do. He started writing. He had been planning the letter all night.

Dear Sarah,

I've thought a lot about our last conversation and I want to tell you I'm sorry. I had no right to condemn you like that but I was feeling angry and hurt.

I still very much regret that you had an abortion but I'm sorry for my part in creating the problem and I wish you could have let me help you as I wanted to.

Apart from that I feel I owe you a lot. I value the time we spent together and I'm grateful to you for many happy moments. I don't think you'll ever know quite how important you were.

The bell rang. He went to the door, furious, and found it was Cassie.

'Why didn't you ring?'

'Am I intruding?'

'No, not at all.'

He put away his letter to Sarah. He had just reached the bit that would say, 'You were unlucky to meet me at such a bad time in my life. It could have been very different.'

Cassie said, 'You're looking better.'

'I really feel the most dreadful fraud. All this fuss and there's nothing wrong with me. Would you like a drink?'

'No, thanks.'

'Coffee?'

'No.'

He wondered why she had called. 'You're looking marvellous.'

'Am I?'

'There's something different about you. You've had your hair done.'

'No.'

'New make-up?'

'No.' She looked embarrassed. 'I'm on a diet.'

'Ah – that must be it.' He didn't know what to say to her: she seemed very strange and remote. Well-meaning but alien, like a foreign business contact.

She said, 'Are you managing all right – on your own?'

'If only I were – on my own, I mean.'

Cassie smiled.

He made a big effort to be entertaining, so she would think there was nothing wrong with him. 'She camps on the sofa, she cooks me meals I don't want, she brings me early-morning tea in bed, and stares at me with spaniel eyes while I drink it. Then we have to plan the menus for the day. Honestly, Cass, I don't want to hurt her feelings but I wish to God she'd leave me in peace. You didn't set her on me, did you, like a watchdog – you and that father of hers?'

'She just likes looking after people.'

'Well, I can't stand it. However, I have a plan. I've told her I'm giving up the flat and taking a long holiday. That ought to get rid of her. She's out collecting holiday brochures now.'

'And what are you really going to do?'

'Just take the car and drive till I stop. I hadn't the heart to tell her. How's Eve?'

'I imagine she's all right.'

'Imagine?' He was alarmed.

'I haven't seen her since ... I haven't seen her for a week so I presume Gavin's managing. I thought he must have got Vicky to help but if you say she's here all the time ... '

'I feel very sorry for her.'

'Eve?'

'No, Vicky. She must be really desperate for some kind of father-figure if she hangs around me when she could be out enjoying herself. I feel guilty for not being more grateful. That father of hers, what's the matter with him, doesn't he care about her?'

'Yes, of course.' She heard herself being too partisan and controlled it. 'I assume he does.'

Vicky, watching Evan shopping, wished he would give her the same attention he gave the food.

'Freshest prawns in London.'

'Is it really all right if I come back home?'

'Shellfish ought to smell of the sea.'

'Well?'

'I've told you – *if* we can live and let live for a change. I don't interfere with your life, why should you interfere with mine?'

'I won't. Of course I won't.'

'Fine. Half a pound, please. But you did last time you lived with me.'

'I was younger then.'

They moved on to the greengrocer.

'A pound and a half of *mange tout* ...'

'Anyway, I don't mind Anna and Christine. In fact I quite like them.'

'And do you like Cassie?' He studied her face. 'Hadn't you guessed? I assumed that was why you wanted to move back.'

'You always look for such complicated motives – I suppose it's your work. I want to move back because I'm sick of sleeping on other people's sofas.'

'I think mangoes will be nice, don't you? Very sexy fruit, mangoes.'

'Why do you need three girlfriends?' She confronted him stubbornly.

'Have you decided never to have more than three friends at once?'

'No, of course not. But you sleep with all yours, don't you?'

'So?'

'Isn't that rather a lot?'

'What a narrow view of sex you have. They're still friends.' She suddenly smiled. 'I think it's a sign of insecurity.'

He enjoyed the challenge. 'Sometimes – with some people.'

Manson found himself wishing that Cassie would go away. She kept asking him what he intended to do.

'Take a long holiday – I've told you.'

'No, I meant what do you want to do about us – when you

come back. Andrew and David will be home soon and I don't know what to tell them.'

He said as kindly as possible, 'I don't think there's any future for us together, do you?'

'No, I suppose not.' She hesitated. 'Not really.'

'All those things you said about Prue ... '

'Oh please. Don't remind me.'

'No, I'm not angry any more. That's all gone. I just think you were so wrong. Far from ruining our marriage, as you said, I think she kept it together. We're very different people, after all, and I think she made a bridge between us.'

'Perhaps.'

He felt she was humouring him. 'Anyway. Why don't you tell the boys we're going to live apart? Blame it on me – say I want to be alone – and we love them as much as ever – you'll know what to say.'

'You talked ... about divorce.'

'There doesn't seem much point. I mean it's not as if either of us wants to re-marry.'

She looked at him strangely. 'No.'

'Why don't we just ... separate and see how it goes.'

'All right.'

'I'll make sure you have enough money.'

'What about the house?'

'Oh – that's yours, of course.'

'But you said – '

'Yes, I think I must have been a little ... I over-reacted. I never meant to sell it.' How unimportant it all seemed now.

'Does that mean you've forgiven me?'

'I don't think I'll ever understand you – but I don't want to punish you any more, if that's what you mean. I've done a lot of thinking since ... It taught me a lot – I'm really going to learn from my mistakes.'

There was a pause. He could see she was moved, but he felt quite unemotional.

'Where will you live after your holiday?'

'You mustn't worry about me.'

'You know you can always come and stay if you want to.'

He almost laughed. It was such an absurd idea. 'Thank you. That's kind of you.'

*

Vicky called from the kitchen. 'How are you getting on? See anything you fancy yet?'

'I think I'm spoilt for choice.'

The brochures lay unopened beside him. He picked one up reluctantly and began turning the pages. The colours were strong and everyone looked unnaturally cheerful.

'Supper's nearly ready,' she shouted. 'I hope you like liver. Only you wouldn't tell me what you wanted and I thought it would be nourishing.'

'Liver will be fine.' He leaned back and shut his eyes.

'The onions smell good, don't they? Don't you think so? That smell's enough to give anyone an appetite.'

'Yes.'

'Even you.'

'Even me.' He got up and paced about the room, looked out of the window. He was desperate to be left alone.

'I've done some bacon as well as you didn't have a proper breakfast.' She came in with two loaded plates, and noticed the discarded brochures. 'Oh – you're not looking at them.'

'No, but I have been looking at them, and I'll look at them again later.'

They took their seats at the table. She said brightly, 'I'm sorry, am I getting on your nerves? I used to get on Gavin's nerves, too, only he always told me. The trouble is, even when I know I'm doing it, I find it awfully hard to stop. I just overdo everything. I can't help it. It drives people mad. My father's always telling me about it.'

'How is your father?'

'He's fine. At least as far as I know. I thought I might go and see him tonight. I expect you'd be glad if I went out for a bit.'

'I wouldn't have put it quite like that.' He was suddenly more sorry for her than for himself.

'It all right, I don't mind. How's the liver?'

'The liver is delicious.'

She was thrilled, like a child who has been awarded top marks. '*Really?*'

Evan was cooking, dressed in a bathrobe. He called out, 'How about a drink for the cook?'

'All right. Just a sec.'

Christine came out of the bedroom wrapping her kimono round herself. As always, no matter how tousled, she managed to preserve the basic gloss and grooming of an air stewardess: it seemed built in. She mixed their drinks with the same air of professionalism and handed him his glass.

'That smells good,' she said, investigating the food.

'So do you. Funny – you never look a mess, no matter what you've been doing.'

'Wish I could say the same for you.' She slipped out of reach just as he was about to give her a playful slap on the bottom. 'You'll have to be quicker than that, I've been dodging passengers all week.'

Manson, listening to Mozart, soaked up the comfort of being alone. He poured himself a drink and started writing. The brochures lay unopened.

My dear Vicky,

I want to thank you for all your efforts to help me. I know I've been very troublesome and unrewarding but I don't want you to feel I'm ungrateful as well.

He thought about her: her eagerness to help, her clumsiness, her goodwill.

I hope you will find somebody worth while to love and take care of you. You deserve to be happy. Don't despair if it doesn't happen at once. I know how hard it is to wait when you are young, but you have your whole life ahead of you and I feel certain there are many good things to come.

Yours affectionately,
Peter Manson

When Gavin opened the door Vicky produced the bottle from behind her back. 'Surprise.'

'Yeah. It certainly is.'

'Can I come in?'

'I *am* working.'

'Ten minutes?' The sight of him was having its usual effect on her.

'Okay.'

She followed him into the living-room and looked round.

'Where is she?'

'Who?'

'Sarah, of course. Isn't she here?'

'I haven't hidden her.'

'I thought she'd moved in.' Perhaps there was hope after all.

'Is that why you called? Look, we told you – '

'You're just good friends.'

'Yeah. Believe it or not.'

She said casually, 'I suppose because I used to fancy you I imagine everyone does. Silly, really. I didn't tell *him* she was here. I thought he might be upset.'

'She's with her husband right now, if you really want to know. Tell him that.'

She was encouraged. 'We used to have a corkscrew.'

'What? Oh, yeah. Sorry.' He fished it out of the drawer. 'This is very nice of you. Just what I need.'

'So you're managing all right?'

'Yeah. Look – I'm not good at this but – I know I gave you a bad time and I'm sorry.'

She knew how hard he found it to apologize and she was grateful. 'Maybe if I'd stuck up for myself, you might have found me more attractive.'

'I think I'd have given anyone a hard time after Prue died.' He poured out two glasses of wine.

'But if I'd been more like her ... '

'I don't want a replacement.'

There was a pause. She wished he hadn't mentioned Prue. But she had to be brave: after all, she had nothing to lose.

'I was wondering ... would you like me to help with Eve in the vac.?'

'No, thanks, I've got Sarah to do that.'

'Oh, is that what you want her for?'

The restaurant was crowded, but he had managed to get their usual table. He thought she looked more beautiful than ever and he had a feeling of desperation: that this might be their last chance to talk. Whatever they decided tonight could be final.

'I did ring you the other night – after I slammed out. But you weren't there. Or you didn't answer.'

'No – I was very upset – I went to stay with Barbara.'

'I suppose she thinks I'm the all-time rat.'

'She was very helpful. She may have found me a job.' The word startled him. 'We agreed I didn't have enough to do and that was part of the trouble – so I'm going to look after somebody's baby part-time.' She paused. 'If you don't mind.'

'Whose baby?' The whole scheme struck him as most bizarre.

'A friend of Barbara's who has to work.'

'Why can't Barbara do it?'

'Oh, she's had enough with her three. Now they're all at school she's looking for a proper job.' Her face was hidden by the menu.

'Can't her friend find a nursery or something?'

'They're too expensive. One-parent families can't afford luxuries like that.'

'So what's she going to pay you?'

'I said I'd do it for nothing.' She emerged. 'You've always said we don't need the money and you don't want me working full-time.'

'So how many hours are you doing?'

'Oh, about thirty.' She saw his look of horror. 'You don't mind, do you?'

'It's all the same if I do, isn't it? It's all arranged.' He felt helpless. Why did she have to be like this just when he was hoping for a new start?

'Only for a few months,' she said calmly. 'It may not work out. We'll have to see how it goes.'

'It's such an unlikely thing for you to be doing.' The understatement of all time.

'Yes, I know.'

There was an uncomfortable silence while they both thought about the abortion.

Sarah said, 'The only other question is – would you rather I went to the parents' home or brought the baby to ours? That really is up to you. It's your house.'

Her coolness floored him. 'I don't know what to say. I've been staying at my old flat.'

Vicky said bitterly, 'So you don't need me for anything.'

'I'm not having a heavy scene with anyone right now. Sarah's helping with Eve and I'm doing a lot of work. That's all.'

Silence. He wished she would leave and let him study in peace.

'Mr Manson's going away,' she said.

'Great.'

'On holiday, I mean. And giving up the flat. I'll have nowhere to stay.' Another heavy silence. 'I thought I might go back to my father for a bit.'

'Why not?'

'Shall I give you the address?'

He didn't want to hurt her but he had to make her understand it was over. 'I'll see you next term, won't I?'

The more they ate and drank, the more they saw each other's point of view.

'You've had a pretty rough time, haven't you? I'm sorry I haven't been more help.'

'You've had a rough time too – I'm sorry.' Sarah smiled at him.

'D'you think we can still get it together?'

'I don't know.'

'Look – we'll have to talk about it. That's why we're here.'

'Yes, I know. But it's very difficult. It makes me feel sort of ... squirmy inside. I want to bury my head and pretend it isn't happening.'

'Is it that bad?' He wanted so much to rescue her – why wouldn't she let him?

'I can't face any more ... head-on collisions. I feel so tired. As if I've been run over. I know it's silly.'

'It's not silly.' He tried to think of the right thing to say, the magic formula. 'You know, you were probably right. About not having the baby. I've thought about it a lot. I shouldn't have sounded off like that. I mean ... we both changed our minds – we weren't sure about it – it's much better this way.'

She said coldly, 'D'you mean more convenient?'

'You're not ... regretting it, are you? Is that why you're going to – '

'No.'

'I mean – you're bound to feel a bit funny for a while, I should think.'

'Yes.'

'And I've been pretty insensitive about the whole thing. I'm sorry.'

She shook her head. 'It's my fault. I should never have let you rescue me last year. I warned you something like this would happen.'

'Something like what?'

'Don't you remember? I told you in the car – it would be all right till the next time. There's something wrong with me. I get these mad impulses to wreck everything just when it's going well ... And I can't resist a lost cause.'

'Could I be a lost cause?' He was suddenly afraid.

'No. You're a winner.'

'I don't feel like a winner right now.' He waited, but she didn't answer. 'It's not too late. We can try again.'

'Can we?'

'Don't you want to?'

The letter to Cassie was harder, much harder. Manson had to rewrite it several times.

Dearest Cass,
I wish I could describe how I felt when I woke up in that clinic and realized I had failed. So much effort, to result only in feeling ill and exhausted – and all to do again. It was such an anticlimax. And being 'saved' seems like a bad joke.

And then, when you said you'd have wanted, even expected a farewell letter. I was so surprised. I'd been sure you would rather think I had died by mistake. Does that show how little I understand you – or merely prove I was thinking only of myself?

He paused. It seemed an impossible task to write all he felt.

Vicky heard herself getting louder. She had drunk more wine than Gavin and it always had that effect on her. Too late to control it now. The disappointment and the bitterness made it worse; or perhaps it just helped to release them.

'It's funny,' she said 'here you are with nobody, and here I am with nobody, and there's Mr Manson with nobody. And Sarah's gone back to her husband. That makes Mrs Manson a clear winner. I always said she had nothing to worry about.'

'How d'you mean?'

'Didn't she tell you? I thought she would have done. She's having a mad affair with my father. Aren't you pleased for her?'

'Yes of course.'

There was some shred of satisfaction in seeing his shock, perhaps even a flash of jealousy.

'Lots of women find him attractive. I can't see it myself, of course. Still, she must be pretty desperate by now.'

Manson tore up two drafts and rewrote his third paragraph. The trouble was, he still felt he was over-simplifying. There were no adequate words to convey the despair he felt: the greyness of the world.

When I took the overdose I was angry and depressed. I felt there was nothing to live for. First I had lost Prue, then you had betrayed me in the worst way possible, then Sarah had failed me, and Vicky had taken Eve away. I was no longer in a fit state to work and so I had no sense of identity, either personal or professional. I didn't think of David and Andrew. I do love them but it's not a strong enough love to support a whole life when everything else has gone.

Brandy and coffee made Sarah look at Geoff more kindly. 'I can't imagine ... not having you around, that scares me – but I don't think I ought to be married, I don't think it suits me. I've done nothing but make trouble since we got married. We were all right before.'

'D'you mean you want a divorce?' He was shocked; she could see that.

'I don't know what I want.'

'Is it ... because of *him*?'

So he still didn't understand. 'Oh no, no, that's all over.'

'Well then. Doesn't that give us a chance? Look, you've never liked the house, have you? We've never been happy there. But we had some good times in the flat. Could you live with me there? We could pretend we're not married.'

'If we have to play games, is it worth – '

'It might help.'

'Yes, I suppose it might.'

'We could let the house, it's much too big for us.'

She sighed. 'I should have been more adaptable.'

'I wasn't very adaptable either. I started playing the heavy Victorian husband, didn't I?'

'Yes, you got all possessive and bossy. And I started yelling about freedom. I never used to do that with you. I didn't have to.'

Both felt the flickerings of goodwill. They smiled at each other.

'Perhaps marriage doesn't suit either of us, if it makes us change so much.'

'Divorce frightens me.' She hadn't known how much until she said it.

'I didn't mean that. Let's just stay in the flat and pretend we're living in sin.'

She looked at her rings. 'Do I have to take these off?'

'No. You're married to someone else and you've left him for me.'

Vicky rang and rang, but there was no reply. She was almost ready to give up when Evan, in bare feet and bathrobe, opened the door.

'I might have known.'

'You said I could come back.' She came in and he closed the door behind her.

'What – *now*?'

'I'm getting on Mr Manson's nerves. I went to see Gavin but I got on his nerves too.'

'So what makes you think you won't get on mine?'

She said bitterly, '"Home is the place that when you have to go there, they have to take you in." Robert Frost.'

'You're in one of your moods.'

'Who is it tonight?' She looked at the débris on the table and pointed towards the bedroom.

'Christine. You really start as you mean to go on, don't you?'

Vicky started to cry. 'There's no need for that. You know it doesn't work with me. I can feel just as sorry for you with dry eyes. Or not, as the case may be.'

'I'm not doing it for you, I'm doing it for me.' She heard herself howling, out of control. She hadn't known that finally losing Gavin would hurt so much, hadn't realized how much she was still hoping.

'Please don't wail, there's a love. She's got an early flight tomorrow.'

She tried to calm herself: he hated scenes. All his tolerance was used up at the clinic. 'Can I sleep here tonight?'

'Of course. Your room's still there. It's even got your name on the door. Vicky's room, it says. So it must be yours.'

She was laughing and crying at once. 'That old thing. You should take it off. It looks so silly.'

'You put it on, you take it off.'

'I was a *child*, when I did that.'

He held out his arms to her and she ran into them. He hugged her tight.

Cassie, alone in her bedroom, stood in front of the mirror admiring herself in a new nightdress. She longed for tomorrow night with Evan but there was a kind of perverse pleasure in having to wait.

Manson was still working on his letter. It was important to get it right.

You have such a strong appetite for life that perhaps you can't understand my wanting to die. Even when you were at your most unhappy over Sven, I seem to remember your writing to me that you wished me and the boys dead, not yourself. That isn't meant as a reproach any more, but it does show the difference between us. I've never wished anyone dead except Gavin and then only to protect Prue. I wish now I had indeed killed him, right at the very beginning, before it was too late.

He stopped. He wanted her to understand, but she seemed so remote from him now. More like a lost friend than a wife. He could think of her with distant affection rather than love.

Perhaps it's worth going through all this twice if only because my attitude has changed. When I took the first overdose I felt that everyone had gone away from me and I wanted to punish them. This time I feel much calmer, as if I am going away from everyone because that's the only way to find peace.

It was late but Gavin was still working. These were the best hours of the day for him. Eve cried and he went to her, book in hand. He was aware that his life had narrowed down to a book and a baby, but he did not mind.

The last part of the letter came more easily: perhaps he had got into the mood. Or perhaps it was just the most important part. But it left him very tired.

It's really very simple: I want to be with Prue. It was foolishness to imagine I could ever have a life without her. For the last few months I've been like a drowning man clinging to a raft, hoping for rescue, refusing to admit I must eventually die. Much better to go now with dignity. There's nothing in life to compensate me for the pain of staying alive.

Don't blame yourself. There was no more that you or anyone else could do. I think you will be happier without me. Take care of Eve and the boys for me and don't let them think too badly of me. Can you remember the early years? There were many happy times, weren't there?

*

The atmosphere was cosy, domestic. Sarah, still in her outdoor things, was entertaining Eve, while Gavin finished his coffee. He looked at her thoughtfully.

'How'd it go last night?'

'All right.' She didn't know how to describe it. 'We're going to have one last try.'

'D'you want to?'

'I'm scared to let go.'

'Think it'll work?'

'I don't know.' Now, in daylight, it seemed a strange decision to have made.

'Are you sure being here with Eve isn't making it harder?'

'Positive.' She tried to intercept him as he went to wash up. 'I can do that.'

'It's okay. You know, this is a lousy arrangement. Eve has a great time but I never see you. If I come home early will you have time for coffee?'

'Lovely. And fruity buns?' She laughed; he looked so puzzled. 'Haven't you read *Kleinzeit*? I'll lend it to you. It's a super book. Have you time to read it?'

'No, but I will.' He seemed reluctant to go. 'I guess I better move.'

'Have a good day.' Suddenly she wanted to tell him. 'He was glad ... about the abortion.'

'Aren't you? Really?' He had reached the door but he turned round to face her.

'Yes.'

'But that's different.'

'Yes. He's also a bit late in the day. Unfair, isn't it?'

Manson disliked being back in the office. He felt everyone was looking at him with concern he didn't believe was genuine, and asking him how he felt.

But it was necessary to be there, for a few days; there were things to be done.

He buzzed Monica. 'Ring the estate agent again and make sure he's taken my house off his books. Ring my solicitor and confirm my appointment for this morning. And ring the other estate agent and tell him I'm not renewing the lease and I'll be out of the flat by the end of the week.'

Finding Sarah in Gavin's flat was quite a shock. Cassie said, 'I only came to see if Gavin and Eve are all right – and obviously they are.'

Sarah was embarrassed. 'I'm just baby-sitting. I took such a fancy to Eve I told Gavin I'd help him out. Really. That's all it is.'

'I don't mind what it is. You don't have to explain to me.'

'I had to explain to Vicky and she didn't believe me. It was awful. The more I tell the truth, the more guilty I feel. No wonder people tell lies.'

Cassie changed the subject. 'Can I see Eve?'

'Yes, of course. She's in the bedroom. I think I've managed to wear her out.'

'That takes some doing.'

'It certainly does. I'm exhausted.'

Cassie went to see Eve. Fast asleep. Already she seemed more exclusively Gavin's child, after such a brief absence. Cassie was not in charge any more.

When she returned to the living-room Sarah was checking her make-up.

'Out for the count.'

Sarah put down the mirror. 'Would you like some tea?'

'No, thanks. I mustn't stay. I've got some shopping to do.' She paused; she wanted to be fair. 'Eve looks very well. You're doing fine.'

'I'm enjoying it.'

'It seems so unlike you.'

'That's what everyone says.'

'I'm sorry, I didn't mean it like that.' But perhaps she did.

'No. I was thinking of my husband.'

The word was evocative.

Cassie wondered how much she ought to say. 'I saw Peter yesterday.' She felt Sarah might not like to ask. 'He seems very well. I hope he's not putting on an act just for me. He's going to give up the flat and take a long holiday, he says. He was full of plans – very cheerful and positive. I don't know what to think.'

She was hoping Sarah would say something reassuring, but at that moment the front door slammed and Gavin called out, 'How about that coffee? I got the fruity buns', before he came in and saw them both. He looked very startled.

'It's all right,' Cassie said. 'I came to see how you and Eve were managing – and you're obviously managing perfectly.'

Sarah said quickly, 'I did explain everything.'

Cassie was amused. 'Why all the fuss? I'm delighted you've got help with Eve – it's a weight off my mind.'

'I thought you'd have enough with your husband at the moment . . . and Sarah wanted to help . . .'

'I said it's all right.'

Suddenly they were embarrassed: they were all protesting too much.

'I'll be off,' Sarah said. 'I've so many things to do.'

Gavin protested. 'But you said ...'

'Another time.'

When Sarah had gone, Gavin made tea for Cassie. He felt strange, seeing her again. The first time since Manson's overdose ... since Vicky told him about her father ... since Sarah took charge of Eve.

He said, 'It really is platonic with us. You do believe me, don't you?'

'Of course I believe you. Anyway, what does it matter if it isn't?'

'It matters that I've never lied to you and I'm not starting now.'

There was a pause. She said placatingly, 'D'you need a deputy baby-sitter?'

'Thanks, that would be great. Just the odd evening – the occasional week-end, maybe.'

'D'you mind if we keep it very flexible? – say you ring me the day before. I don't want to get into a routine – the way it used to be.'

'Because of Dr Lewis.' He enjoyed watching her reaction. 'It's okay – Vicky told me. I'm happy for you.'

'Are you?'

'Yes, of course. I hope he'll be good to you, that's all.' He didn't like the way Vicky had described her father.

'What d'you mean?'

'You deserve the best.'

'Thank you.'

Cassie needed kindness, he thought. Would this man be kind to her? Having hurt her himself, he felt fiercely protective.

'It's pretty sudden, isn't it? When did it start?'

'When Peter was in hospital. I feel a bit guilty about that.'

'Just like us.' All the memories flooded back. Had he really appreciated her?

'I must have a thing about people being ill. It seems to "turn me on".'

'You were anxious and you needed comfort. Why not?'

'Yes, but it's more than that. Oh Gavin, I'm so happy.'

'Yeah, I can see you are.' She looked more attractive than he had ever seen her. Radiant. He felt a twinge of grief.

'I feel very guilty but there's no reason why I should. Peter's adamant he doesn't want to come back. Oh – it's the sort of thing I thought would never happen again and it has. Just when I'd given up hope. I can hardly believe it.'

'Terrific.'

She smiled at him. 'I'm so happy I want everyone else to be happy too.'

Geoff said angrily, 'It's no good. I simply don't believe you're looking after a baby. You're off with some man, aren't you?'

'What's got into you?'

'I don't know. I've been thinking about it ever since you told me what you were going to do.'

'You said you didn't mind.'

'What else could I say?'

'And I wanted to come back.'

'Did you? Really?'

Impasse. She wouldn't make any concessions and he couldn't believe a word she said.

'You've told so many lies, I don't know where to start. D'you know why you do it? I'd like you to tell me the truth for once.'

'I am looking after a baby.' She was patiently spelling it out.

'What baby?'

'Prue's baby.' She saw his look of fury. 'You asked me. Well, why not? I'm being useful, for a change. Gavin has to study. Mrs Manson has other things to do, why shouldn't I help? I've done enough harm, isn't it time I did a bit of good?'

'What is it about that family? You just can't stay away from them.'

Cassie seemed reluctant to sit down, although Manson was pouring a drink for her. 'I won't stay long.'

'You're not disturbing me.'

'No? Peter – I'm sorry – I don't want to worry you but I had to see you before you went – because of the boys.'

'Why? What's the matter?'

'I think we should both tell them – not just me.'

'But Cass, you're so much better at that sort of thing – I thought we'd agreed.' He felt panic at the prospect of any fresh demands being made on him.

'Yes – but I think it would be better if we were together. When are you coming back? Will you be back in time for the school play in three weeks?'

'Oh Cass – how can I tell?'

'Haven't you any plans for returning?'

'No.'

'Oh.' She seemed oddly bereft. 'I know you want to be free but is there any way I could contact you?'

'Why would you want to?'

'I might need to.'

'But if I'd died you wouldn't have been able to.' He liked the finality of that.

'Peter, please – anyway that's past and didn't happen.'

'It might have.'

'It's hypothetical.'

'I could get run over tomorrow.' He was thinking with satisfaction how they would all reproach themselves.

'So could I, so could any of us.' She seemed impatient with him.

'The point I'm trying to make is that if I were dead – you wouldn't be able to reach me and I'm sure that you'd manage perfectly.'

'If you insist on being morbid – yes – but you *are* alive and I need you to be with me when I tell the twins about us.'

'Do you?'

'Yes.' She glanced at her watch. 'I must go.'

'Don't rush – have another drink.'

'I can't – I mustn't be late. I'm going out to dinner.'

She got up. He felt a sudden panic. He might never see her again and perhaps she could still say something magical and save him.

'Cass.' It was a cry for help, but she didn't hear it.

'Please ring me when you get where you're going.' She kissed him lightly on the cheek.

Geoff went on so long that Sarah gave up.

'I think I'd better go out.'

'Where?'

'Just out. It's our first evening and already we're about to have a row. If I stay we will.' It was not like her to evade a scene, but she was weary.

'Where are you going?'

'Just to cool off.'

'Back to *him*, you mean.'

'No.' If only he could understand how angry interrogation made her, even if it were justified.

'How can I believe you?'

'I'll be back later – when we've both calmed down.'

'No. We've got to settle this now.'

'I've told you before – I'm too tired for any arguments.'

He was killing the last of her feeling for him and she was encouraging him. Now he threw the unforgivable at her.

'You're not too tired to look after someone else's baby when you've got rid of your own.'

Cassie was pleased when she didn't find Evan's key under the brick. She thought he must be home early. But when she rang the bell, Vicky opened the door.

'Oh, Mrs Manson. Hullo. Do come in.'

Cassie felt at once an intruder. Seeing Vicky as hostess in Evan's home seemed to wipe out all the trouble they had shared over Eve, while reviving their antagonism over Gavin.

'Dad should be home any minute. Can I get you a drink?' Vicky led the way into the kitchen where Cassie had been so happy.

'Yes. Thank you.'

'What would you like?'

'Campari soda, if there is any.' There had been the other night.

'I expect there is.' Vicky searched. 'Yes. Here we are. I bet you're surprised to see me here. Only when Mr Manson changed his plans I had nowhere to go, so I asked Dad if I could stay for a bit. I don't think he expected me to move back quite so fast.' She handed Cassie her glass.

'Aren't you having a drink?'

'No. I don't really like drinking. I used to have a Scotch with Gavin but I've gone right off that.' She was talking rather fast.

'Maybe I'll have a tomato juice.' She added ice and lemon and Tabasco to it as Cassie watched her. 'Pretend it's a Bloody Mary. He's awfully hard to help, isn't he? Mr Manson, I mean.'

'Yes.'

Vicky sipped her drink. 'Oh – before I forget – I found your pendant on the sofa.'

'My what?'

'Isn't it yours? I thought with a C on it, it must be. It's Gucci, isn't is? They're terribly expensive.' She dangled a solid, dark-blue initial on a silver chain in front of Cassie.

'It's not mine.'

'Oh, good, then I can say I don't like them. I didn't want to offend you. I expect it's Christine's – she'll probably call for it. Oh – I suppose it could be Anna's – C for Carlson, I mean. I don't know whether people put the initial of their surname or their first name on these things – do you?'

'No.' Cassie felt frozen inside.

'Dad can sort it out,' said Vicky confidently, smiling at her.

'Who are Christine and Anna?'

'Hasn't he mentioned them?' She seemed alarmed. 'Oh, Lord, forget I said anything, please. He'll tell you in his own good time.'

Cassie pulled herself together and said sharply, 'Why don't you save him the trouble?'

Gavin led Sarah into the sitting-room. He was delighted to see her again.

'I've just put Eve to bed. Have you time for a coffee?' He wanted to make up for her rapid exit when Cassie was there.

'Oh yes, I've plenty of time.' She seemed very agitated.

'What happened?'

'Is there any whisky left?'

When Evan came in he found Cassie and Vicky sitting opposite each other in hostile silence. He felt the atmosphere at once but decided to ignore it. He would deal with it later, if he had to. But his heart sank a little: was Vicky up to her old tricks again already?

'Full house.' he said cheerfully.

Vicky sprang up. 'Hullo. You're late.'

'Yes. I was delayed. Hullo, Cass.' He kissed her on the cheek: a defiant gesture to tell Vicky about his loyalties.

'Hullo, Evan.' She barely responded.

He said to Vicky, 'I wasn't expecting you.'

'You said I could come back.'

'Today?'

'When you let me stay last night I thought you knew I was bringing my stuff today.'

'I didn't realize you were in such a hurry.'

'Aren't you flattered?'

Silence. He felt all the old nightmares resurrect. His life would not be his own.

'Have you given Cassie a drink?'

'Yes.'

'Then perhaps she'd like another.'

'I did ask her.'

'Would you, Cassie?'

'No, thank you. I think one's enough.'

Vicky turned to him. 'Shall I get you one?'

'No, I'll do it myself.' He poured whisky on ice. 'You know I definitely get the feeling I've walked in on something. I don't suppose anyone's going to tell me what, but if the fridge packed up this minute, you two could make ice all by yourselves.'

Cassie stood up. 'I think I'd better go.'

'If I slip you two quid,' Evan said to Vicky, all brisk and jovial, 'will you go to the pictures?'

'It's her home, isn't it?' Cassie said, picking up her handbag.

Vicky looked from one to the other apprehensively. 'I'm going to study. I told you.'

Evan raised his voice. 'It's also my home and I'd like a say in what goes on in it. Does anyone object to that?' He glanced at Cassie. 'If you want to be private, we can talk in the bedroom.'

'No, thank you.'

'I don't mind,' Vicky said. 'I'm used to it.'

'Or we can go out.'

Sarah couldn't stop talking about it. She was so indignant.

'It's ridiculous, a baby, no one can be jealous of a baby.'

'Sure they can.' Gavin refilled her glass.

'Oh, but not Geoff. Maybe he didn't believe me. We had a big thing about all the lies I tell.'

'Do you?'

'Yes.'

'Have you told me any?'

'No.'

'Was that the first one?'

'I don't remember.' She began to laugh. The casual way he accepted her was wonderful. She chose to forget that Geoff had been accepting once.

Gavin was also amused. 'I always tell the truth, so we should cancel out.'

'Always?'

'Nearly always.'

Sarah went to sit beside him. 'Oh, I *am* glad you were here.'

'Where did you say you were going?'

'Just out. When I've cooled off I suppose I'll have to crawl back and eat humble pie.'

'I can't see you doing that.' The door-bell rang. 'Oh, hell, who's that?'

'If it's Peter, I'm not here.'

'Why should it be?'

'Everyone else has called.'

Gavin went to the door. Sarah relaxed on the sofa. She felt unaccountably safe in Gavin's flat, as if nothing bad could happen to her there. Then she heard Geoff's voice.

'I'd like to see my wife.'

'Who are you?'

'Don't bother play-acting. Just get out of my way.' He came in, pushing past Gavin. 'What took you so long? I've been waiting half an hour. I thought you'd have been in bed by now.'

'You followed me.' She was outraged.

'How else can I find out what's going on? You're never going to tell me, are you?'

Cassie and Evan came out of the flat and walked aimlessly up and down the road, like children with nowhere to play. Evan tried to take her arm but she wouldn't let him.

'Come on. There's a nice pub round the corner.'

'I don't feel like a drink.'

'It will do you good.'

'I said I don't want one.'

'Ah – you don't want to be done good to. All right.' They walked for a while in silence. She kept turning round so that he had to follow her. 'Are we going to walk up and down all night? Because I don't know about you but I've had a heavy day and I'd like to sit down.' He unlocked and opened his car door. After a moment Cassie got in. He walked round and got in beside her. 'What was all that about?' She didn't answer. 'Come on, let's have it out. Don't ruin the whole evening.'

'There's not much left to ruin.'

'There's as much as you want.'

Silence. She could hardly speak for pain but she was afraid he would think she was merely sulking.

'It's not very pleasant to find out from Vicky you've already got two mistresses.'

He said lightly, 'They're not mistresses. I can't possibly afford a mistress.'

'All right – bed partners. Whatever you call them.' She tried to smile but she was so angry and humiliated she wanted to injure him.

'I call them friends, as a matter of fact.'

'You've got two of them already – what the hell d'you need me for – just to make a hat trick?'

He sighed. 'It's extraordinary how alike you and my daughter are – what mathematical minds you've got. One is okay, two is greedy and three is disgusting? Is that it?'

Cassie tried to think, to control herself, to be reasonable. Was there still hope? She couldn't bear to lose all she had gained: it was so new and she had invested so much hope in it. 'Why didn't you tell me yourself?'

'For all kinds of reasons. Because it's private – I haven't told them about you either. Because it's not something to be ... confessed, like a criminal record. Because I've only known you a week. Because I thought you might be hurt – and now you are.'

He put his hand over hers and she trembled.

'I'm a very jealous person.'

'I'm sorry, that must be very painful for you.'

'But you don't give a damn.'

'Darling, listen. I wasn't trying to hide anything but I wasn't trying to broadcast it either. I thought you'd assume at my age there'd be other people in my life. I'm not a monogamous person. That's one of the reasons I got divorced.'

'I see.' It was almost too much to bear, that all this could happen again. How often did she have to hear it?

'There are other people in your life too,' he said gently.

'Not so's you'd notice.' The bitterness nearly swamped her, but she made a supreme effort. 'Tell me about yours.' She was curious as well as hurt.

'All right. Anna used to be a nurse, that's how I met her. She married a rich man much older than she is. He travels a lot and I see her when he's away. Christine is an air stewardess and I see her when she's in town. Her boyfriend lives in New York.'

She had asked to be told; she had needed to know. Now she couldn't think what to say. It sounded so cosy. She was the outsider.

'Yes, well, you're all very lucky and I'm just old-fashioned.'

'Did it hurt more because Vicky told you?'

'I don't know. Yes, probably.'

'D'you think she did it on purpose?'

She didn't want to condemn his child. 'It seemed to slip out. I can't tell.'

'She's probably jealous. She may not even realize. I've had a lot of trouble with her before like this.'

Cassie was just managing not to cry. 'I was so happy – but I've only got myself in another mess.'

'Darling, don't. I've known these people for years – we're only just beginning. Let's give it a chance.'

'I want to.' The understatement of all time.

They went on staring at the windscreen for a while. Then they looked at each other and suddenly embraced.

After Geoff had gone, Gavin said, 'I think he'll be back.'

'I don't. Sorry I let you in for that awful scene, though.' She was ashamed of all the ugly things Geoff had said and she knew she had driven him to it. Now her boats were well and truly burned. The only way to freedom, perhaps.

'That was a scene? Hell, when you've been thumped by your father-in-law, having some lady's husband yell a little doesn't seem like much. Besides, I'm glad you're here. Stay as long as you like.'

'Can I really?' She liked his warmth and resilience but she did not like what she had done to Geoff.

'Sure you can. Only I better sleep on the couch.'

'Why?'

'Because I'm not feeling so tired any more.'

'But you know too much about me.' How could he accept her when she had been so hideously honest?

'Maybe I like what I know.'

Sarah took off her rings, on a sudden impulse, and laid them on the table. Her hand looked very bare but more recognizably her own. Gavin covered it with his.

'You're going to miss the money.'

'Rotten sod. Yes, I am. Oh, Gavin, do we know what we're doing?'

They looked at each other very straight, suddenly aware of tensions, attraction, the challenge of newness. A sense of adventure beginning.

'You're going to share a flat with a violent sadistic monster with a weakness for older women.'

'And you're going to share a flat with a congenital liar who collects men like insurance policies – given half a chance.'

There was a pause. Both were wondering what odds they had: how much depended on her being Manson's mistress and him being Prue's husband. Neither could say it. Or were they purely themselves? Could they start again?

'Sounds like a pretty good deal,' Gavin said.

The challenge excited her and she leaned across the table to kiss him. But before they could touch, Eve cried from the bedroom. They both collapsed into laughter.

Standing at last beside Prue's grave, Manson wondered why he had ever been afraid to come here. It was so peaceful, a place of beauty, and she was waiting for him. He could see her so clearly he wondered why other people did not comment on her. The longing to join her was overwhelming: he marvelled that he had wasted so much time in the charade of life, when the only reality was here.

In bed again with Evan, drowsy after love-making, Cassie felt peaceful and generous towards the whole world.

'What *are* we going to do about Vicky?'

'Don't worry. I'll have a word with her.'

'I think she's going to be a problem.' But she could recognize Vicky's pain.

'She'll be fine as soon as she gets a new boyfriend. That's all it is. Only of course right now she can't believe it will ever happen.'

'I know the feeling. Believe me, I sympathize with her.' She would always identify with Vicky: they had both been rejected, both wanted what they could not have.

Evan kissed her. 'You talk too much.'

'So do you.'

Driving back to the flat, Manson nearly had an accident. All he could see was Prue and he swerved only just in time. First he swore at himself for the absurd reflex: it would have been easier that way. But no; there was the other driver to consider. He might have been killed or injured; or he might have lived on with a death on his conscience, never knowing he was a benefactor. Even at the last, one must not be irresponsible.

Sarah, Gavin and Eve shared a messy breakfast. Sarah felt relaxed and cheerful, lightweight, as if she had no problems. She could not remember when last she had felt like that.

Gavin said, 'D'you want to fetch your stuff today?'

'Ugh.' She made a face. 'I thought I'd put it off as long as I can.'

'I'll come with you. We can take Eve and make a day of it. With any luck he'll be at the office.'

She was already at ease with him and their night had been a success. Now she felt gratitude as well. She hugged him. 'You're incredible.'

Manson parked carelessly on a yellow line for the first time in his life and left the car door open. After all, what did it matter? And he felt a great sense of urgency now.

Upstairs in the flat he set out the pills and water. He would not chance whisky again; he might be sick, and this time he had to get it right. He thought briefly of Cassie, Sarah, the boys, but they all seemed very small, like images seen through the wrong end of a telescope. They belonged to another life; and they were nothing to do with him.

There were a lot of pills, more than enough, but he had to be sure, so he took them all. Then he lay down on the bed to wait for Prue. He was happy.

MORE ABOUT PENGUINS
AND PELICANS

Penguinews, which appears every month, contains details of all the new books issued by Penguins as they are published. From time to time it is supplemented by *Penguins in Print*, which is our complete list of almost 5,000 titles.

A specimen copy of Penguinews will be sent to you free on request. Please write to Dept EP, Penguin Books Ltd, Harmondsworth, Middlesex, for your copy.

In the U.S.A.: For a complete list of books available from Penguins in the United States write to Dept CS, Penguin Books, 625 Madison Avenue, New York, New York 10022.

In Canada: For a complete list of books available from Penguins in Canada write to Penguin Books Canada Ltd, 2801 John Street, Markham, Ontario L3R 1B4.

AN EVIL STREAK

Andrea Newman

'A marvellous *tour-de-force*' – Margaret Drabble

Alexander Kyle, a sardonic and perverse academic, is engaged in the translation of Chaucer's *Troilus and Criseyde*. Whether his motives are evil or merely frivolous, his attempt to play Pandarus in masterminding and corrupting his niece's love life becomes an obsession, bordering on black comedy – and tragedy.

As in A *Bouquet of Barbed Wire*, Andrea Newman has written a novel that startles the reader with its power and extraordinary insight into human behaviour, combined with superb artistic effect.

'Its readability has an uncommon hold, and the narrative brings unexpected bends, dips and heights ... The book itself glows with inner balance. Buy it' – *The Times*

ANDREA NEWMAN

A BOUQUET OF BARBED WIRE

Peter Eliot Manson is in love – with his own daughter. Confused, he hides behind a guilty affair with his secretary. Within a few short summer months a whole family is turned inside out.

As viewers of the successful television adaptation will remember, *A Bouquet of Barbed Wire* gains the tense momentum of a thriller as the convoluted relationships lead to tragedy.

THREE INTO TWO WON'T GO

Andrea Newman turns the eternal triangle on its head. The angles are not all equal, three into two won't go – and somebody has to lose.

ALEXA

Christine is a musician whose marriage has dulled her life. In answer to a call for help her friend Alexa, the novelist, arrives in the household, only to tangle with the husband, Paul ...